Something In The Neighborhood Of Real

Craig Schwab

Outskirts Press, Inc.
Denver, Colorado

v4.0

Cover Painting by : Israel Issi Dayan
Orange Stain Visual Productions
www.orangestain165.com
issi165@017.net.il
(646)283 0166

Outskirts Press, Inc.
http://www.outskirtspress.com

ISBN: 978-1-4327-5201-9

PRINTED IN THE UNITED STATES OF AMERICA

Dedicated to my brother Frank and Tommy Huber

The following musicians kept me company while writing this book:

Louis Armstrong
Miles Davis
Bill Frisell
Brian Eno
The Beatles
Bob Dylan

The following writers taught me how to express myself on paper:

Kurt Vonnegut
John Irving
Jack Kerouac
Richard Russo

The following people are my constant reminder of what's real in life:

Eileen Schwab
Alison Schwab
Kevin Schwab
Brian Schwab

Keep smiling and Rock On.
Craig Schwab

"Every man is obsessed by the memories of his own youth"

Umberto Eco

This is almost a true story. Many of the names are real except one of the main characters may or may not have lived.

It could be a mystery.

Prologue

When on a carousel, it can feel like you are in a child's dream. Round and round the entire world is seen in passing moments of glory, wonder and promise. For some it is a ride offering a series of brilliant memories, while others experience a sense of dizziness, longing to get off. The choice is never as easy as it seems. The ride can come to a screeching halt, or can propel us in to a state of shocking reality. Smiling and waving to loved ones can remind us how temporary the shining lights. Such is the beauty and sadness of memory in the neighborhood of real. Where time allows us to embrace all we did, and will do, in our next breath.

Darkness surrounded by unanswered whispers. Prayers that we hope will open opportunities and secrets never meant to be said out loud. On and on the ride goes filled with ups and downs, colored stallions, stand alone lions, and tigers. We hold on while reaching out for answers we are not yet ready for. All aboard the carousel, where reality can be an escape or a rude awakening.

Watch your step getting on; no one gets off until the music ends.

Chapter One

It was a time of simple status symbols. You could not determine from house to house if any family had more than another. It was a time of unrest. The future would paint a brighter picture for some and a bleaker picture for others.

It was a time of vivid imaginations. Children played outside all year round. If there was something missing in their lives, they invented it or made it up. This is a story about making things up even if most of everything that happened was real.

Billy Moran was ten years old when I met him. We did not know at the time we would always know one another. This is important to understand because friends come and go in our lifetime. Knowing someone for your whole life, from a certain era until you are old and gray, is rare. You never expect to know someone for so long that they can validate everything you say, or dispute it. Billy Moran and I were destined to be friends for life. So it is that a life sentence is not always a horrible thing.

The only way to begin is from the beginning. Shortcuts take too long to explain.

On the day I met Billy Moran, it was nearing the start of

the school year. In New York, as was the custom nationwide in America, most schools when we were young started on the same day. We called it 'the Start of the New School year'. I do not recall a differentiation between public school, private school or special school children. Everyone had differences; but in more ways than can be imagined, we were all the same.

I should clarify the time frame for you the reader, so as to define exactly when the beginning started. It was after the death of a President by assassination. It was after the arrival of a band from England who would change music. It was before people started choosing sides on a war that was never a war. It was before man walked anywhere except here on earth. Somewhere in this time frame Billy Moran and I became friends. As I said, we were ten years old. We had a lifetime ahead of us that many people would say advanced mankind for the better. Billy and I would dispute that.

There were no cell phones. No fax machines. No Internet. No E-mail. When Mrs. Moran needed to find Billy this is what she would do:

BILLY!!!

The fact that Billy was sometimes three blocks away did not matter. If someone heard his mother yelling for him, like a telegraph line stretched across the heartland word would reach him. Neighbors knew neighbors. Storeowners knew everyone. Even bus drivers would wave from their windows at people as they passed by on the Avenue. Hiding was not an option, you could always be found; but in a different way than kids today with their modern gadgets.

Billy Moran's father was the one who introduced us. This is what he said after taking Billy up to the park to meet new friends:

"This is Billy Moran, can he play ball with you?"

I suspect now that my reply may have been thought rude. In retrospect, I think if I had said anything else I have my doubts we would have remained friends. I replied, "I don't know. Is he any good?"

At the time, being good at playing ball was based on three essential ingredients:

1. Can you catch?
2. Can you throw?
3. Can you hit?

Not necessarily in this order. There was no facilitating by parents to make it easier for a child to adapt. Mr. Arthur Moran showed Billy where children played ball. He introduced him to us. He sat for a moment on a park bench then went home to do whatever it was parents did. Billy stood for a moment quietly looking at us as we sized him up. He answered yes to each of the essential ingredients for playing ball. I advised the other kids:

"The new kid's on my side!"

And thus began a friendship that would never end.

Chapter Two

I never heard anyone except my parents call me by name as a child. Everyone had nicknames or was simply spoken to as if names did not matter. For the sake of good order, I will tell you I was born Jonathan Francis Kiddrane. My friends called me Jono for reasons of which I am clueless. Later in this same decade I would become known forever as The Sundance Kidd, but I do not wish to get ahead of myself.

On that first day, Billy Moran held his own on the ball field. He hit the ball a few times and struck out swinging a few times. He caught the ball on the ground, and a fly ball or two. He also watched a ball sail over his head like it was a bird. This is what I said to Billy Moran when he missed the ball: "Nice play, moron!"

No one that day knew that Billy Moran and I were bonding in ways few could understand. Billy did not get down on himself when he missed a ball. He did not get angry when he watched a ball sail over his head or through his legs. He even laughed out loud after throwing it over my head and I screamed like an idiot telling him he was a moron. Winning was not everything and losing was just another way for the other team to boast until the next day. When the next day came, I still picked Billy Moran for my team. This is what I said – "I have the Moron."

At the tail end of a summer, in the heart of New York City – playing ball was a preparation for the Fall Classic. The World Series. Fathers would read newspapers while sitting in their lounge chairs and mothers prepared dinner while singing along with songs on the radio. When the school year started, kids in my neighborhood did not have tales to tell about exotic vacations or trips to Disneyland. To us, Disney was just another television show on Sunday nights. It would later become a name associated with escape, but again, I do not wish to get ahead of myself.

Once the school year began, what happened on the ball field by way of friendship stayed on the field. There were no associations made between the neighborhood kids and the new kids who showed up in class. When the Principal ushered Billy Moran in to the classroom, I did not look up from my desk. I already knew him. I had no reason to be introduced again. On the first day of school, a group of boys who called themselves "the park boys" gathered around Billy at lunchtime. Billy and I had played ball in the park for the better part of a month before school opened, but we never saw "the park boys" in the park. They did not stay near the places, like the ball field, that we considered the park. We would later discover that the park had many areas we knew nothing about. I must confess, in the first month since being introduced to Billy Moran his nickname, 'moron', took on more meanings than we ever associated with the word. The 'park boys' jumped on this variation of his last name with bravado and hopes of humiliation. Just how many 'park boys' there were in the neighborhood was always up for speculation, but five of them went to the same school as Billy and I. On this particular day in school they decided to surround him, typical of the gang mentality popular with that sort. The biggest one shoved Billy against the cafeteria wall while he was carrying his lunch on a tray. Billy managed to grab hold of everything on his tray after being pushed, except his container of milk. The milk fell to the floor, making a loud splashing sound. It went: **S P L O O S H!**

The biggest "park boy" was named Tommy Hargrove. He was known around the neighborhood as the kid to stay away from unless you hoped to be a member of a gang or wanted to have your head bashed in. I did not think Billy wanted to join a gang. He already had friends and we played ball together. I did not think Billy wanted to have his head bashed in, either. There were a few of us ball players readying ourselves in case things got out of hand.

"So you're the new kid?" Tommy Hargrove said in a voice demanding respect.

Billy looked down at his fallen milk container. The milk laid in a puddle in front of him and he watched as the other "park boys" scattered on their toes around it.

"I asked you a question!" Tommy Hargrove said in an even louder voice.

It is important to note that teachers and security guards were not a part of the cafeteria scene during this period of American history. Maybe one or two teachers were assigned "cafeteria duty", but it was their lunch hour as well, and most times they would sit in the back of the room drinking coffee and discussing topics no one else cared much about. The fact that an altercation was taking place near the front of the cafeteria was oblivious to them. On the other hand, kids noticed things in a different light. Growing up was a lot like cars on a large highway. You needed to avoid large trucks, and it was established early on that some cars went faster than others.

Billy was still immersed in trying to figure out how he was going to drink milk with his lunch. Tommy Hargrove shoved him again, demanding his attention. "Are you some kind of moron?" he said, looking around at his boys for a laugh. They all seemed to know when they were expected to laugh in harmony. Each of the park boys guffawed and shuffled around, nodding their heads in agreement. It is important for you the reader to know that Billy was not tall, by the usual standards he may have actually been considered short. He had no distinguishable differences except that it could be argued one leg was longer than the other. He could have been described as someone who walked with a limp, or perhaps as someone who walked with an attitude. It was up to anyone's discretion to make his or her own observation. On this particular day, Billy Moran walked with an attitude. The cafeteria crowd was typical for an American school; made up of groups of people who made a big deal out of who sat at what table. It was an unspoken code. During an altercation of any kind, the cafeteria changed from a huge commune to a war zone. Billy Moran was about to make a point, and an entire school would be placed on notice.

Billy had not looked up from staring at the fallen milk. The milk had become for him a symbol of transgression. It was Billy's father who told him: "There are two kinds of people in this world, good and bad. Nothing can change that. Not their height or weight. Not their color or religious beliefs. Good and bad is all that matters. Always fight the bad and never let them get away with anything." It was a simple lesson Billy's father would share with anyone who would listen. As we grew closer throughout life,

Billy's father would teach many lessons; but on this day, while Billy stood hypnotized by a puddle of milk, while this latest victim of the park boys transfixed an entire cafeteria, wondering what would happen next, Billy Moran made a name for himself.

I looked around the cafeteria, trying to find people I could count on for help if matters got worse. I do not think it even occurred to me that Billy would not need help. When Billy did look up from his tray, there was a look in his eyes that up until that day I saw only when he was disappointed in himself for throwing the ball over my head, or striking out. He knew he had to do something. The tray was lifted in to the chin of Tommy Hargrove with such force that he fell back against a table, hitting his head. The other park boys were so taken by the act that they seemed frozen in time. The two on either side of Billy went down with equal force after being punched in the stomach. The two standing behind them were still mesmerized by the speed of what had happened, and they did not see Billy's hands coming at them until they were both hit, sent to the floor beside the others.

The entire cafeteria seemed to stand in unison, amazed by what they had just witnessed. Two teachers stood speechless for the moment, watching the whole room react to the event. That is what it became known as for the remaining years of Billy's time in school:

THE EVENT

The teachers asked what happened. They stood looking around the cafeteria at anyone who could describe what had just transpired. Five "park boys" were on the floor in various positions holding parts of their bodies moaning. Billy stood looking at the crowd. With everyone standing, he managed to find my eyes in the crowd. Without saying a word this is what both of us were thinking: **HOLY SHIT!**

The teachers quickly surmised what must have happened. The "park boys" must have slipped on a broken container of milk. No one in the cafeteria on that day would say differently.

There was an annual ritual related to playing ball. Every year, a baseball glove needed to be prepared for the season. A new glove required preparation that bordered on obsession. Dickie Blues got a new glove every year. His preparation process was legendary. As we would prepare for April's inauguration of each baseball season, there was chatter about what Dickie Blues would do to make his glove ready. No one as far as I know ever inherited a Dickie Blues glove. There was speculation he kept each glove to remind him of something only he could appreciate. I only had one glove during my youthful baseball playing days. It was a brown Rawlings Brooks Robinson model. Brooks Robinson was the third baseman for the Baltimore Orioles. He was nicknamed the human vacuum. At the end of every season I placed a baseball in the pocket of the glove and tied it tightly closed with a shoestring. When a new season began the glove was taken from beneath my bed where I stored it for winter. Once the shoestring was untied the glove was a sight to behold. It would slowly unravel itself, like a budding flower looking for sunshine. And when it was fully open, the baseball removed, I would hold it up to my nose; taking in the fresh smell of leather. It was a perfect ritual. To make the glove ready for play, I would soak the entire glove in Vaseline. The baseball was placed again into the pocket and tied closed with the same shoestring. I left it on the windowsill in my room overnight to dry. The leather year after year became softer, and the glove fit better and better over time. Dickie Blues had a different way of doing most things. His glove preparation, despite it being proof of his possible insanity, always required an audience. Normally, the preparation of one's sporting equipment wasn't shared with friends. I never witnessed my brother, Hank making his glove season ready. We shared a tiny room and I never once saw where he kept his glove or how he prepared it when put away or taken out for a new year. I never saw his glove on our windowsill or caught a glimpse of him applying any special care to it. Once on the ball field, it was usually thought that his glove was blessed by the gods, but I needed to perform miracles to make circus catches in the outfield. He would merely take the field and year after year stick his glove out and make plays that caused us all to stare in wonder. The preparation of my glove was a form of avoiding bad vibes. He never made a bad play. It was as if the rest of us were cursed with being average and he was gifted with something special. Every ballplayer is superstitious in one way or another. At the start of baseball season, everyone would show up on the field ready to start playing. Every sport had a begin date that was generally agreed upon. The weather had little to do with our seasons. Snow nor rain or the still cold winds of winter could deter our April 1st baseball season. New bats would be held and swung at the open air around the dugout. Small talk would ensue about getting ready to beat anyone who dared to challenge our team. Without being too obvious, everyone would occasionally look over their shoulder, awaiting the arrival of Dickie Blues. It was in many ways an unspoken code; the season did not officially begin until Dickie Blues arrived with his new glove. This particular year, Dickie arrived with a glove that caused widespread jealousy. He unveiled it from inside a sports bag. He was the first and only kid to own a sports bag when we were young. We gathered around him to take in the look and appearance of the glove.

It was different than anything we had ever seen. It was sky blue. He made a point to mention that it matched his sky blue Chuck Taylor converse sneakers. It was beautiful. Each of us was allowed to hold it. I held it up to my nose, taking in the scent of blue leather that was unmatched by anything I had ever known. I was convinced that blue leather was fit for royalty. After we were finished marveling at the glove, Dickie Blues began his preparation process. The very first thing he did was toss it as far as he could throw it. It landed with a loud thud around second base. He ran as fast as he could, slowing down as he neared the glove and kicking it as hard as possible. This process of kicking went on for close to ten minutes. He then picked up the glove and held it over his head, studying the glove for what he hoped were newly made defects. He dropped it on the ground in the outfield grass where he jumped up and down on it for another good ten minutes. He then walked to home plate, picked up a new bat and, tossing the glove in the air, began smacking it as hard and as far as possible. No one ever said a word as he prepared his glove. It was an act that caused awe more than anything else. On this particular day after studying the glove numerous times, shaking his head after each inspection, the preparation process took on one of the most bizarre actions we had ever witnessed, even for Dickie Blues. He walked with his glove to the outfield where he exited through a chain link fence. He walked to the edge of Interboro Parkway. He stood for a moment watching the passing cars. He then dropped the glove on to the highway. We ran to the outfield fence staring in disbelief. Still, we admired what we wanted to believe was a form of dedication that touched upon art. Several cars ran over the glove. One car's tires dragged the glove for a quarter mile. Dickie Blues charged after the car along the highways edge while every one of us ran along the outfield fence cheering. He stepped on to the highway as cars veered to avoid hitting him. He leaned down near the yellow line that separated lanes, oblivious of the screeching tires from cars coming to a complete halt around and near him. He held the glove over his head. He studied it with car horns honking and drivers screaming all kinds of obscenities at him. He looked at us standing along the outfield fence in silence and shock. He sneered at the drivers and then, looking back at us, he smiled. The glove was ready. He screamed from the highway; "PLAY BALL!" A new season could begin.

Chapter Three

My father made connections as a deliveryman for the Daily News. He would bring home tickets for ball games, major motion pictures and events around New York City. Seeing the Yankees play in Yankee Stadium was an amazing treat. My brother and I especially enjoyed the surprise tickets to movies at the Ziegfeld Theater. My mother would get dressed up and we would go to opening nights. On several occasions we would turn the block off 6th Avenue and see the movie stars getting out of their limousines, the spot lights shining everywhere. It was one such night that we attended the opening of a film that would change everything. The name of the movie was "Butch Cassidy and The Sundance Kidd" starring Paul Newman, Robert Redford and Katherine Ross. My father loved westerns. He was dressed in one of his finest suits. My brother and I wore matching shirts, which only happened when my Mom wanted to show us off. We watched Paul Newman with his wife waving to the crowd. We waved at them like we were the only ones they saw. Robert Redford was next and he made my mother blush by blowing her a kiss. Katherine Ross arrived and she looked elegant and tall.

After all the stars were inside, everyone with a ticket was ushered inside. We sat way up top in the balcony, a mile from the screen. Everyone was standing and watching the stars milling around downstairs. We could not see them, but as the crowd pointed and waved it was more and more exciting. The lights dimmed and everyone applauded. For the next two and a half hours, I could see why my father loved westerns. Whenever we would go to the movies, my father would tell my brother and me: "You stand on line for two things in this life, James Bond and a good western." We had no idea what he meant until we saw Butch Cassidy and The Sundance Kidd. He was smiling from ear to ear throughout the entire movie. Even when it got corny and Paul Newman was riding Katherine Ross on the handlebars of a bicycle while some song called "Raindrops Keep Falling on My Head" was playing, I could see my father was genuinely happy. He whispered in to my ear, "See what I mean about a good western?" I nodded my head, stuffing my face with popcorn. He once said, "You can always enjoy a western because the good guys wear white hats and the bad guys wear black hats. You can go to the bathroom, get something to eat and not miss a thing." It got a little confusing watching Butch and Sundance, because they were bad guys, I think. Everyone was pulling for them right up to the end no matter what they did – like rob trains, banks and shooting people. It was fun to sit with adults in the dark and watch them cheer these things. It didn't matter, because from that night on, I wanted everyone to know my name. On the way home in the car I told my brother my nickname and he made fun of me. I told my father and he cheered after looking through the rearview mirror while holding my mothers hand all the way home over the 59th Street

Bridge, down Queens Boulevard and back on to our street. On the night we saw the greatest western in the world, we were a happy family; and I was forever The Sundance Kidd. The second "D" was for "Dangerous!"

Chapter Four

For our remaining years at school there were no further incidents in the cafeteria. Anyone in the know would understand that a statement was made, and in its wake everyone was safe for the time being. Bullies would come and go in the future; there would be other incidents with Tommy Hargrove and the park boys that would take place outside of school. Billy Moran in one day had created a safe haven for us all.

Time goes by in the wink of an eye when you're young. No one cared about time unless it meant the school bell would ring, letting us back out in to the free world. We learned about discipline and respect from our parents; and God help any kid who needed to hear it from the nuns or priests in school. For the record, Tommy Hargrove and his gang needed to stay after school on many occasions because their parents were not able to teach or live by example.

As the years passed by, Billy and I were inseparable. We went everywhere and did everything together. Friends are what we were, and friends we would always be. But a story about friendship must have other elements as well, and since I have told most of this story so far about Billy, perhaps it is time to talk about something else: my family.

My parents were unique in their own ways. As I said, my father drove a truck delivering the Daily News to stores around Yankee Stadium, which was and is still located in the Bronx. The Bronx had a reputation when I was a kid of being one of the most dangerous places to live in New York. Being a fan of the Yankees was difficult, especially if you were raised in Queens where it was assumed you were a fan of another team. Perhaps it is necessary that I explain a few things about being a fan of baseball in New York during this period in history. In the 1950s, there were three teams playing for the hearts of baseball fans:

1. New York Yankees
2. New York Giants
3. Brooklyn Dodgers

Each of these teams had an intense fan base that could almost be compared to a gang, if you think about it. On any day between April and October, there were arguments that promised a certain death to anyone who wasn't wearing the right hat at a particular stadium. My father was a Yankee fan. My mother was a Yankee fan. Where we lived had nothing to do with our allegiance. It was a tradition passed down through the ages like blood.

The Daily News was delivered three times each day. There was the morning edition, (the one my father delivered by truck), the afternoon edition and the evening edition. It was not so much that there was more news, or better news – it's just how it was done. On occasion my father would ask if I wanted to join him on his delivery runs. It meant getting up at 3 o'clock in the morning, jumping on his truck as it went by on Myrtle Avenue, sitting up front as my father screamed over the sound of the engine about the day's upcoming news. Except for the reporters, my father knew the news before anyone else in New York. On school days I could tell the other kids things their parents did not know yet. It made me popular. It made me feel special.

Being with my father as he drove his truck on to the Grand Central parkway towards the Major Deegan Expressway was always an adventure. Newspaper trucks, it seemed, could go as fast as they pleased. They could switch lanes without signaling. They could be waved past tollbooths like they were armored cars carrying the riches of the world.

Once on the streets of the Bronx, my father would instruct me as to how many bundles to toss out the side door of the truck. The bundles were encased with wire that required gloves so you did not cut your hands open lifting them. I would toss the bundles on the street in front of the stores as my father slowed down. It was important to toss the bundle in such a way as to not cause the bundle to tear open and send papers flying every which way. It took practice. My father told me I was a natural.

As the truck entered the Grand Concourse portion of the Bronx, and he steered the truck on to River Avenue – the cathedral of baseball, Yankee Stadium, could be seen in all its glory. It is perhaps a tad sacrilegious, and I did promise my father I would never tell anyone he did this – but as we passed the Stadium, my father made the sign of the cross. The first time I saw him do it, I was certain we were going to crash and die a fiery death.

The fact we did not crash and the fact that my father would smile when looking over at me after doing it, started a ritual that would last a lifetime. My father would say –

"Here's to the team, son!" Soon I, too, would make the gesture, never telling another living soul about our sacred allegiance.

All good things, as the saying goes, come to an end. I would learn from my father on those morning delivery runs about history according to a parent's point of view. What was reported in the newspapers was not always the truth. How a story was told was not always how it happened. Most of all I learned how as a young boy, before I had any appreciation for what was important in life, the two rival baseball teams in New York; the Dodgers and then the Giants abandoned the city for the West Coast. My father told me one day they were here and the next they were gone. First the Brooklyn Dodgers did it, leaving an entire borough of New York City forever broken- hearted. My father, a Yankee fan, got misty-eyed talking about it. He said, "When the Giants left, they did it after beating the Yankees in the World Series. Imagine beating the best team in baseball and leaving the city that loved you." I can't say I understood his sentiment, almost whispered in a reverent tone. I understood it better when he said; "They took Willie Mays with them." Willie Mays was, for argumentative reasons, the best centerfielder who ever played the game. My father told me Willie Mays looked like he was on ice skates when he ran. He told me with tears in his eyes how he saw Willie Mays catch a ball once that until the day he died could never be forgotten. I remember one night as we passed Yankee Stadium saying to my father "Hey Dad, I wonder how Mickey Mantle's doing?"

The Mick was the Yankee centerfielder. He followed Joe DiMaggio before him and made himself a hometown hero. I did not know then that heroes were made out of flesh and blood and did not fall from grace until they left the game, until after they died.

Chapter Five

I graduated from school with Billy Moran in the same year a man walked on the moon. It was the same year the rival team from across town, the New York Mets, won the World Series. It was called the Summer of Love by many people, as hundreds of thousands of kids called hippies camped out on a farm in upstate New York listening to music and doing things that opened a few eyes and ears.

For years, there would be three things that everyone would say they either saw or attended personally:

1. Neil Armstrong stepping down on the moon.
2. The New York Mets winning the World Series.
3. Woodstock.

For what it's worth, I saw two out of three and heard the music from the other played on the radio. In the late 1960s, radio became a god no religious leader could control or silence. The music became a force to be reckoned with; seemingly overnight it was, as John Lennon had said "bigger than God." Cars were equipped with AM radios. The AM radio stations played Top 40 music across the land. Music, in the beginning, was for everyone to enjoy together. The top songs consisted of those that were most popular, according to records bought and number of times played on the radio. But there was something more: there was another side to radio that would soon light the world on fire. It was called FM. Tuning into a station on the FM frequency required a passion for adventure; hearing these new and different sounds opened the world's ears to the music being made by a new generation.

On clear nights emanating through the vastness of space shared only by Neil Armstrong as he stepped on the lunar surface, music could be heard echoing in the air like sprinkled gold from the heavens. As word of the other frequency spread through the neighborhood in the summer of 1969, life was changing in ways many people to this day cannot fully understand. The American people were standing up for things they had taken for granted in the past. Children were making themselves heard in ways no one could have imagined. Billy Moran and I were headed to high school, where there were no uniforms worn and the rules were written down without any way of being enforced, or preventing the coming storm.

Chapter Six

In a city like New York, all communities were like cities of their own. My father's paper route changed the summer before I started high school. Who would have thought that he would deliver to stores with another stadium in the middle of nowhere? Shea Stadium – home of the Mets. The arch rivals of the Yankees and the media darlings since winning the 1969 World Series. I have to admit the whole thing enchanted me – even if I couldn't believe it happened. It was like some kind of miracle. So it was that I would continue throwing papers off the back of my father's truck in the wee hours of a new summer day, in an entirely new neighborhood. The thing about it now looking back was those people loved their team so much, I think I was jealous in a strange way. It was in that summer that I met someone who would also mean a lot to me, as I grew older. Some one who was bigger than life itself, and it was my Dad who introduced us. Who would have guessed my Dad could know so many cool people? But there we were delivering newspapers one summer morning, after being out on the route since 3am and while sitting at a red light – the truck idling and a sound coming through the air like a bird singing a song. I remember looking at my father – his head just shaking and his face grinning. "What's that, Dad?" I said looking out the side door of the truck. He looked at me and said, "That, my son would be the man himself, Louie Armstrong. Satchmo's home." I had no idea what a Satchmo was. – "Louie who?" I said with a growing sense of magic coming through the early morning sky. My father said smiling, "He's the Father of Jazz, son! He's only home on certain days. We could go and visit if you like." I had never heard of jazz and I was definitely up for meeting someone who was the father of anything.

My father turned on to Louie's block and there he was – standing on a small balcony just playing his trumpet like he had no cares in the world. The first time I saw Louis – it could not have been more than 6am and the sun was slowly making itself known in the sky. Louis and his shadow playing his trumpet cast a glowing beam of light on its own. My Dad pulled up to the house and got out waving. "Hey Louie!" my father screamed up at Louis Armstrong – the father of Jazz. "Hey yourself!" he yelled down to my father. My Dad pointed to me slowly getting out of the truck – "this here is my boy!" It was the first and last time I actually heard my Dad say something that seemed he was proud of me being his son. Louis waved us inside – "Come on up in here! Let me take a look at this boy!" he yelled in a raspy voice. I had never heard a voice like that before. We climbed the stairs to his house. We waited a moment before he came to the door, smiling and inviting us inside. He called my father "Frankie boy." I had never seen anyone so full of life. He ushered us in to his living room and we sat on his huge white couch. There was a piano and the coolest of cool paintings on the walls. One picture was especially great – it showed a man playing a saxophone and was different from any other picture I had ever seen. Louis excused himself and I asked my Dad how he knew someone like this. My Dad laughed saying he and Louis went way back. It didn't tell me much and I never asked him again what "way back" meant. Everyone, it seemed, knew Louie. "Where did he go, Dad?" Again my father started laughing like I had never seen him laugh. "He's turning on the microphones, most likely – he loves to tape conversations of everyone who visits. It's a hobby of his!" Sure enough – Louis came back holding a handkerchief and laughing like everything was a riot. He wiped himself with that handkerchief over and over again, and when that handkerchief seemed to be finished another would appear out of mid air.

He was the Houdini of handkerchiefs. He made coffee for my Dad and poured me a glass of milk. His wife Lucille came in and I was startled by her sense of joy in seeing my Dad. She gave him a hug and a big kiss on the cheek. She said, "Let me make something to go with coffee." Off she went and in came a dog – even the dog was friendly. "This here is the General", said Louis, looking at me on the carpet playing with the dog. I followed the dog in to the hallway and out to the kitchen, which was unlike any kitchen I had ever seen in my life. The cabinets were the bluest blue! There was Lucille singing away and happy as can be about having guests, so early in the morning. There were gadgets on the counter I had never seen before. The stove was huge! It had six burners and there was something cooking on each one. I walked back inside and Louis was laughing like crazy with my father buckled over in stitches. "Come on over here, son, tell me what you're about?" We talked for what seemed like hours. Then before leaving Louis went upstairs and came down smiling, holding a record in his hand. He wanted me to have it.

There was picture of him on the cover playing his trumpet and holding his handkerchief. He said – Wait till you hear this!" He pushed a button and I could not believe my own ears-- there I was talking to Louie Armstrong, my voice coming out of speakers in the ceiling.

Louis – Tell me what you're about?

Jono – I'm about 5'6" and growing everyday.

Louis – Oh so you're a growing boy?

Jono – Everyday.

Louis – And what you doin' with all this growing up?

Jono – I'm getting taller and older by the minute.

Louis – You better not grow by the minute – my ceilings ain't that high!

And laugh Louie did, like no one I've ever heard since. We left after wishing Louis, Lucille and General the dog the very best. They stood on their stoop waving like they were happier to see us than any visitors on Christmas morning.

My Dad started up the truck and we drove away from Satchmo's with both of us grinning, feeling like we'd already had a perfect day. The sun was only awake a few hours and we had been to the moon and back. I could not wait to tell Billy I met a legend. He would never believe it. It was the coolest thing ever.

Chapter Seven

The day I met Louis Armstrong opened me up to the many different ways my father taught me how to love life. He told me there would be times when all seems lost, but I should keep my wits about me and hope for the best. I was too young to understand fully what he meant at the time, but I was learning. I never had my very own record before, and on this day Louis gave one to me. I could not wait to go home and put it on the stereo. I should give a little background here before I go on. I knew about music from listening to the radio. My dad had given me and my brother our own radios; they were each the size of a shoebox. My radio was a shade of green I have never seen again anywhere. I discovered music on my own, with a little help from deejays who cared more about music then the commercials they had to read in between songs. You could tell a real deejay from a fake one; a real deejay made you feel like you were sitting with him in his living room. He would say things like, "Wait till you hear this one!" and I would immediately pay attention. One deejay I listened to was discovered by accident; I was looking at the way the radio dial lit up in the dark and I pulled the antenna all the way up. I noticed there was a button on one side that said FM. I had no idea what FM stood for, but when I pressed the button the static was louder than any noise I had ever heard.

It wasn't normal static; this sounded like something from outer space. While turning it down, I accidentally hit the station dial and there was suddenly a man talking. I couldn't make out every word;, but he was really into explaining something about the music he had just been playing. I had never heard anyone talking so proudly about music before. He played a song by a group called The Chambers Brothers, called Time Has Come Today. Only this song was nothing like the version I had heard once on an AM station; this song seemed to last for what seemed like an hour. No kidding! – it just kept playing and I think I must have lost track of time. I fell asleep holding the radio, using it as a pillow. The best I could make out was the deejay's name was Ben Kelsa. This guy really loved music; and, better than that, he liked to play it for as long as possible. The station I found Ben Kelsa on faded during the night, but I vowed to find him again. I knew he was out there on the air waves somewhere; I just had to find the right star to point the antenna toward. The discovery of new songs on the radio would become a lifetime ritual; it was a practice that cost nothing but time and gave me an appreciation of music that would never leave me. When I got home I slowly took the album Louie gave me out of the album sleeve. Taking records out of the 12"x12" cardboard sleeve was an act of pure discovery. There was a distinct sound to the removal of vinyl from a record sleeve, it slipped from the confines of an enclosed darkness into a new light. In the palm of your hand it felt like an undiscovered treasure. The smoothness of the vinyl had a glow that when held against the light made shadows on the walls. I had watched my parents place records on the living room console stereo many times, and I knew that they had an appreciation for music they enjoyed listening to. Frank Sinatra, Dean Martin and big-band tunes would fill my house with the sounds of a concert hall. Sometimes I thought it was corny to watch my parents with their friends dancing to songs while holding their glasses of liquor high in the air, singing and laughing along with the music. Still, the regard for the music was always a pleasant surprise. Late at night, when everyone was feeling mellow, the tempo of the music would change and like magic it would fill in the background while my parents and their guests talked about things that meant nothing to me. Poised in my bedroom looking through a thin crevice of a door ajar I would watch the records spinning on the turntable. The console was on the other side of my bedroom wall and I could easily see every record spinning at an exact 33'1/3 revolution. It was mesmerizing; and many a night it was the last thing I would see and hear before falling asleep. I knew an album was a delicate object. I watched as my father would hold each record between the upheld palms of his two hands, studying the label for the side he wanted to hear. The precise manner in which he placed the record on the turntable was an art form I longed to learn. The way he would slowly take the tone arm and place the needle on the first track of a record was like watching a surgeon with a scalpel. I would look into my father's eyes as the first sounds of a song emanated from the stereo; it was a look of absolute satisfaction. A slow grin would form at the corners of his lips and it was always followed with a sigh of relief. The first moment of the music was a constant reminder to me of how everything in life requires adjustment. I always felt the sound was an introduction to something new and exciting. When I held

Louie's album in my hands for the first time it almost felt as if I were embarking on a journey; a journey I was invited to take by Louie himself. I placed the needle onto the first track and after the slow crackle like a door being opened, it took me on a new adventure. It would be the first of many adventures I would take with as many artists I could assemble; in a collection filled with albums and songs to last a lifetime.

Chapter Eight

On one occasion my father dropped me off at Louie's house, telling me he would return shortly. He wanted to get the truck back to the depot early and would return with his car. It felt strange ringing Louie's bell without my Dad. He was my father's friend, not mine. How could it be fun for him and his wife to entertain a kid? I watched my father's truck disappear around the corner and walked up the steps. As usual it was before dawn and I could not believe that regular people were awake at such an hour if they didn't work. I rang the bell and waited for someone to answer. I rang it once and when no one came to the door – I was hesitant to ring it a second time. Maybe they were asleep like everyone in the world should be at 5am in the morning. I sat down on the steps and prepared myself to wait for my father's return.

Louis: Whatcha doin' sittin' like a lump on a log son?

I couldn't see him, but his distinctive voice was certainly somewhere.

Louis: Hey son – get your self 'round here now?

I looked up at the house on the patio where I first saw Louis Armstrong playing his trumpet. He wasn't there. I looked up at the windows. He wasn't there. I turned and there he was standing by the garage door laughing like only he could.

Louis: Lucille and I stayed up all night stargazing in the yard.

I had never heard of anyone "star gazing" before. He told me to follow him 'round back in to his yard. I had never seen a yard like it. It was something that did not look like it belonged in the middle of a city, no less in Corona, Queens. There were trees I had never seen before. There was a little spring with water splashing down around rocks. Lucille, Louie's wife was sitting in a lawn chair and smiling when she saw me. I did not know anyone who could smile at 5am or any time for that matter like Lucille could.

Louis: Come on in here – sit on down there.

I sat down in the chair next to Lucille and Louis went over to a round concrete bar yelling he was going to "fetch me a soda pop."

Louis: Where'd Frankie Boy run himself off to?

Jono: He wanted to go pick up his car. He said it would be alright for me to stay here?

Louis: Of course it's alright. That father of yours, he alright.

Jono: Yes sir.

Louis: And you spending this time with him – can't beat that.

Jono: No sir.

Louis: Look at that sky son? You ever see something like that?

I looked up through the beautiful trees and felt mesmerized by the surreal feeling of standing in a garden belonging to the Father of Jazz.

Louis: What's the matter – cat got your tongue?

Jono: No sir, I've never seen trees with leaves like these.

Louis: Of course you ain't – this here is Lucille's Japanese Garden. These trees were flown in here special for us.

Jono: Wow.

That's all I could muster the strength to say, Wow.

Louis: People forget to enjoy life. Don't you forget that.

Jono: No sir.

Louis: I make music for a living. You know that? It's beautiful music. Everyone in the world wants to hear Louie sing and play his horn. But you know what – look at that sky up there. We can't play anything as beautiful as that. Can we now? Not a chance – see this tree? We can't make anything as beautiful as that. Can we now? Not a chance – nope not a chance. But Jono my boy – you got only a few times in your life to learn this one lesson. Are you ready?

Jono: Yes sir.

Louis: Friendship is the one thing you can't turn your back on. Hell – people can hear me playing the sweetest melody you ever heard, it won't stop them from getting up and walking right on out of the club. The same people can hear one of my songs playing on the radio – and SWITCH! Turn it off. But, you got yourself a friend, that's forever.

Jono: Yes sir.

Louis: You got a good man for your Daddy. Good man. He's my friend and your father.

You got yourself a friend like that?

Jono: Yes sir.

Louis: What's this friend's name?

Jono: Billy, sir. Billy Moran. Only I can call him Moron.

Louis: Let me get this right? You got a friend only you can call moron?

Jono: I mean it in a good way sir. He calls me Kid. Like Butch Cassidy and the Sundance Kid.

Louis: He can call you kid and you call him Moron? This is some kind of friend.

Jono: Yes sir.

Louis: I had me some names too. Satchel Mouth because of how I look – and that became Satchmo. I love that, I really do. So this "Moron" friend of yours – how long you know him?

Jono: Since I was a kid. I mean a boy.

Louis: You are always going to be a kid, ain't you son?

No other adult could have understood what I was talking about. Lucille sat in her chair looking demure and princess-like.

Louis: It used to be a man had to know his place. You still need to watch your Ps and Qs – but I'll tell you; listen to a radio show like The Make Believe Ballroom sometime and you'll know what I mean about being taken to special places just by closing your eyes and listening to the music.

Jono: I know about make believe.

Louis: Do you now? What you know about make believe?

Jono: That if you wish hard enough for something, your dreams can come true.

Louis: You right. Don't forget it.

Jono: Do you think dreams come true Mr. Armstrong?

He laughed so loud I swear lights went on in the houses surrounding us in the back yard.

Lucille shook her head smiling. She looked over at me and said, "You sure enough opened it up now son."

Louis: Look around this yard son. You been in my house? Now what you think this is? It's a dream. A beautiful dream it is. When I was half your age – I was lucky to have the clothes on my back. Did that make me stand around saying "oh poor poor Louie" Not a chance. Did it make me want to go around robbing people? Not a chance. You go down that road and you might as well stay lost for a million years! Did being poor make me hate anyone who had what I wanted? Not on your life! I got me a horn. Money loaned me by some wonderful people. You know what gift they gave me? Not the money to buy it. Not even the horn. They gave me something more precious than that. They believed I could do something if given the chance. You can't put a price on that son. Nowhere you go on this earth can you hope to find anything better than that? Now – some people gonna go and call it the work of God. What God has to do with anything is in that sky and in these trees. He is much too busy to worry about Louie and his horn. That was up to me! And son, you need to find what is up with you! You find that and you have it all.

I stood looking at him standing in his yard with the sun rising, holding his handkerchief, ranting and raving with a feeling of something I never saw again in any one.

My Dad came in the yard smiling holding a copy of the Daily News under his arm.

He said, "Louie, you're going to wake up this entire neighborhood. I heard you clear out on to the street. I followed your voice right on in here."

Louis: Frankie Boy! Been talking to Jono about the meaning of life.

My Dad looked at me and rubbed my head. On that day, it felt better than any hug or kiss. He handed Louis his paper and told him we needed to get home so I could get to school on time.

Louis: A boy needs his learning! He needs to go to school.

I wanted desperately to tell Louis that standing in his garden and being in his company was better than any school I could go to. I watched my Dad standing with Louis by the little spring with water coming down over the rocks – all lit up in colors slowly fading in the daylight. I watched Louis shaking my father's hand. I watched how they stood next to one another. My father all of 6'4" and Louis Armstrong smaller; but in that light, their shadows were the same size. My father walked over to me – put his arm around me and said, "I'll see you Louie! Lucille, you take care of him now"

I kept turning my head listening to Louis laughing and saying "S'all!"

We got in to my father's car and I asked my father what "S'all" meant?

My father started laughing, saying "that's New Orleans talk son – "That's all!"

There are lessons to be learned everyday. You do not understand what you learn until years later. it is re doing. They are doing One day while in the second grade Sister James announced to the class we could color during recess. This was a big deal because it meant we could take out our coloring books and crayons for a full thirty minutes. While we colored, Sister James would play music on a record player she kept hidden in a coat closet. Secretly, I think Sister James wanted to be a singer or a deejay. She would belt out songs, dancing in a way that would have made Elvis Presley envious. On the day I remember best, Sister James was singing "Hound Dog", by Elvis making it nearly impossible to concentrate on staying between the lines in our coloring books.

She walked and danced part of the way up and down the aisles stopping to comment on different pictures kids were coloring:

"Stay in the lines Johnny."

"No one has red and blue hair Billy."

"Don't press so hard Marie."

"Use more than one color for the dress Linda."

When she got to my desk I heard her gasp. She picked up my coloring book just as Elvis was finishing his last howl of Hound Dog. The record lifted off the turntable and the soft clicking noise of the tone arm could be heard filling the room.

Everyone noticed Sister James when she was annoyed. It scared us in to a silence that resonated with anticipation. "Class", she said in a low monotone voice, "Jonathan is making a mistake we must all avoid." I had no idea what could be wrong with my picture. I stayed between the lines. I changed colors to make it colorful. She said, "Stand up and explain to the class why this man wearing a suit in the picture has a black face?" It was a picture of a man standing in front of a crowd of people making a speech. I said, "He's the President of the United States."

She said, "There is no such thing as a black President. Children, we have to be realistic when we color, it allows us to show we understand the world as it is."

She tore out the page telling me to start over on a new picture.

I told this story to Louis. He was silent for a moment than he did what only Louis could do. He laughed wiping his forehead, shaking hid head while saying, "Yes, yes yes."

He looked at me and with eyes of concern told me, "Kidd, she was right and wrong at the same time. It is something that people do everyday."

I was confused. I asked him, "Do you think there could be a black President?"

He got up to grab another handkerchief. He laughed louder,

shaking his head saying "Yes, yes, yes." Then he hesitated for a moment looking at a bunch of African sculptures on a shelf near the television and stereo in the corner of the room. It will not happen in my lifetime, but maybe yours."

"But, how could she be right and wrong at the same time?"

"Half ways because it never happened before and her knowing like I do it may not happen while she's alive."

The silence after my asking him this question was followed by the same kind of sigh Sister James made in class that day. He shook his head without uttering a sound, and then he said, "It would have to be for the right reasons. It would need to be because he or she earned it. If someone gets anything because of what they are instead of whom they are it will always be questionable if they deserve it."

I looked at him, knowing he knew immediately that I had no idea what he meant. Shaking his head again in an almost exaggerated gesture, he winked at me. "Ok, here's what I mean, all people deserve to be happy, but it is not guaranteed. You have to earn the right to be respected. But, it comes with a price. You can never expect to have respect from everyone. If a black man ever becomes President of anything, he needs to know it was because he earned it. It has nothing to do with the time being right or because of his color. People need to believe in something, you cannot make people pretend the time is right for anything." He looked out the front window out on to the street. He sighed again before adding, "No one deserves anything at all unless they earn it. If you wake up tomorrow thinking your time has come, it better be because you finally figured out a way to play all the right notes at the right time." I cannot say Sister James and Louis would have understood one another. Maybe Sister James wanted me to be realistic. Louis wanted to believe in dreams.

Chapter Nine

Another time I stopped by to see Louis with Billy. He had heard me telling him so many stories he wanted to see how close a friend Louis was to my Dad and me.

I was hesitant, feeling it might be an intrusion to visit without calling or asking my father first. It was a Saturday afternoon after a New York Mets game at Shea Stadium. I knew Louis was home because I had seen him while helping my father earlier in the day.

The Mets were not the team Billy and I cared about, but they had played the San Francisco Giants. Any opportunity to see Willie Mays play was a joy not to be missed.

We sat in the last row way up over left field, in the nose bleed seats as everyone called them. Anyone who loved the game of baseball knew that seeing Willie Mays in centerfield was as close to heaven any fan could get. On that day Willie Mays leaped in the air so high to catch a ball we thought he could defy gravity. He hit a home run and stole a base so easily he had Met fans scratching their heads. No one booed Willie Mays; even though the Giants had left New York for California every fan deep down appreciated everything Willie Mays could do on a ball field.

After the game while walking to the train, Billy got it in his head that we should visit Louis. I told him it might not be a good idea.

"Just what I thought you would say. You made all that stuff up about meeting him. You don't even know where he lives. Do you?"

I hated when Billy became combative. It was a challenge, though, and one that I knew I could not ignore.

"This has nothing to do with lying, Billy. It's just not proper to drop in on someone like Louis Armstrong."

"Liar! Liar! Pants on Fire! You told a lie and now you or someone you know will die!"

"That's the most retarded thing I've ever heard! I don't want to intrude on his privacy."

"Yeah, yeah, forget it. Just don't go telling me anymore of your stories about him."

"I was there this morning. He's having company and we are not invited. It would be like barging in on him."

"Lets go home Kidd, just don't bullshit me about your pal Louis Armstrong."

He started up the stairs to the train as I stood on the street feeling torn between invading Louis's privacy and ignoring Billy's request.

"Ok Billy", I shouted up to him, "If we do this you have to promise not to say or do anything stupid?"

"Like what?"

"How do I know? You have your moments of being a jerk, you know."

"If you pull this off, I will never call you an asshole again."

"When did you call me an asshole?"

"It's happened."

"Recently?"

"I don't remember. I won't do it again."

"Some friend you are for even thinking such a thing."

"That's what friends are for."

"Let's go."

We walked down Roosevelt Avenue towards Louis's house. I needed to adjust my bearings a few times since I had only traveled to his house in my father's truck. Every time I thought we should turn on one block or another Billy would chime in with a snide remark.

"You're lost, aren't you?"

"Shut up Billy."

"You have no idea where he lives."

"Shut up Billy."

Finally I recognized one of the candy stores where my Dad delivered the paper and we turned on to Louis's block. We heard music playing loudly from the backyard. I told Billy not to make fools out of us as we neared the entrance to the yard past the garage where Louis had his car parked. Billy recognized the song immediately saying, "This Louis friend of yours likes the Beatles?" It was a song called Honey Pie.

We entered the yard after I again warned Billy to be cool.

I waited, trying to think how I was going to explain our showing up unannounced. There was a loud conversation taking place. I saw Louis standing in the middle of the yard holding his trumpet and using it to point at someone he was talking to. Billy nearly fell down when he recognized who it was standing behind a concrete bar in the corner of the yard. "Hey… calm down Billy", I said.

"Do you know who that is?"

"Yes Billy, like I've been telling you, it's Louis Armstrong."

"No him!" he said pointing to the man standing behind the bar.

I turned to see who Billy was talking about and I confess I was thrown for a moment.

"Who is it?"

"You really are an asshole."

"You told me you would never call me that again!"

"It's John Lennon!"

I turned again, realizing Billy was shaking like he was seeing a ghost. I had to listen for the British accent before realizing Billy was right. Louis was louder now, yelling over a new song. He said, "You have to listen! Hearing is not enough!"

John Lennon was shaking his head in agreement, yelling back over the music, "Rock and roll requires a different set of ears!" Louis fell to his knees, clutching his trumpet and letting out a loud laugh. He wiped his brow with a handkerchief, yelling back, "Rock and roll, Johnny my boy, is the blues played with electric!"

"Well it's here to stay", John Lennon responded as the song playing came to an end.

Louis looked over to see Billy standing with his mouth open and then over at me.

"Young Jono, what you doing here?"

I was taken by seeing an actual Beatle standing in front of me. I stuttered as I spoke;

"I'm er sorry Louis, but um this here is Bill…Billy Moran my friend."

Louis looked at Billy standing with his mouth open, "Billy Moran, your moron friend?"

"Yes sir… we were at the ballgame and he asked if we could visit?"

"Of course you can visit Louis, anytime."

He got up from his knees laughing and pointing his trumpet at John Lennon. "This here is a friend of mine, John Lennon."

John was helping himself to a cold drink behind the bar, "'Ello boys, how 'bout a soda pop?" Billy walked with his knees shaking, nearly falling down after tripping over a lawn chair. He took a bottle of orange soda from John Lennon, holding the bottle with both hands. He said in an almost unrecognizable voice, "You're John Lennon."

"So I am, so I am and over there young man is the father of jazz himself Louis Armstrong." Bill turned awkwardly and fell again with his bottle of orange soda.

Louis was giggling uncontrollably, "He really is a moron eh Jono?"

I apologized to Louis as I ran over to help Billy get up.

"Why did you tell this jazz guy I was a moron?"

"It's a long story."

"Well you're an asshole even if I promised not to call you that."

"It wasn't an insult my telling your nickname."

"I don't have a nickname! I let you get away with it because you're an asshole."

We both looked up to see Louis and John Lennon laughing at us.

John said, "You can always tell best friends when you see them."

Louis laughing responded, "That's right Johnny. Jono's Dad and I go way back and now I get to see his young boy all the time.

It's poetry in motion, you know what I mean?"

"Sure do. Paul and I carried on the same way until this fame thing got in the way. Now we argue more than we need to."

"It happens in every close band. I don't understand it, but I've seen it a thousand times."

"Hey where are the guys anyway?"

Louis laughing said, "I'm willing to bet anything Lucille got them to her cooking. It gets anyone who comes over."

Billy stood staring at the two music giants and casually whispered to me, "Did he say other guys?"

"I don't know, why?"

"One Beatle in person could make us the talk of the town, but more than one, I might have to have a heart attack."

I had to admit Billy had a point. The Beatles were the biggest sensation in music since Elvis Presley. I could not imagine that, even just for Louis, there were not a million reporters clogging the streets waiting to take photos and ask ridiculous questions.

I decided to ask Louis, "Excuse me Louis; I hope I'm not intruding, but if Lucille is cooking, we sure could use a bite to eat?"

"Of course you're hungry! No one intrudes on Louis, not Kings, Presidents or the FBI!" Both Louis and John laughed out loud as we were ushered in to the house through the kitchen door. At a round table in a room off the kitchen sat the remaining members of the most popular rock band on earth. Lucille was in the kitchen with all burners blazing away. She took one look at me and made such a fuss it was embarrassing.

"Jonathan!" she yelled hugging and rubbing my head. "Look who's here everyone! It's our friend Jonathan!" The Beatles, now assembled at the table including John, sat shaking their heads and smiling at me. Each one had full plates of food in front of them. "Ello Jonathan!" they each said in a way that made me think I was dreaming. She looked over at Billy, "And who do we have here?" Louis chimed in, "That's the famous Billy Moran Jonathan is always talking about!"

"Welcome Billy!" Lucille said giving him a hug that nearly knocked him over.

"Come on in here and get something to eat." She was thrilled to have so many guests. We sat on chairs so close to one another it was like we were sitting on one another's laps. George Harrison was discussing a recent trip to India where he said, "Everything is sacred if you respect where it comes from." Ringo had the best accent, even if they were all from the same place. He said, "Well George, if I knew everything was sacred I would have more girlfriends."

Everybody laughed and it seemed just like sitting with family for a big holiday dinner. Billy got past the shock and started talking a blue streak about his piano playing. Paul said, "We should get this lad in our band and make some music!" That had everyone smiling and I knew right away it would be a day Billy or I would never forget. Over the years I had sort of gotten used to Louis having people to his house. Sitting with The Beatles made me remember something Louis had told my father about fame and fortune. He said, "All these people you meet can see their names in lights every night of the week. But, they are not happy until all those lights burn out and they can sit with friends, smiling, laughing, joking and talking. Don't you ever forget it!"

Louis said something to Lucille in a whisper then casually went upstairs. She looked at me with a concerned look on her face; I knew instantly something was wrong. I went over to her, she asked me to go upstairs and check on Louis. I climbed the stairs listening to Billy and his new friends going on about the powers of music.

At the top of the stairs I hesitated, not wanting to disturb Louis if he had gone to take a nap. If he wasn't feeling like himself it was best to let him get the rest he needed. He always said to my father, "Everyone needs to know when to take themselves out of the game."

Louis traveled all over the world and when he came home he enjoyed seeing friends, most of all he liked taking some time to unwind. I looked in the bedroom and it was empty. I heard the beginnings of the song, "When You're Smiling", one of Louis's best songs. I tiptoed to his office at the end of the hallway. He was busy taking clippings from newspapers and magazines and taping them to his reel-to-reel boxes. It was form of meditation for Louis; he once told my Dad, "Frankie, those papers you leave me have the saddest stories I ever read. I cut out the words I like and turn them in to something that can make me smile." I had seen some of his finished tape boxes. Every one was unique and special to him. He noticed me standing in the doorway and gestured with his hand for me to join him. We were sitting in his music room, his private sanctuary. A new song started, "We Have All the Time in the World", and we sat listening to the song while I watched Louis meticulously placing words and pictures on his private canvases. There were hundreds of clippings cut out of magazines and newspapers from all over the world.

"Look at me smiling in that picture Jonathan! It's from Japan. I was never around so many happy people in my life. They love Jazz music and they love Louis."

I picked up the photo, which was part of an article I could

not read. Every word looked like stick figures. "It's written in Japanese. A man there interviewed me. Isn't it beautiful?" I shook my head, having never seen any language except English.

We sat listening to the music and he whispered, "Lucille asked you to check on me?"

"Yes sir, she told me to make sure you were resting."

"Let's keep this to ourselves. That woman worries herself too much. When you go downstairs you tell her I fell asleep."

"Won't she hear the music?"

Laughing and shaking his head, "You sure do know Lucille with her super hearing!"

"I don't want to lie to her."

"It will be our little secret Jonathan."

"Yes sir."

"Now start taping these words on that box right there."

"What should it say?"

"It says the truth! Louis Loving Life!"

We sat for a few minutes as I tried to place the words exactly the way Louis liked them. I told him I should let Lucille know he was fine. He agreed, but before dismissing me he said, "Those are fine young men down there. They came all the way from England to visit Louis."

"Yes sir."

"Yes, yes, yes, fine young boys. You know I knocked them out of the number one record slot?"

"Yes sir, with Hello Dolly!"

"That's right, Louis has still got it. Put those young rock stars back on their heels."

He was shaking his head saying "Yes, yes, yes", laughing and making an ordinary tape box in to a work of art. He looked at me as I got up to leave, "I hope those young men don't get themselves all carried away."

"Carried away sir?"

"You remember what I told you about fame and fortune?"

"Yes sir."

"It's worse than you can ever imagine today. Those fine young men are already losing the magic that made them in to the biggest names in music. I have seen it happen too many times. They are older than their years in some ways and younger than they will ever understand. That Johnny is a regular guy. I could see it in his eyes when we were in the yard. He loves music like I do and cannot get enough of it. I think he will be the one to know when to say enough is enough. Yup, he will know when to take himself out of the game. I pray he stays away when he discovers how happy daily life can really be. Listen to me preaching about such things! I cannot stay away from the music and the crowds. You know, innovators are men and women with something special who wake up one day to see they changed the world." I let Louis talk, having learned from my father what it was like to listen to a man praying out loud. I thanked Louis for letting me help him. I went downstairs to the sound of Louis playing somewhere Live, and The Beatles still in the kitchen laughing with Billy. Lucille met me at the bottom of the stairs. She was standing with her hands on her hips. She said, "He's making his collages and listening to music?"

I thought about trying to keep the secret like Louis asked me, but there was no fooling Lucille. I shook my head in agreement without saying a word.

"That man cannot rest." She walked back in to the kitchen. I decided to take the dog, General, out for a walk. I let her run free in the back yard. I heard a commotion out on the street. Lucille was hugging all four of the Beatles who thanked her for the best home cooked meal they'd ever had. A huge limousine pulled up in front of the house and they got in as I stood by the garage watching them leave. I let General scamper around the yard a little longer. I ran to the backdoor leading in to the kitchen, and the dog followed close behind. Once inside, the kitchen miraculously was fully cleaned; every dish put away and the counters bright and sparkling like no one had touched a thing. I heard the piano playing in the living room. It was Billy playing a song for Lucille. I knew Billy took lessons and every Thursday night he would play for his parents at Durows restaurant to the delight of the entire crowd. I stood in the hallway outside the living room thinking how people who can play a musical instrument are the luckiest people on earth. When the song ended Lucille applauded. I entered the room knowing just what to say; "That wasn't half bad for a moron."

"Hey!"

"Now boys don't go breaking the spell of this special day."

We both laughed and I went so far as to pat Billy on the back saying, "Good job."

We thanked Lucille and asked her to let Louis know we appreciated their hospitality.

On the way back to the train Billy and I did not talk much.

I wanted to ask him a million questions about his chatting with John, Paul, George and Ringo. Instead, we walked in silence most of the way mentioning a few times,

"What a day huh?"

"Yup, what a day."

We had seen Willie Mays play the outfield for the Giants

during the afternoon. Every step he took was like seeing a star shining in broad daylight. We had visited Louis Armstrong and met the biggest rock band on earth. It was night fall when we got off the train. We stood waiting for a bus that would take us back to Real. Waiting for the bus we both knew we could never tell anyone about what happened.

Billy said it first, "No one would ever believe us."

Chapter Ten

We had a ritual for meeting in the park. It wasn't planned, just a habit we had fallen into, as friends sometimes do. Billy always managed to be waiting before I arrived. He lived three blocks away from the park; but I lived just across the street. He told me something his father had once said about corporate people and getting to work on time. He said, "People who live the closest get to work last." We discussed this detail at length for days. One morning, I arrived to find Billy sitting on our park bench reading the Daily News, enjoying jelly donuts and a cup of coffee. The Real Bakery was on the corner across from the basketball court. On mornings when I did not help my father deliver the papers he brought home rolls, donuts and the best damn crumb cake ever made. Billy was reading the paper and stuffing jelly donuts in his mouth like they were his last meal.

"Slow down man, you're eating like there's no tomorrow!"

"They should bottle smells."

"What smells?"

"Every smell, but more than any other, the smell of a bakery when you first enter it in the morning."

"You scare me sometimes."

"I'm serious, nothing else in the world smells like a bakery in the morning."

I sat watching him eating his jelly donuts. I thought about what he said and could not disagree. "You know, on mornings when my Dad brings home breakfast from the bakery, the smell fills the hallways and then it lingers in the entire apartment. The smell drifts through each room and with the smell of fresh made coffee, it is a nice smell."

"I told you. If they could bottle that smell people would be happier."

"Why do you think that is, Billy?"

"What?"

"Smelling and feeling good?"

"It's the five senses, sight, taste, and hearing, touching and smelling. I have been sitting here now waiting for you and thinking about it."

"What time do you get here? I live right across the street and I never get here before you!"

"Today, I got here at 6:30. I saw your Dad at the bakery. He paid for my breakfast."

"He didn't say a thing about it to me."

"Yeah well we got to talking about last night's Yankee game. He sure does know his baseball."

"They can't get a break these days. When was the last time they won a game?"

"You see that's what I said and he set me straight."

"How?"

He said, "It's not the result as much as the game itself. I thought about that too while sitting here. I get angry when they lose. I look to blame the hitting; the pitching. It's the manager's fault. But you know something, it's not the game as much as it is, I don't know he said it so perfectly."

"He gets upset sometimes too. And then he almost watches each pitch like it was a moment in time. It gets weird you know? It's like everything happening in every day life can be forgotten. Louis once said he got that way when he played his horn. Everyone needs something to keep them happy."

"Yup, baseball, music and jelly donuts."

"You cannot put jelly donuts in the same league as baseball and music."

"Why not?"

"It's not equal."

"Who says?"

"I say, anyone would say so."

"Then you don't know what you're talking about."

The Real Bakery was on the corner of 80th Street and Myrtle Avenue. It was a staple of the neighborhood. Marty Gaston worked at the bakery. He was a friend of ours and we hardly ever saw him because he practically lived at the bakery. Sometimes we would sit on a concrete wall across from the bakery and marvel at the things Marty had to do. He would sweep up the sidewalk or shovel the snow in the winter. He would carry loads of supplies off a truck and in through a side door.

"Some day he's going to be the owner of that bakery."

"Why would he want to own a bakery?"

"Maybe he's addicted to the jelly donuts?"

"I doubt it. Maybe he likes what he does?"

"Sweeping and carrying boxes? Who enjoys that?"

"He's been at it for quite some time."

As we sat there that morning I said, "Maybe he's addicted to the smell?"

"Who?"

"Marty Gaston."

"Maybe we should ask him?"

"He would never admit it."

"What do you mean?"

"No one owns up to their addictions."

"We're talking jelly donuts and the aroma of fresh baked cookies, not heroin Billy."

"It's the same thing."

"What! First you compare baseball and music to jelly donuts, now you say the same thing about heroin?"

"You hate it when I'm right."

"No I hate it when you're crazy!"

"It makes perfect sense and you know it."

"Maybe, they really are good jelly donuts."

Billy sat reading the paper. He decided to read out loud a few stories he found interesting. Some of the stories made you wonder about the world.

"Did you hear the new Gibson Stratocaster album?"

"No. Why?"

"It says here it's the best record released since Pet Sounds by The Beach Boys."

"That's some guys' opinion and besides, nothing will ever be better than Pet Sounds."

"Yeah you might be right. But this record sounds like we should hear it."

"What's the article say about it?"

Billy liked when I asked him to read something out loud.

"Gibson Stratocaster and The Chords have hit pay dirt again. Their second album brings to the surface a unique sound that only this band can make. It is not so much a record as a novel with music. Gibson Stratosphere, who's real name is Ira Schwartz, writes lyrics that touch upon our modern world. Each song is reminiscent of the sound of waves crashing on a beach, honking car horns, thunderstorms; the best and most unique being a twelve minute conversation between band members about watching different things. The title of the album "Watching Different Things" is brought to a climax when the title song leaps in to the foray of jazz oriented guitar licks and drum solos. The songs on this record challenge the listener to find different things interesting that we might take for granted everyday. The first single, "Flag Poles" is a tour de force of lyrical brilliance. In the song, Gibson Stratocaster and The Chords may well have written an anthem that defines our nation's current chaos."

"Their last album wasn't that special."

"Yeah but maybe a band needs to work things out before reaching a masterpiece."

"You haven't even heard the record and you're declaring it a masterpiece!"

"It says here the record will change your life."

"That's the problem with you Billy; you can't believe everything you read."

"I'm going to buy it and I won't let you hear it!"

"Good. You'll be changed and I will stay the same."

"I'm going right now to buy it."

"Where?"

"Like there are a million places to go? Action Records of course."

"I'll go with you."

"I'm telling you you're not listening to it with me."

"Fine."

Action Records was a record store on Myrtle Avenue. To get there you needed to take a bus or walk about five miles. Billy was in the mood for a walk and I tagged along. On our way we discussed music and the audacity of some music critics to declare anything the best they had ever heard.

"How can you say something is the best if you haven't heard everything to compare it to?"

"Music critics hear everything. They know about these things."

"Impossible! Take Louis for example, he's the best that ever lived but that doesn't mean everyone who wants a jazz record is running out to buy his music."

"It's the sound man, you can't ask people to like everything they hear."

"So how can a critic say a record is the best ever made?"

"It's a figure of speech; and besides, he can say whatever he wants."

"That's my point! I can hear something you completely enjoy and hate it!"

"It only proves you're deaf."

"You can't stand to admit that a critic is just someone with an opinion and a place to share it."

"I'll give you that. But, there are times when they are right."

"Billy? The article is saying a record released today is better than Pet Sounds by The Beach Boys. You told me a hundred times that's the best record ever made."

"So you can see why I need to hear anything that someone says is better."

"You mean you're not buying it because you're a fan? You're curious?"

"Maybe."

"It is amazing, don't you think, that curiosity can make people do things?"

"Like what?"

"You name it! People seem to be doing a lot of stupid things these days."

"For example?"

"Like last night for example, I couldn't sleep so I took the dog for a walk in the park. Over near the park house the park boys were making quite a racket. The police came a few times and the park boys scattered in to the woods behind the swings. As soon as the police left, they were back at doing what ever it is they do. I was by the ball field so I could see them but they couldn't see me. I noticed the park boys were chasing a bunch of girls with water balloons. The park girls were getting drenched from those balloons. I was sitting on the bench. I always let my dog off the leash so she can run free. I was watching my dog enjoying its freedom and taking glances over at the park house. A bunch of the girls came running over to the water fountain near the ball field. They were wringing their clothes dry and cursing up a storm. Two girls helped one of the others jump up on to the water fountain. She was straddling the water fountain while the others helped her stay up there. She removed her panties and started urinating in to a balloon. They were giggling so loudly my dog ran over and they didn't even notice. They must have been drunk or on something I guess, because each one of them did the same thing until they had a half dozen balloons filled with urine. They snuck around the back to the park house and I heard the splashing sounds of those balloons. Those park boys must have been pissed. Excuse my pun."

"You saw this happen?"

"Like I said, people do all kinds of stupid things these days."

"That's not stupid. That's disgusting!"

"Yeah well, revenge is a bitch."

Entering Action Records was like escaping in to another world. The latest hit albums were always hanging on little frames that hung from the ceiling. At the back of the store the owner stayed behind a counter that was filled with an assortment of records and stacks of spindles used to put into the holes on 45rpms so they could be played on your turntable. I mentioned to Billy as we rummaged through the various racks of albums looking for the latest Gibson Stratocaster and The Chords record, "Someone should package the smell of vinyl records." He nodded his head in agreement. After briefly taking in the smell, any self respecting music fan would become quiet. The search for music was the equivalent to getting lost in a forest while looking for the perfect tree. We could spend hours lost in a record store, at times whispering in reverence when finding something special: "Have you heard this one?" The music playing in Action Records that afternoon was something we had not heard. Several times I caught Billy looking up at the front counter and then over at me in a silent nod of recognition. Asking the guy behind the counter what was playing always went one of two ways. If the guy was in the mood to talk he would tell you everything you needed to know about a certain record. If he was into the record he might turn into a raving lunatic saying "You haven't heard this record? What right do you have coming in to my store if you don't even know this record?" Billy and I were enjoying the record being played, and one of us was going to need to ask the guy behind the counter about it. Billy went through the racks, holding each record in front of him like he was reading the most important document ever written. I was doing the same thing in the jazz section, which I realized was like visiting the adult section in a book store. I caught the guy behind the counter looking at me as I held up copies of Louis' records, studying them for comments and pictures. I held up a copy of Kind Of Blue by Miles Davis and the guy behind the counter yelled over the music "Be careful with that!" I put it back in to the rack and looked over at Billy who was smirking. Billy was looking at Beatles records, which annoyed me because he already had everything they did, and some of them five or six copies. I asked him once why he looked at records he already had. He looked at me as if I were crazy, saying, "You don't know anything about record collecting, do you? There might be a song released on one record that they didn't put on another, or there might be a defect on the cover that makes it so special that its better than finding the Holy Grail." I let Billy have his way while I looked through a rack of records that were labeled "One Dollar Specials." Sometimes the best records could be found in a rack filled with albums no one else liked or wanted. I heard Billy ask the guy behind the counter, "Excuse me, can you tell me what record is playing?" There was a silence as I looked over my shoulder to see what kind of response Billy was going to get. The guy looked down at Billy from the counter and took a deep breath. "Son, you're listening to the best record ever made in these parts since I first heard music emanating from my dear mother's radio when I was a little boy. She kept that radio on the kitchen counter in our small apartment over the Schwab's drug store on Sunset Boulevard. It was her only companion because my father was a working man and a quiet man. I sometimes think the voices on that radio were the only people she could talk to. Ah, my dear mother was a fine lass. One day she says to me, "Jimmie me boy, when all else fails there's always music." And here I am now, my dear young man, behind a counter in a record store surrounded by the voices that were my mother's best friends." I watched Billy's facial expression, which was something caught between awe and shock. Billy nodded his head and smiled. The guy behind the counter was no where near finished. It was quite obvious that Billy had caught him between a tender moment and a memory he wanted to share. I asked Louis once if he visited record stores to check out how his albums were selling, and he laughed, telling me most of what he wanted he could get from his business partners and other musicians. Louis did tell me something that stayed in my mind as I watched Billy listening to the sermon from the guy behind the record store counter. Louis said, "A lot of record store people may be aliens from outer space. They know things no one else could possibly ever know about music and mostly everything else. If there ever comes a time that there are no more record stores, you rest assure the government found out about these aliens and think the world a better place for it. Only thing is, there are good aliens and bad aliens and I do not want to live in a world without good aliens who live in record stores and believe they can save the world." Watching Billy staring at the guy behind the counter and then at the man himself, I was convinced Louis was right. This guy did not have any human-like features common to the rest of us. His eyes blinked non-stop like he was receiving instructions from another place and time. His arms seemed capable of handling more things than mere humans could do in a single gesture. They were holding records and moving around his head in a way that made him look strange. He casually placed sunglasses on while holding everything and talking at the same time. I was convinced he knew I was on to him. He glanced in my direction without missing a beat in his story. It made me aware that sometimes asking a person in a record store was like asking for a testimonial in a place of worship. "Me dear mother had few friends. That radio on the counter and little things me brothers and sisters could do for her to make life easier. There were eight of us and that never stopped me mother from caring for each of us in a special way." Billy took a sideways glance to see if I was witnessing everything.

The guy behind the counter continued, "Me mother was an angel. I now know in me heart she was sent here to save us. I profoundly forgive all her transgressions. It was not her fault with the upbringing she experienced. So she relied a tad heavily on the liquor at times. Me father did not give her much time or notice. …. She was most happy when that radio played something that rescued her from the world. One year me brothers and sisters put what little money we could from panhandling and singing on the corner to buy her a new radio. A fine radio it was, bigger than the one she had but do you want to know something strange? She never opened that new radio. It stayed in its box until the day she died. She dusted the box like it was a fine piece of furniture. Any one who visited would get the same story. She would hold up that box and say "Did you see what my children gave me for Christmas?" Twenty two years of me brothers and sisters buying her things and that boxed radio was the treasure she could not forget." The guy behind the counter turned away for a moment as if to wipe something from his eyes. When he turned around he was holding an album. It was Gibson Stratocaster and The

Chords "Watching Different Things." Billy looked over at me and I felt my jaw drop. The guy behind the counter said, "This record will change your life. You can read about it in today's paper. The guy who wrote the article quotes me."

Billy took the album from the guy behind the counter. He held it in his hands after looking at the front cover. There were no words on the front cover. There was a black and white photograph of Schwab's Pharmacy. The script for the word "Schwab's" was beautiful. There were two small windows on each side of the store's front door. In each small window, nearly unrecognizable, were the words "Watching Different Things" and in the other "Gibson Stratocaster and The Chords." There were crowds of people in front of the store, each of the pictured men were smiling. On the back cover, also in black and white, was a photo showing a bunch of people inside the drugstore standing around as if they were at a party. Billy paid the guy behind the counter and we left, feeling in some way that we had discovered the best album ever made. We looked at the front and back cover all the way home, trying to figure out if there were hidden meanings.

"It's a statement about the times, Billy", I said after studying the back cover.

"How so?"

"You know sex, drugs, rock and roll."

He grabbed the album from me, asking how I got that from an old 1940s photo.

"It's easy man, Gibson Stratocaster is saying how once upon a time we could all assemble at one time in a drug store like it was party place and now everything is behind the counter hidden from us. All our freedoms are being slowly taken away from us. We are all watching different things while being told we need to watch the same things or we are not welcomed by society."

"You got that from this picture?"

"And the lyrics to the songs we heard in the record store. Weren't you listening?"

"I was too busy listening to the preacher behind the counter."

"Well I was listening to the songs at the same time and man if Gibson hasn't created some kind of biblical statement about the times."

"Like what?"

"I'll have to spend some time with the album alone, but I heard a line from a song that goes "When you think you know what you want, you're half way there to getting it."

"What song is that in?"

"I don't know. I'll have to spend time with it alone."

"Yeah well you're not borrowing my copy."

"Of course not, I have to have my own copy. Some things you have to hold knowing they belong only to you."

"I'm not walking back there with you."

"I think this record requires I spend some time alone."

"You really are strange when it comes to music, Jono."

"Yeah, I'm always watching different things."

"My parents are going to love this album cover."

"My parents too, maybe that's another thing Gibson is trying to say?"

"What's that?"

"It's all the same even when it is different. The people on this cover are from another era but they all seem happy about what it is they are doing. They are doing nothing, except being with one another and enjoying life. Maybe that's the secret message from the record?"

"Are you going back there today?"

"I need to get $3.99 from my mom for the record."

"You better hurry, it might be sold out."

"How come we haven't heard about this album on the radio?"

"Even deejays can't listen to everything."

"But they're supposed to know about records that can change your life."

"Yeah well, their lives might not need changing; and besides, lately they have to play what the sponsors tell them to."

"Do you think that will change? The deejays not being able to play what they please?"

"I think it will get worse. Some day there just might be so much choice but everything will be packaged in a way that no one really will have a way of finding anything."

"That would be pretty bad."

"Yeah, imagine too much choice being a bad thing?"

"Diversity made in to a curse. That's crazy."

"Welcome to the modern world, Kidd."

We walked and talked about a record we had not yet really heard. There was a curiosity about finding something we both felt needed further investigation. I told Billy I would see him in the morning and I ran the rest of the way, asking my mother for $3.99 to buy a record that promised to change my life. She told me I had to take out the garbage and clean my room. I never did those chores with such gusto before in my life. She handed me a crisp five dollar bill, telling me to bring home the change. I went back to Action Records right before the guy behind the counter started to close up for the day. I walked in and right up to the counter and asked for Gibson Stratocaster and The Chords' new album. He looked down at me from the counter smiling. He said, "I knew you would be back."

I took the copy of the record and held it under my arm as I paid for it. I walked home quickly, wanting to spend as much time as possible with a record that promised to change my life.

Chapter Eleven

It was a June morning, and school would end in a few short weeks. I was preparing for the big visit to Louis's house because my Dad said – "Louis says his birthday is on the 4th of July!" It was just like Louis to decide his birthday was on a day when there were fireworks going off in the sky and celebrations with barbeques. I couldn't wait to get over to Louie's house and celebrate. Lucille looked worried. A princess should always smile, I thought that day. My father went upstairs to talk with Louis. I stood around with so many people; all of them looked worried. I thought, "It's the 4th of July! Why is everyone so sad? Sure enough, Louis's voice came howling down the stairs. He descended the stairs on a chair waving and smiling. People started to pep up and soon enough Lucille was bringing in food from the kitchen and the music was blaring in every room. It was the best 4th of July ever! My father drove my Mom, my brother and me home after staying long enough to watch the fireworks going off in the night skies over Corona, Queens. He did not talk much. I wanted to ask him what was wrong. Usually when we left Louie's he was talking so much and laughing it was like listening to the happiest man on earth.

On July 6th, it came over the radio. It was on the front page of all the newspapers. My father did not talk about it. The newspaper bundles that night were never so heavy. I threw them off the truck and my father kept quiet. My Dad had lost a friend who was a friend to everyone who got to know him. My Dad was a friend of the Father of Jazz. I was his son along for the ride.

Chapter Twelve

Local heroes fall in to obscurity like the changing of store fronts and street names over time. There were a few people it turns out who recognized we had an actual music hero in Real. A larger number of people cared less whether he became a household name or a flash in the pan. Billy and I liked Gibson Stratocaster records because he wrote songs about the places we knew and visited every day. The fact that Ira Schwartz never reached radio royalty by having one of his songs appear in the Top 40 did not matter to us. His band was pure rock and roll. So pure it could not be tainted by popularity. When we chose to listen to music without outside interference, meaning the radio or television – just us and our turntables or cassette players, most times we would inevitably play something by Gibson Stratocaster and The Chords. During a time when it was sacrilegious to mix songs by The Beatles, The Stones, The Who, The Kinks with an unknown artist like Gibson Stratocaster, a few FM stations would challenge every thing considered musically acceptable. It was Ben Kelsa who had the audacity to invite Gibson Stratocaster and The Chords on his overnight radio show. Maybe because it was after midnight and most people were asleep, on his one and only radio concert Gibson Stratocaster played one of the best shows no one may have heard.

In his best "look what I found" voice, Ben Kelsa introduced Gibson and his band mates that night with the fanfare of having discovered the saviors of rock and roll. I taped the show feeling I was capturing rock history.

Ben always started his radio shows with an obscure jazz song. It was always a song that somehow set the tone for what was to happen throughout the night. On the night of the best concert no one heard, Ben Kelsa started his show with Jitterbug Waltz by The Charles Mingus Sextet. Ben shared the significance of his choice before saying, Ladies and gentleman, I have found the future of rock and roll and his name is Gibson Stratocaster. For the next hour without commercials, Gibson Stratocaster and the Chords rocked on like they were playing for their lives. They opened with a song from their first album, Down in the Cemetery Holes; which, if anyone was listening to the lyrics, knew was about Harry Houdini's grave located in the heart of Real, New York. In between songs Ben interviewed the band:

Ben – You guys do not have an actual recording contract?

Gibson – I think we are a band before our time.

Ben – What do you mean?

Gibson – We play for the love of the music and don't require recognition.

Ben – How do you expect to survive without getting paid?

Gibson – Bohemians don't rely on cash.

Ben – (laughing) You have to eat!

Gibson – We all live with our folks, so we do eat.

Harold – (the drummer) Occasionally.

Ben – So you're not starving artists?

Sam – (bass player) I wouldn't say we're starving, malnourished maybe.

Ben – (laughing) Just a diet of Twinkies and Yoo-Hoo?

Gibson – Some days if we're lucky its hot dogs and orange soda.

Ben – I have a copy of your album on cassette. Are their actual LPs available?

Gibson – No. I record our music exclusively on tape.

Harold – We all know at any moment we can be erased. Vinyl is too permanent.

Ben – (laughing) I was listening to Down in the Cemetery Hole, off your first album. Is that a personal experience you refer to in the song?

Gibson – Everything happened in Real for a reason, Ben.

Ben – So I can quote you as having actually fallen in love with a statue of Harry Houdini's wife?

Gibson – It's all on the record.

Ben – That is without doubt a very strange confession!

Gibson – Rock and Roll Ben.

Ben – I've done my research and I discovered Gibson Stratocaster is not your real name?

Gibson – Real names are tied very closely to parental roots, which is what rock and roll is against.

Ben – So you don't want me to tell the listening audience your real name?

Gibson – It doesn't matter since no one knows me one way or another.

Ben – (laughing) So if I say, Ira – what's it like being a rock and roll star?

Gibson (laughing) I might fall down laughing.

Ben – Can you play us another song?

Gibson – It would be our pleasure. ONE TWO THREE FOUR!

Ben Kelsa was true to his word that night. He did not over extend his knowledge of music or try to exploit an unknown band. He even sang along with the band on their song "What Goes Round Comes Round." In my bedroom I too sang along with full throttle abandonment. I woke up my mother, who was none too pleased to hear me singing –

No one knows me
The way that you do
I'm right here for you
Like a song on the radio
You taught me a lesson
When you said goodbye
Now it's you and your broken heart
How does it feel to know?
What goes round comes around."

My mother did not expect to find me standing on my bed at 3am holding a hairbrush like a microphone with my eyes closed and singing as loud as I could. She did not utter the usual lines that accompanied my antics: Wait till your father gets home.

Instead, to her credit she waited until the song was over. I opened my eyes to see her standing in my doorway with her arms folded. She said, Are you finished?

I stepped down from the bed trying to apologize without saying a word. I had a cassette player which did not have a recording feature. To capture the show that night I had to put a microphone up to the speakers of my stereo. On the cassette for years to come whenever I played it I could hear our conversation in-between the last song by Gibson Stratocaster and The Chords; which was never released anywhere else as far as I know. The song was entitled, "Have Mercy on a Poor Soldier's Heart." Over the lyrics which went: "It's my choice / I don't expect you to understand / I want to do my part / Have mercy on a poor soldier's heart", you could hear my mother and I talking.

Mom – Is that my hairbrush?
Me – I think so.
Mom – You're not spitting on it?
Me – I hope not.
Mom – Is this almost over?
Me – I don't know.
Mom – You have school in the morning.
Me – I'll turn it down.
Mom – Good night.

My mother understood about things without really understanding what it was she understood. Most parents are pushed to the brink of their patience during a time of change. I did turn down the stereo and because I was recording it, the remaining part of the concert no one heard is less audible. The hiss on the tape makes the remainder of that night's history making event hard to hear. A few weeks later while helping my Dad deliver the newspapers, after the headlines had detailed the death of a jazz king who was my father's friend; there was a small article about Gibson Stratocaster being drafted. The article said; Ira Schwartz, lead singer of little known local band Gibson Stratocaster and The Chords was drafted in to the Army. His final concert was aired on the Ben Kelsa show last week. He never mentioned he had been drafted. His final song that night was "Have Mercy on a Poor Soldier's Heart." I played that tape for many nights after reading the article. Ira Schwartz never became a household name. He was wounded shortly after getting to Vietnam. In an interview with Ben Kelsa on a show that aired almost a year to the date after the concert no one heard, Ira Schwartz, confined to a wheelchair for the remainder of his life, told Ben, "I would be dead except the bullet that hit me in the chest was stopped by a harmonica I had in my shirt pocket." I never heard or saw another article about Ira Schwartz or his namesake Gibson Stratocaster. One night while sitting in the park I was playing the cassette copy of the concert no one heard. A man walking with a limp came by with his dog. He calmly passed me while I sat on a bench. He stopped for a brief moment and looked at me. Before leaving the park he came over to where I was sitting and said, "Best damn concert no one ever heard." He walked down the stairs and disappeared before I could realize who he might have been. In retrospect I like to think Gibson Stratocaster is alive and well, out walking his dog after midnight.

Chapter Thirteen

Billy's father said one day, "Each person survives his or her storm differently." Billy and I looked at one another, not certain we understood the meaning. The decade of the 1970s would prove to be the most enduring and life changing decade of our young lives.

It began quietly enough, and then things started to happen which some may consider spiraling out of control, or as we saw it – a step out of time.

We played organized ball for the first time. The bar leagues proved to be our introduction in to the adult world. We played softball for a bar called "Mike's Tavern." The team's owner was a seven-foot tall German man named "Mike." He loved his ball players. The team members were a group of men and boys who could easily have been cast in a movie defining the era.

Billy was our pitcher, with a delivery because of his size and shape that drove batters crazy. The ball seemed to leave his hands from another dimension. Batters would swing at the ball and miss at the last moment. Billy Moran became known through out the league as a secret weapon.

Catching was a kid from the neighborhood named Pete Trent. He was introduced to me as "The Boob." Being accustomed to the affection associated with nicknames, I shook his hand when we met saying "How's it going, Boob?" I did not know I was being set up for a practical joke as no one ever called him by this nickname out loud. From the beginning there would be bad blood between us. At first base, Dickie Blues played with an abandonment that bordered on insanity. As I said before, Dickie was someone Billy and I knew from the neighborhood. It was his idea for us to join the team. At second base, Bryan Folly was ten years older, in his late 20s. He carried a comb on to the field, more interested at times with how he looked than how he played.

At third base, my brother, Hank – whose real name was Frank, but for some reason everyone called him Abdul, played with perhaps the only real athletic talent on the team. At shortstop was another older generation character named Joe Friday. He had more women watching him play than any matinee idol. He shared the position with a cousin my brother and I only saw occasionally, Jimmy Trailer. Jimmy, like my brother, had natural talent and only showed up when his other team on Long Island did not have a game. I played leftfield and I am probably remembered as the guy who made circus catches. It was usually because I was actually too slow to reach the ball in time. I would catch up to the ball by leaping or jumping awkwardly. The owner loved it. In centerfield was Albert A. No one knew Albert's last name; it was rumored he was once in jail for chasing his wife with an axe. It was a strange comfort knowing we had an *almost axe* murderer playing center field. In right field, there was Roland Gunner. He played with the most intensity of any one I had ever seen. He would grit his teeth throughout the game, smashing the ball when at bat and running with awesome speed. At the end of each game blood would cover his lips and teeth from the pressure he placed on himself. In softball, there are ten players. Someone who was usually chosen to fill in the gap behind second base played the tenth position. The choice for this position was always up in the air at game time for our team. On occasion, it was played by someone we did not know or in keeping with it being a bar league, any drunk that showed up to watch would find himself with a glove, standing behind second base.

It was after a game played on a Sunday afternoon in August of 1972 that Billy and I would be introduced to someone who would haunt us and enchant us for the remainder of our lives. After a game, it was customary to return to the home team's bar and "empty the keg." Most of us on the team had never drunk beer or any other alcoholic beverage. Watching some of the older players drink mug after mug of beer was awe-inspiring. After our first game, we returned to Mike's Tavern and were immediately introduced to the cast of characters that made up the bar scene. We never imagined that a bar maid could become the fantasy figure of every one standing around watching her move gracefully up and down the bar. We never imagined that people could sit in the same place and drink themselves in to a state of oblivion. We never imagined that a jukebox could become the center of attention for so many strangers, turning them into both life long friends and babbling idiots. Billy and I normally did not drink, but on the first day we did decide, out of courtesy, to toast our first victory. Our team had a nickname; we were called the Jagermeisters. A "jagermeister" was German liquor that tasted like licorice. The owner of the team would start a chant, and every one in the bar would down a small glass of this horrible tasting liquor.

He would stand on the bar – all seven feet tall, making him look in our growing condition of intoxication like Thor! He would hold his shot glass erect, nearly touching the ceiling of the bar and shout:

"Zig-a-zagger – Zig-a-zagger"

Everyone in the bar holding their glasses aloft above their heads would yell in reply:

"OY! OY! OY!"

He would repeat the chant even louder a second time!

"Zig-a-zagger – Zig-a-zagger"

The bar would respond in loud response:

"OY! OY! OY!"

This would continue until the entire bar was a crowd of raving lunatics.

In unison everyone would down the shot glass of "jagermeister" screaming in harmony and half disgust – "YEAH!"

It being our first game and first victory, the celebration was an extended one. Billy and I lost track of time and space. At one point Billy went to the bathroom, and I heard him screaming above the crowd, "HEY JONO! IT'S COMING OUT WHITE!" The madness continued until it was proclaimed we had indeed finished the keg of beer. To which the owner tapped another keg and the celebration continued. Billy and I, in some semblance of child-parent allegiance, realized we needed to get home. It was the latest we had ever stayed out in our lives. Walking back, or should I say stumbling back through the park, we sang at the top of our lungs and laughed harder than we would ever laugh again.

Chapter Fourteen

We stumbled our way home to Billy's house after running partially and falling down numerous times. We exited on to Myrtle Avenue after laughing our way through "Freedom Road" which was a small patch of highway that connected our neighborhood with Richmond Hill where Mike's Tavern resided. Once on the avenue, we tried to assemble a story to tell Billy's parents explaining why we were so late getting home.

The story was, in our state of mind, ingenious.

Billy's mother as expected was standing on the steps of his house looking for him to come home. Billy's father was in the house, later telling us – "the rite of passage for every man requires freedom." We first took this to mean he knew we had stumbled our way from the bar by making our way on Freedom Road. It was a shared secret for the remainder of his father's life, how much wisdom could be held without leaving the comfort of his home.

This is what Billy's mother said to us as we tried desperately to walk as straight as possible down his block: **"YOU BETTER HAVE A GOOD EXCUSE MISTER FOR GIVING ME A HEART ATTACK!"**

We did not know she had been sick and could not imagine our being missing for a few hours could cause her any pain. Billy's mother, standing all of 4'8" was looking at us with more concern than anyone we had ever seen. We had devised our story and were committed to using it, but we never anticipated that her questions would lead us towards introducing someone into our lives that we would never forget.

"JUST WHAT DO YOU HAVE TO SAY FOR YOURSELF, MISTER?" Mrs. Moran stood with her hands on her hips, her foot stomping. Her stance made us find the level of sobriety needed to hide our condition.

Billy spoke first, carefully enunciating his words so as to sound sincere and sorry.

"Mom, we had no idea it was this late." The second the words left his lips; I knew he had opened a can of worms.

"No one had a watch! There were no clocks anywhere?" I had anticipated the reply and was ready for an explanation. I took a deep breath, praying quietly to myself that my voice would speak in unison with my thoughts, "Mrs. Moran, it was my fault."

This time Billy was readying himself for his mother's response.

"How could it be your fault? Did you twist his arm to stay out all night?"

Billy jumped in immediately replying, "Ma, we thought we were getting a ride."

This was not a planned response. The statement took me by surprise, realizing I had no rehearsed line to add. His mother for a moment seemed stumped by the answer, and for a brief second there was a silence that made me aware of the pounding sensation in my brain.

She took a step back and looked at me, then at Billy. After what felt like an eternity, she asked in a calm voice: "Someone promised to give you a ride?"

I could not believe it, Billy had found a way to make it sound like it was someone's fault besides his or mine. It was a stroke of genius. The hesitation as to which of us should reply took longer than either of us could imagine. Billy broke the silence –

"Ma, we won our first game today, and we had no idea how we were going to get home. This guy promised to give us a ride. He never showed up, so we had to walk through the park at this late hour."

It was a mouthful of white lies unlike anything I had ever heard before. The fact that in a few seconds we would be telling the biggest lie of our lives never occurred to us. Billy's mother appeared sympathetic standing on her stoop at nearly 4'o'clock in the morning with birds starting to sing in the trees around us.

"Who would make such a promise and leave two young boys out in the middle of the night?" Somehow, we both knew the storm had passed from us on to an unnamed, (and until that moment, unknown) person.

As I write this, I must confess the following exchange of information may have been turned around. I honestly forget whether it was Billy who spoke first, or if it was I. In either case, we were about to invent an individual who as I said would become a part of our lives forever. Billy's mother looked at me, and then at Billy. "I want to know who would promise my son a ride home and then choose to not show up." Her foot began to stomp again and her hands on her hips became more pronounced. We had to think fast and we had to be certain we both agreed before giving our answer.

I said a name, looking to silence her inquisition, "Bob."

That was my contribution.

It should have been enough; she could now forever hold "Bob" in contempt for causing her so much concern and nearly giving her a heart attack.

But, Mrs. Moran stood with a look of growing impatience. The next question from her lips, and Billy's response, would be the one word that would stay with us until we were old and gray.

I apologize, I am certain now – it was Billy who invented both our nemesis and our greatest friend. He reared back a step, clutching at my arm so as to not fall down and said:

"Googenblatt, Bob Googenblatt."

I can still feel my eyes searching the side of my head thinking how in the world, in our condition he could come up with a name like "Googenblatt."

Even now, as I write and expect you the reader to fathom such an event with belief, I think, "Why didn't he say, Smith – Jones – anything but Gooogenblatt."

But "Googenblatt" it was and in retrospect, it had to be. The name seemed to catch his mother off guard. She had never heard of such a name in her life. Her pose on the steps of Billy's house seemed to relax. She was happy to see her son was alive and well. She took a step down closer to us both standing at the front gate and told us: "I am going to have a thing or two to tell this Bob Googenblatt when I meet him."

Our plight for this night was over. The worst had passed. The inquisition had ended. We were free to move on. Billy's mother came down the stairs and hugged him. She reached up and rubbed my head. "Are you going to be alright walking home alone?" she said with a concerned voice. I nodded my head and stepped back away from the fence. I watched Billy's mother with her arm around him usher him up the stoop into their house. I walked the three blocks to my house, aware that I no longer had a headache. It was a strange and glorious day. Billy Moran and I had survived our introduction in to the world of adult indulgences; we had drunk ourselves blind, and walked it off. We had found a friend named Bob Googenblatt who was more real than anyone we actually could see with our own eyes. Our lives would never be the same.

Chapter Fifteen

In the early years of the 1970s, Billy Moran and I played ball, went to high school and talked bout our friend Bob Googenblatt. When I visited Billy's house his mother would ask how Bob Googenblatt was doing. As time went on, we invented a life, giving him not only credibility but also legendary status. We decided Bob went away to college. This allowed us the freedom to never have him meet anyone. Bob Googenblatt went away to college in Anchorage, Alaska. He was studying marine biology. We told Billy's mother one day that he was teaching penguins to spy for the military.

"Did you hear that, honey", she yelled from the kitchen to Mr. Moran," Bob Googenblatt is working with the military." She was as proud as any mother would be. It got to be more than a game because secretly we suspected Billy's Dad was on to us. One day we decided to make Bob more real than a conversation. Both of us sat down at the typewriter his father used and wrote a letter from Bob Googenblatt to Billy. This is what the letter said:

Dear Billy,

It has been awhile since I have been home. You would not

believe how cold it can get here in Anchorage. One day I took off my ski mask and sneezed – my face froze to the ground! The police had to come and chop away the ice from my nose. I was out talking with the Penguin Pack, which is the name of our secret service group and I swear this one Penguin I'm training started talking. I am the first one to reach this level of communication. Everyone was so pleased. The President might fly up here and pin a medal on me. If I have to fly down to the White House, I will call you and Kidd and maybe you can come see me meet the President. I am not allowed to communicate often, as what we are doing is Top Secret. Please only tell people who you really trust about where I am and what I am doing. I am not allowed to tell my own parents where I am and what I am doing. I know I can trust you. Tell Kidd I heard about his joining the Army. Is he sure that's what he wants to do after getting out of High School? I have to go and feed the Penguins, they get real upset if you're late. Take care and stay warm!
All the best,
Bob Googenblatt
C.A.H. Road
Anchorage, Alaska

We read the letter out loud a few times. After the fifth read through we were so convinced of its authenticity we promised to write more letters as often as possible. Even the address was a stroke of genius as far as Billy and I was convinced.

C.A.H. seemed very official. It stood for Cold As Hell.

We took a bus and mailed the letter from a different neighborhood. It was genius! The letter arrived and Billy made certain to tear it open in front of his mother. We had rehearsed the reading so well he could read the entire content verbatim.

His mother's reaction was better than we planned. She took it after putting on her reading glasses and looking at the envelope saying, "All the way from Alaska."

Mr. Moran was not as easily convinced. He studied the envelope and looked at Billy with suspicious eyes. He asked if he could take the letter downstairs to his office. Mr. Moran's office was in the back of the basement. Inside the office was a desk containing the tools of a writer. An Underwood typewriter sat in the middle of the desk. The typewriter was always in use by Mr. Moran. He composed letters to all the daily newspapers. There wasn't an editorial page Mr. Moran did not read and have a comment about on any given day. Next to the typewriter was a magnifying glass that would make Sherlock Holmes envious. Mr. Moran took the envelope and letter downstairs. Mrs. Moran was practically singing "All the way from Alaska" like it was a number one hit song on the radio. For whatever reason, that first letter never resurfaced. Artie Moran, Billy's Dad, never said a word. It was like he was on to us, but appreciated our creativity.

Most everything you read about looking back is tainted with misery. Billy's Dad one day told us only a few people can find a silver lining in the rain. He had a way of making statements that caused Billy and me to talk about him like he was a Rhodes Scholar. Mostly we agreed he was a poet. Billy's Dad had a way of expressing himself that bordered on brilliant. There were poets everywhere walking around Real on a daily basis, you needed only to listen. One in particular came from an unlikely source. Everyone knew this man that we had declared a poet; but it was Billy's Dad who labeled him such before we could appreciate his daily rants and raves.

We never knew the man's last name. Still, he was a part of the daily landscape in Real. He was as reliable as the grocer, the pharmacist and the bus drivers who were part of the world we called home. Everyone knew him as Charley MandM. He was the Real mailman. No matter the weather or gloom of the day, Charley MandM delivered the mail.

His last name came by way of children defining him by his profession. On any block Charley delivered mail you could hear a child proclaim – here comes Charlie the Mailman. Over the years for some unknown reason, his last name was shortened to MandM. As we got older Billy and I referred to him as Mr. MandM. Back then in any neighborhood someone you saw everyday became a part of your world; people took notice of one another in ways no longer practiced. This was on a day that would go down in Real history as one of the coldest days ever. Schools were closed. The radio advised people to stay home from work. Snow began falling after midnight, continuing in to the next afternoon. The drifts of snow were so high on some blocks that other essential members of society who get taken for granted, the sanitation department, could not even maneuver their trucks safely. The main streets of Real were covered in nothing but snow as far as your eyes could see. Billy and I, like any young kids, were thrilled to have a day without school. My brother and a group of his friends declared themselves entrepreneurs, and made a small fortune shoveling sidewalks and driveways. Billy and I were not as enterprising. We wanted to explore Real in a way not normally seen. We climbed over drifts of snow and made our way to Myrtle Avenue. Standing on a hill of snow in the middle of the biggest main street with no cars able to get through, we declared ourselves the Kings of Real. We shouted at the top of our lungs "WE ARE THE KINGS OF REAL!"

Our words echoed down and around the neighborhood like we were yelling through bullhorns. We laughed, yelling louder and louder as our voices filled our kingdom.

From far off down Myrtle Avenue we saw a figure walking toward us. He was carrying a leather satchel and singing. His singing caused us to contemplate his sanity. What kind of fool would walk straight down the main street of any neighborhood singing while weighed down by a leather satchel? Christmas had passed and we had both discussed at length the whereabouts of Santa Claus once December disappeared.

His voice became louder and louder until we could clearly make out the song he was singing. We both agreed standing atop our drift of snow near the entrance to Forest Park that it was an odd song choice for such a dreary day. The words to "I Only Have Eyes for You" by The Flamingos filled the air around him, his voice getting stronger as he neared us. It was Charlie MandM and he was delivering the mail despite the weather and a declaration by the Mayor of New York that we were in a state of emergency. As Charley got closer, he looked up at Billy and me standing atop our hill. He did something that day which made no sense at all. He knelt down in the snow and said, "May I pass into the Kingdom of Real me Lords?"

Billy looked at me and I back at him as if we were in a fairy tale. Charley, covered in snow, knelt with his head bowed to the ground; sincere about his intentions. Billy took a deep breath, smiling, he said, "You may, my young squire!" Charley stood up smiling; he bowed his head and continued walking to the beginning of his route. He stopped for a moment to greet Huntz, the grocer, Mike the baker, and James the druggist. The four of them stood in the middle of Myrtle Avenue looking up and down the abandoned landscape. They waved to Billy and me. It was a day that most people would define as a horrible day; but Billy and I would disagree. To us it was a day The Flamingos sang in a snow storm and Charley MandM delivered his mail to the waiting world. By the next morning the snow was piled on both sides of most streets, and people were digging themselves out of what the newspapers said was the worst blizzard in years. It never occurred to me after all Billy and I said to one another that day, how the newspapers were delivered just like the mail without anyone taking notice or caring how it was done. I did not see my Dad until a few days after the storm. I asked him how he managed to maneuver through the snow. This is what he said, "Some things you just do without worrying how to do it." My Dad and Billy's father had a way with words.

Chapter Sixteen

Mr. Arthur Moran was a freelance writer. He had other jobs working for the City, but none were as important as his job writing letters and his weekly columns for the Daily News. Billy and I would contemplate the fact that in many ways our fathers were connected. Billy's father wrote for the paper and my father delivered it to the millions of people who read it everyday.

When we were in Billy's basement the click-clack of the typewriter emanated from the back office. If Billy's father was not working on his daily column called "Around Town", he was writing letters to the editors of every other newspaper he could find. Nothing got past Artie Moran. He would emerge from his office on some afternoons smiling from ear to ear. He would be holding an envelope between his knuckles, "So there are no fingerprints", he told us. Inside the envelope were carefully devised comments to the editors of newspapers about their stand on "issues relevant to modern society."

Some of the letters were brilliant statements about the ignorance of government decisions, corporate ideals and if he was in the mood a comment or two about "Hollywood Hogs", which was what Mr. Moran called famous people who did things "just to get their names in the paper."

On certain occasions he would read aloud from one of his letters; which from the opening sentence had Billy and me rolling on the floor in laughter. "Dear Meathead!" some letters would start, leading us towards a barrage of comments against someone or something. Another would start, "Dear Crack head" or "Your Honorable Stupid face." The letters were a way Mr. Moran explained of "keeping fresh his opinions and not falling victim to the idle nonsense other writers called journalism.'

The High School years went by like a flash of light. The only memorable events for four years were the growing unrest about a war that wasn't a war, and the sudden awareness that there were more than boys in the park where we played ball and hung out everyday. One day we were a bunch of guys playing football in the winter, baseball in the summer, basketball in the fall and standing around like geeks on parade in the spring. Every season had a purpose that lasted the number of required months and like clockwork we would gravitate to the portion of the park set-aside for us. The ball field doubled as our playground for winter and summer activities. In the summer, we would play baseball. When winter rolled around we elongated the field and made boundaries for playing football. In the fall we went over to the other side of the park and used the basketball courts. Every sport when we were young, in the neighborhood of Real, New York had a season and an exact purpose. In the spring of 1972, at the rightful age of 17 years of age; the ritual practice of sitting around and waiting for baseball season to start went through changes. It had been customary since we were 8 years old or so to assemble on the benches at the top of the stairs after entering the park from Myrtle Avenue. The trees were beginning to show their luster. Only a jacket or sweatshirt was needed to keep warm. In 1972, sitting on our park benches were a "bunch of girls." They didn't belong in the park. Girls walked around the perimeter of the park. They stayed home with their mothers and learned to do things our mother's did. Cooking. Cleaning. Shopping. Soap operas. The thought that they were sitting now on our turf, in male territory, was quite disturbing. The group of us who still looked forward to following the ritual routines of our youth met one night in the ball field. It was March, and in March there wasn't much yet to talk about concerning sports. The only professional ball players needed to report to spring training were the pitchers and catchers; and we did not pay attention to their comings and goings unless either the Yankees or the Mets got someone exceptional. So nothing was happening in the spring of 1972 in the sports pages that would keep us up at night. The conversation instead was about what we were going to do about the sudden appearance of females on our turf.

What could they want?

How did they know our names?

Who knew them and why had he betrayed our sacred trust?

Where were we going to sit and talk if they were going to be around everyday?

How did this happen?

Every generation goes through its own trials and tribulations. The changes happen sooner for some generations than for others. We were maybe a tad behind the times when it came to deciding the world is big enough for more things than sports. We had attended the mandatory school dances. We knew what it was like to stand around and look across the gym at girls. They would look – giggle – look again and giggle some more. I hated school dances. The music was awful and at least once you had to dance with some girl who said she liked your smile. I hated smiling too. But, as my father pointed out during one of our midnight runs delivering the papers : "It's all in the game." The only game I cared about until the summer of 1972 required a bat and ball, a helmet or a hoop. We were in a strange place as the summer played out and new desires were born.

The meeting in the spring of 1972 included all the regulars who had over the years become a part of our "crew." We were a "crew" because we were not a gang. It was as simple as that – no further explanation is required except I'll give some insight because you either fully understand or maybe you didn't grow up in a similar situation.

A crew was a bunch of guys who did not smoke cigarettes, drink beer to get drunk or sniff glue to get high like gang kids did. As crewmembers we were what some might call "squares" or "geeks." We did not know we were anything but "cool." Once girls entered the equation "cool" took on a whole different meaning.

As the crew assembled, my brother and I entered the park after I had been out delivering newspapers with our Dad. My brother, whom I have not said much about up until now, was a good guy. We were in many ways best friends but we did not know that then. We took for granted that we hung out with the same crowd of people. My brother is a year and half younger than me. He liked playing the same sports I enjoyed. We watched the same things on television except for a few shows that had us fighting and threatening bodily harm sometimes. For example, he liked shows like Star Trek and I liked Kung Fu. He liked "Lost in Space" and I liked a show called "Then Came Bronson." We did not know it at the time, but these shows were affecting us in ways that would make us each unique or strange, depending on your definition. My brother's name was Frank, but he had several nicknames. One name I gave him early on in life. I couldn't pronounce his name when were really young, so for some unknown reason Frank came out sounding like "Hank." He would be known as "Hank" forever. My mother called it "a term of endearment." My father had a better way of explaining it. He said one night – "Well we know Jonathan will never get arrested for cursing." We were sitting at the table having dinner and both my brother and I looked up with interest. My father hardly ever included us in table conversations. We listened and the parents talked about all things parents talked about. My mothers looked up from her plate and with a look of wife-like ponder said, "What are you talking about, honey?" They actually called each other "honey" and "darling", and every once in a while my father would call my Mom "Butch." Parents are weird. He reared back in his chair and said, "You can't get arrested for saying "Huck You!" He would laugh after these kinds of statements so loud he had to cough. My father's cough was a barking sound that as he laughed would get worse and worse. My mother would get up and start pounding my father on his back and they would both be laughing and coughing and pounding away. I didn't think it was that funny. I couldn't pronounce certain words and it was not something to make fun of. However, it was from that night on – that my brother and I got to use the term "Huck You!" when ever we were yelling at one another. Our own father had declared it was ok to say. It got so every one in the crew used it too. We would add each other's names after the phrase like "Huck You Billy!" Even other parents thought it colorful. Billy explained to his Mom one day that it had to do with liking books by Mark Twain. He told her, "You know Mom, Tom Sawyer and Huck Finn!" She looked confused and then became animated and thrilled that we were so creative. Mr. Moran was not amused when he came up from his office in the basement and Mrs. Moran greeted him with a "Huck you Honey!"

Times were indeed strange and they were bound to get stranger as the summer of 1972 progressed.

The other guys assembled that fateful morning with the usual flair for showing up.

"Huck You Billy!" I said as he entered the park munching on some kind of concoction I had never seen before. "What is that?" He looked at my brother and me shaking his head. "It's a rice krispies bar. My mother made it!" I had seen pictures of such a thing on the back of a cereal box, but never knew anyone actually made them. It looked like a bowl of cereal on a stick. We shared a "you're stupid" – "no you're stupid" intellectual conversation for a few moments before others started to arrive.

"Huck You Dickie!"

"Huck You Roland!"

"Huck You Mikey!"

"Huck You Freddie!"

"Huck You Tommy!"

The "huck you's" went on until every one was sitting on the bench, readying ourselves for what to do about being invaded. That's what we considered the girls were, "invaders."

I brought it up in the only way I knew how. I wanted to put it right out there and discuss it like rational intelligent adults. I said, "Who invited the chicks?" There were a series of stares as we sat on the bench in the dugout. There were intelligent and thought provoking comments immediately. Mike, who lived next door to my brother and I, looked at me and said "What chicks?" Freddie, who lived around the block from my brother and I, chimed in with the best response of all; he said, "We have chicks? What about the eggs?" No one quite understood what he was asking and no one bothered to answer him. I was aggravated as usual when talking about anything except sports with these guys and I further elaborated. "I'm talking about the girls who have come up here and started poking their noses in our business!" This got their attention. Roland, who was the most intense ballplayer we knew, who worked out before we even knew what working out meant said, "What do they want? What's our business?" This made me stand up and start walking around on the field. "Come on guys – someone made friends with these girls and now they won't leave us alone!" It was Dickie who said, "Who wants them to leave us alone?" It was as if he had requested a vote. The guys looked at one another and started shaking their heads in agreement. As it turned out, no one wanted the girls to leave us alone; apparently, everyone was sort of enjoying the attention. I was the only hold out. "Come on guys! How can we play ball with girls staring and making silly comments?" Again, it was as if I was speaking a foreign language. No one cared whether they stared or made silly comments. "Am I the only one who cares about how good we play?" I pleaded with them. It was on that day, without anyone knowing it, that our chances of being taken seriously as ball players disappeared. It was like we were preparing ourselves for the big game and the crowd took over the field. From that day on, the girls would be accepted as part of the game. They came – made funny remarks, laughed – and the crew became something else.

Chapter Seventeen

There were some strange people in Real, and some were a lot stranger than others. Gertrude McGuffey was strange. She was in her seventies. In appearance, she dressed in the proper fashion suitable for a woman of her age. The only mark of strangeness when seeing Gertrude in local grocery stores or out and about on the street was her face. She used cosmetics in the same way a clown might use make-up to put on an exaggerated expression. The way she looked caused people to stare; and when she spoke it was more apparent she suffered from some kind of neurosis. Her voice patterns could cause people to cover their ears. She could not control the sound level of her words; they always came out sounding like a shout. The house she lived in was a neighborhood eyesore. The yard was overgrown in such a way that it seemed to be in a constant state of Halloween. On her property there lived a small army of cats. These cats were so abundant that on late night walks their cries and carrying on sounded like a siren. It was no secret that neighbors had offered to help Gertrude clean her yard, but she would dismiss their requests with an eerie smile or shrieked comment that made people leave her alone. She would go about her business of placing bowls of tuna fish on her porch and on window ledges around the house. The sound of sirens and the smell of tuna fish were a constant reminder of her eccentricities.

It was an early Saturday morning when Billy rang my bell asking for help. In typical fashion the request came before I could see him marching up the stairs to my parent's apartment. "I'm not doing this alone", Billy's voice echoed up the stairs as I stood on the top landing waiting to see who was calling for me. I shouted down the stairwell, "What are you talking about?" He stood at the bottom step and replied, "My parents volunteered us to help Gertrude McGuffey."

Your parents volunteered us?

They said; get a friend to help Gertrude McGuffey clean out her house. I came here knowing you're the only one I could ask.

Gertrude McGuffey? The clown lady?

My parents think she's a nice lady with no one to help her.

What are we supposed to do?

She wants it cleaned up.

Why?

I didn't ask why. It's something she has to do.

When?

Today. I am on my way there now.

As we neared the house it was obvious we were about to take on a task which equaled a line from a popular television show: we were about to "boldly go where no man had gone before." Just climbing the stairs to her house was a feat more challenging than the job itself. For years, especially around Halloween, there was an unspoken fear when with friends anywhere near her house. Kids from streets as far away as Ridgewood and Woodhaven could be heard daring some one to ring the McGuffey bell. The house looked haunted. To ring the McGuffey bell and run was a rite of passage in Real and even some of the surrounding neighborhoods. The fact that Billy and I never did it was a testimonial to some form of warped respect; every one knew Billy's parents were friendly with her and for some reason it was never made in to an issue when we refused the dare. Standing on the porch, Billy and I took in the aroma of tuna fish while witnessing the scurrying of cats in every direction. "I'm telling you right now Billy, if she has indoor cats, I am out of here!" She came to the door in a floral dress that looked like it belonged in a movie about Japan. Her make-up was on her face in a way that reminded me of Betty Davis in 'Hush Hush Sweet Charlotte'. I took a step back off the porch and Billy, knocking in to me, nearly caused us to both fall down the wooden steps.

"What do you want?" she asked in a booming voice. It didn't sound like it came from her but like something that came from a ventriloquist. I looked to see if there was any one standing behind her with a hand up her back making her speak.

"Hello Mrs. McGuffey. It's me, Billy Moran, Arthur Moran's son. He told me you need help cleaning your house."

And who is that behind you?

"My friend Jonathan Kiddrane. He offered to help me."

I punched Billy in the ribs feeling I was being set up. Billy took the blow and fell forward a few steps almost knocking Gertrude McGuffey back in to her house.

"Do you have seizures?"

Billy looked at me and I stood silent. "No Mrs. McGuffey, I tripped trying to get inside so we can start right away." He turned to glare at me. I offered no expression of any kind.

"I like enthusiasm young man. Well let's get started. Come on in."

Entering the McGuffey home was terrifying. I took a last look at the clear blue skies outside, feeling I would never see the sun again. Standing in her living room, which was the first room after the door closed behind us, was a picture of the most disturbing kind.

Everywhere we looked, there was clutter at such a level it felt overwhelming. Piles of papers on tables, buckets filled with water of some liquid substance suitable for science projects. On an end table there were books stacked like a tower, almost touching the ceiling. The ceiling was filled with cobwebs from one end to the other. There were two arm chairs on each side of a massive sofa filled with opened cans of tuna fish. There were insects crawling in and out of the cans in such a way that they looked like thread torn from the upholstery. There were curtains across one wall thick with mildew and dust.

"I suspect you will want me out of your way! I'll go grocery shopping while you clean up!" She went to the front door with her purse, dressed in her kimono dress without telling us where to begin. I looked at Billy and said exactly what I knew I had to say; "How do you want to die?"

Billy had a look of horror on his face looking around at the room we supposed to clean. He said without looking at me, "Let's kill my parents first." I felt obliged to relieve him of any ill feelings toward his mother and father. They were trying to be thoughtful friends. It was certain they could not be held accountable.

"Listen Billy, you do upstairs. I'll do downstairs in the basement. We'll leave this floor to do last since I have no idea where to begin. He agreed without either of us knowing what

was waiting for us. We shook hands as he peered up the stairs leading up and I looking down at the prospect of what lay below. I approached the steps leading down to the basement after trying to find a light switch. Not finding one, I held on to the side walls aware I was shaking in a way I can not describe. I found the last step on the stairs, shuffling my feet to adjust to the darkness. My head bumped in to something and I stood motionless trying to catch my breath. The object hit my head again. I reached up to protect myself grabbing hold of what turned out to be a light bulb hanging on a wire. I felt around the bulb feeling a small string. I pulled the string and light filled the space around me. It took a moment for my eyes to adjust to my surroundings. Before me were row upon row of stacked newspapers. The stacks were all of the same height. On each stack was a handwritten note detailing the contents: *NY TIMES – JAN – DEC 1940*
DAILY NEWS – JAN – DEC 1953

The stacks were organized in a manner that was not in keeping with the mess on the first floor. Disturbing the stacks would destroy a carefully orchestrated dedication to detail. I could not fathom any one collecting so many newspapers and having the mindset to categorize them in such a detailed way. I walked from row to row looking at the precise logic of each stack. My fears turned to admiration. I turned on several more lights hanging from the ceiling. I walked through each row, 10 rows with 10 stacks in each one. The newspapers went back to the 1880s: *New Yorker Staats-Zeitung Jan – Dec 1868*

I was awestruck by the thinness of the paper. As I tried to remove the top paper it crumbled in my hands like dust. I had to show Billy what I found. There was no way I could dismantle a room filled with so much….history.

I made my way to the stairs and went to the second floor. At the top steps I whispered out for Billy to hear me. "Billy, you've got to see what I found in the basement."

The loudness of my whisper filled the musty air around me. I opened a door at the top of the stairs and found Billy sitting in a pristine clean room on a rocking chair reading a book. "What are you doing?" He looked up from the book he was holding in his hands, "Do you have any idea who Gertrude McGuffey is related to?"

I looked around the room at books neatly placed side-by-side; there were volumes that looked to be the same book stacked from floor to ceiling on shelves. The room in contrast to the first floor was spotless. There was not a speck of dust to be seen anywhere. It smelled like opening a box in school filled with books. I always found the opening of those boxes to be the highlight of a school year; I may not have liked to study the contents, but the smell was worth the gamble every time.

Standing in the Gertrude McGuffey library was the best smelling place on earth. "Kidd!" Billy said holding the book up to me, "She's a McGuffey!" I looked at the cover having no appreciation for what it might be. Billy had over the years inherited a love of books far more advanced than anyone our age. His father was a reader. From his father he discovered a fondness for all things written. In Billy's house every room had a bookcase. In his basement, like Gertrude McGuffey – stacks of book shelves stood as room dividers. I looked again at the cover of the book as Billy stood up removing another just like it from a shelf. His voice was shaking as he spoke, "My father has a set of these. They were the books used in the late 1800s and early 1900s in schools across America. These are the first books of American education. She must have two, maybe three thousand copies of each volume."

Billy, why are we whispering?

He smiled looking at the shelves, "Books make you whisper. It's like being in a church."

What are we going to do?

He looked around at the bookshelves and then at me with wide-eyed confidence, "We have to clean out the house, only I cannot figure out what to do."

"Billy, you have to see the basement, it's got newspapers stacked to the ceiling. They go back over 100 years ago." We decided it would take us weeks, if not months to clean out the books and newspapers. Every room on the second floor was filled with volumes of books. There were Bibles that looked like they were handwritten by the original apostles. There was a room filled with poetry books dating back to the 19th century. In Gertrude McGuffey's bedroom which was immaculate in appearance, books lined one wall with handwritten stories, poems and family history.

In another room shelves displayed what appeared to be brown cardboard folders. I took one of the folders from the top shelf on one wall. It was a music record. I had heard about 78rpms but had never seen one. The record itself was much heavier than a vinyl one. I looked around the room, noticing shelf upon shelf of these records. I removed several, aware after only taking a few from their sleeves that everything was in alphabetical order. It was a room filled with treasures no one looking from the outside could ever imagine were hidden inside. I yelled for Billy to come quick after pulling a record from a middle shelf. "Why are you yelling?"

"Look at what I found!"

Billy was appreciative of recorded music having a sizable vinyl collection himself.

"Get out of the way!" he screamed, taking in the immensity of my discovery.

A look came over his face and his eyes became glassy. He removed a brown covered sleeve and held it in his hands, opening the fold of the record slowly. I heard his gasp.

"What is it?"

I knew Billy for what can be argued to be a lifetime, and I had never seen him so enthralled about anything. Not even his secret admiration for certain girls or even jelly donuts for that matter could compete with the look on his face.

It should be mentioned that childhood friendships start at an age when forever begins. The years growing up confined to your parents' living space do not count. I always thought that life's real self discovery started when you could go out and play without parental supervision. It was not until your parents allowed you to discover things on your own; then and only then did true time begin. I had known Billy since true time began and here he was standing in old lady Gertrude McGuffey house, with the possible threat of doom and disaster looming on the first floor, getting emotional over holding a piece of plastic.

"It's not plastic you idiot! It's pure virgin shellac." His voice began to get lower as he held the record. He began to say things I had difficulty understanding.

"She's a collector of things that no one on earth owns anymore. This record if you look closer is smaller than the others. These records were released in various sizes. The early records were experiments, not only by each artist but by the record companies who released them. The sizes were essential to capturing sound in a way they hoped was better to listen to. This 7" disc on the Harvard Disc Record label is very rare. Just the title alone can cause record collectors to collapse. 'I Never Trouble With Trouble until Trouble Troubles Me' by Arthur Collins and Byron Harlan."

Tears appeared in the corner of his eyes and for a moment I was embarrassed seeing him get that way over a record. He continued his search by pulling out several more records and removing them from their sleeves. "Look at this in pristine condition, these labels are long gone but they represent the history of recorded music. My father talks about these labels like they were lost books of the Bible. Look at this on the Conqueror label perfect in every way, 'Starving to Death on a Government Claim' by Cowboy Ed Crane. And this one on the Challenge label 'Forked Deer' by The Clinch Valley Boys. These are better than finding the lost china of the Titanic; look at these labels -- Oxford, Silverstone, Super tone, Edison and Victor. You have no idea what this is worth. I am not talking about money; I am talking about the historic value." I watched him but had no appreciation for the manner in which he was carrying on. He held up two records that caused his hands to shake. 'Too Pooped To Pop' by Chuck Berry! Do you see this? It's thought to be the last 78rpm record ever released." He took a record out of one sleeve that looked different from the other hard covered shellac discs. He looked like he was going to faint.

"What is it?"

"It's Elvis Presley, the original pressing on acetate of him singing 'That's Alright Mama'. I need to lie down. I'm feeling light headed."

The only thing we could do on the second floor was marvel

at the collections stored meticulously in every room.

"We need to clean something, Billy."

Walking past the master bedroom like we were inside a hidden museum, I heard Billy gasp again.

"What now?"

Billy was staring at a frame on a wall between the master bedroom and the record room. I looked closer at the small photo inside an enlarged frame. I felt myself let out a gasp. Billy nudged me saying, "Told you."

"Do you think it is real?"

"Of course it's real. No one bothers to put something like that in frame for no reason."

"It's the holy grail, Billy."

In a soft whisper he responded, "Yup."

We were both collectors of baseball cards. Any kid worth his own weight collected something. Baseball cards and comic books represented the treasures of our youth. It was not so much the value of any one card or comic book, but the ability to boast about having what was deemed collectable. There were no books or magazines defining certain things as more valuable or collectible; natural born collectors just knew instinctively what was desired and necessary to own. Every generation has something worth owning. In the neighborhood of Real, baseball cards, comic books and records were the objects of our desire. Only one kid in the neighborhood that we knew about had our generation's holy grail. His name was Michael Kleaner and he owned a copy of Mickey Mantle's rookie card. It was not so much about it being rare as it was about having the one card everyone wanted. We did not envy Michael Kleaner for owning it. We hated him. As Billy and I stood looking at the card in the frame on the wall, his voice again reached depths of sincerity I found momentarily embarrassing. He said, "My father once talked about it in a whisper. He said 'Honus Wagner' the same way Harry Houdini probably said abracadabra. If you had that card all your worries about everything happening in the world would disappear."

In a simple 8x10 frame on a wall in Gertrude McGuffey's house was a Honus Wagner T206 baseball card. It was in mint condition. I do not remember any other time in our lives when we stood as silent as that moment. We stared at the card the same way people might look at a painting by Van Gogh. Works of art come in all shapes and sizes.

After Billy and I checked out all of the rooms we went to the basement. He walked as I did past each neatly stacked row of newspapers saying "Wow", "Oh My God" and his best observation was "It's too perfect to touch."

I understood what he meant. In the nearly three hours we were inside the McGuffey house, we felt like we were in heaven and hell at the same time.

Without uttering a word we looked around the basement and walked calmly to the first floor. There were no whispers when we took to the task. "Holy Shit", was our main statement as we tried desperately to define a plan. We opened the windows behind the sofa after carefully taking down the red velvet curtains that covered the wall. "Don't get anything on your head! You'll go bald!" screamed Billy as the curtain fell to the floor. We jimmied open the windows after fighting with them for an hour. The room had not seen sunlight for years, no less fresh air. Once opened, we both stood with our heads outside the window taking in air like we had been drowning.

Turning from the windows we took in the room draped in

light. I looked at the armchairs not wanting to touch anything on them. The cans of tuna fish were foul smelling with what we determined were maggots crawling in and around them. We had never seen maggots but these crawling, sucking ugly worm like things fit the description.

Billy took a deep breath and said, "We can leave now or toss the entire chair out the window in to the yard." It was a brilliant decision that would require precise handling of what we knew and believed would kill us if touched. Carefully, I stood behind one chair after measuring the window width with a quick eye. "It will fit, but if we miss there will be hell to pay." Billy stood in front of the chair looking down at the cans of moldy tuna and crawling maggots. "Why do I have to be in front?"

"Hey, it's your fault we are here!"

We agreed to reach on three. I was to grab the top of the chair and Billy had to lean down to grab the legs: ONE – TWO – THREE!

The chair was in our hands. The maggots, sensing a change in their daily foray of eating began to move about in an alarming way. Moving to the window, we had forgotten to move the sofa away from the wall. I stood taking in the error of our haste. Billy, who was nearly face-to-face with the now leaping maggots, was not of the mindset to take in anything. "Just throw it!" he yelled. The chair sailed over the couch and for a brief moment we stood in a state of frozen time. The toss was made with such force it caused the cans to dislodge from the chair cushions. Every where we could see, were flying cans of tuna fish and the now desperate maggots. The speed that the human body can move during certain incidents has never been properly timed; but Billy on that day leaped up a flight of stairs without his feet once touching a single step. I was not as lucky.

In my rush for escape I ran to the front door. It was locked. I turned and found myself standing in a swarm of maggots. "Billy!" I screamed, discovering a sound emanating from my throat I never thought possible. "Help!" He was hesitant to come down stairs. From the top step he yelled, "It was nice knowing you!"

"Get down here and do something!"

He came half way down the stairs looking at me trapped on my toes with my back up against the front door.

"They're hungry little suckers ain't they?"

"Don't give me that! Do something!"

It took us several minutes to come up with our next big plan.

Billy climbed over the railing on the staircase and stood on a fire place mantle. From his perch he looked at me saying, "It was your idea to throw the chair out the window!" "This is no time for blame! Just do it!"

He rocked the mantle on the fire place until it came lose from the wall. Balancing himself, he grabbed hold of the staircase banister and kicked the mantle over on to the ground. It caused a huge sound that felt like an explosion. I covered my head not knowing what to expect. When I opened my eyes the mantle was in the middle of the living room floor. The maggots had scurried away in to a new feeding frenzy. They were climbing legs of the arm chair in the far corner of the room still filled with cans of tuna. I ran to the staircase. Billy and I took in the view of the now dislodged fire place mantle. Connected to the fire place was a metal rod. "What's that piece of metal for Billy?" "Oh No" he said in an alarming voice. "What?

"It's a gas line."

In the more than five hours we were in the McGuffey house, we discovered she was related to one of the most important families in the history of American education. She was an historian of the most eccentric type. We had managed to nearly blow up her house.

Carefully and slowly we made our way to the middle of the living room. The cans of tuna were now imbedded in the carpet giving off a stench that made us both take our shirts and pull them up over our noses. Our plan was to lift the mantle back in to place.

ONE – TWO – THREE!

We lifted the mantle with our arms stretched to all possible levels of strength; once upright, we stood with our noses covered, slowly removing our shirts from our noses attempting to distinguish the smell of gas from tuna. We sniffed at the air like blood hounds. Convinced we had not caused a leak in the metal rod now bent behind the mantle, we returned to the staircase to contemplate our next move.

Billy broke the silence, "She asked us to clean out the house right?"

What are you thinking?

We cover everything in newspaper. We smother the maggots. We cover the smell of tuna."

Then what?

I didn't think the plan out that far.

"Sounds good."

The moment I heard myself saying the plan sounded good I knew I was filled with dread.

It took us another hour to completely cover everything in the living room with newspapers. We ran up and down the basement stairs carrying arm loads of Gertrude McGuffey's life long tribute to recorded history. It was an option we both felt was worth doing. With nearly 4 decades worth of the 19th century dumped on to and in to every crevice of the living room, we both without discussing our next move began to jump up and down on every thing and anything in our path. This was followed by leaps from one piece of furniture to another. All the while we were performing this macabre dance we had not noticed Gertrude McGuffey opening the front door. She was standing at the front door in what can only be described as a state of shock.

The newspapers were ripped to shreds from our jumping on them. The older lesser maintained editions were turned in to almost liquid-like putty. Standing now in silence, we wanted to see if Gertrude McGuffey would fall down dead or decide to call the police. Instead, she did a remarkable about face adding as she left, "I had no idea there was so much involved. I'm going to the movies."

She slammed the door behind her. Billy and I now stood dumbstruck covered in newspaper and a pasty film. I lifted my shirt to smell the pasty film, it smelled like tuna fish. We found shovels in the basement. We took to shoveling the debris out the open windows in to the yard. We were careful as we neared the carpet, making certain any thing left alive would not jump out at us for revenge. The pile of papers when everything was finally tossed outside reached to the windows ledge. We tossed the end tables and lamps outside as well. We both noticed what appeared to be 50 cats sitting on the McGuffey fence watching everything we were doing. We closed the windows so nothing could crawl back inside.

I looked around for a light switch. Finding one I turned it on almost hypnotized by a massive chandelier hanging from the ceiling. To our amazement the chandelier was so bright it felt like we were in a spot light. It looked so clean that it defied logic. The cobwebs I had seen earlier were only visible in the four corners of the room, which I reached up and dragged down with the handle from the shovel. The remaining hours were filled with sorting through things in the dining room, which when closely examined amounted to dishes that needed to be boxed up and piled in a corner. The kitchen upon closer inspection was nowhere near as bad as we once perceived it to be. We washed the dishes in the sink and placed them on the counter to dry. It took us nearly twelve hours in all to clean the first floor of Gertrude McGuffey's house. A woman we discovered who was in some way related to the original scholars of America. A woman who was meticulous in ways we would never understand. When Gertrude McGuffey came home she stood taking in our work. She covered her mouth to gasp, forcing us to believe we had failed. She then turned to say, "I had forgotten there were windows in this room."

Billy looked at me and shrugged his shoulders. She looked at the boxes of dishes. For a moment she stood facing the fireplace mantle and then said two words we never thought we would hear. She said, "Thank you." As tired as we both were, we wanted to ask about the rooms filled with shelves of books and the basement with rows of newspapers from the last 100 years. Without asking her anything, we bowed our heads acknowledging her "thank you" and smiled as she handed us both a crisp twenty dollar bill. Exiting the McGuffey house, we stood on the porch for a moment in silence. Night had arrived and no one could ever dare Billy Moran or Jonathan Kiddrane to try anything ever again.

The next day I heard from Billy neighbors came in to the yard with shovels wearing masks. They put all the debris we had tossed out the window in to a waiting sanitation truck. They told Gertrude they would feed the cats. She seemed relieved someone else would perform a task she felt it was her duty to take care of for so many years. With tears in her eyes she thanked everyone. Once the yard was cleaned up the house looked like any other. Inside, Billy and I knew were rooms filled with treasures few would ever see.

Chapter Eighteen

Tommy Hargrove had all he could take sitting on the park bench near the swings.

He had grown tired of waiting for her. He did not know her name. She did not know his name. She told him one night, "It's best if we don't get too close." The way she said the word "close" haunted him because he was afraid of intimacy. He was becoming impatient as he sat waiting for her. He begged her one night to tell him her name after she sat in silence staring at the cars passing on the highway. Sometimes she would talk in a sing-song voice, saying gibberish things that made little sense. He had gotten accustomed to her needs. Like himself, she wanted someone to listen. Tommy discovered if he listened, without interrupting her, it let loose a hunger like nothing he would experience again. The way her mind worked made Tommy's head spin. She would stand with her thoughts looking at the passing cars and share her fears. She would scream out in to the darkness, "I am ready to confess!"

When she stood at the top of the steps entering the park, she looked like an angel. On the night Tommy was about to give up on her she arrived out of breath and excited to see him. She started shouting, "Time was love meant something to people! It was a necessary beginning! Men courted women. I like the word "courted. It has certain eloquence." Tommy was mesmerized by her. He had no idea what she was talking about but he could not take his eyes from her dream-like gaze. She laughed when she said anything that she knew might be misinterpreted. She continued after laughing at the look on Tommy's face. "I should have been born when women wore petticoats. Undergarments as it were – all that frilly satin and lace dictated respect. Now its one hand in strip poker and a girl's half naked. It must have taken women hours to get naked when courting was in style." She laughed, turning around and running her hands through her long red hair. Tommy listened to her in the half lit shadows of a lamp post on the bench behind the swings in the park. She was his bedtime story with a promise of much more if he shut up and listened.

He once thought she was the first drug addict. His reputation left a lot of people wondering what kind of lifestyle he lived, but little did anyone know the bullying of others at school, around the neighborhood, and in the park was an act. The real Tommy Hargrove needed someone to love him. No matter how mundane, simple or corny that sounds, Tommy Hargrove, deep down was lonely without any friends. The members of the gang he supposedly led were the real derelicts of the neighborhood. The violent streak Tommy was capable of resorting to was the only thing that provided him any respect. The streak was not something he was proud of showing. While others may have thought it cool, to pretend to support the bullying of others was nothing more than a masquerade.

For Tommy, it was easier to punch someone than to display his weaknesses. His weakness was hidden beneath a hard nosed attitude. His attitude was a product of something Tommy could only speak about with her.

It was a perfect union, the kind of match made of trust. On

this particular night she let out a laugh after tossing a cigarette she never smoked but enjoyed holding. She held her arms high over her head and screamed, "Call me Lila!"

The name Lila echoed through the empty park. She slowly walked to where Tommy sat on the bench. She whispered, "Tell Lila you want her." Tommy was hypnotized by her demand, he whispered, "I want you." She came closer, "Tell Lila you need her." Tommy sat gasping for air, "I need you." Standing in front of him staring right in to his eyes, "Tell Lila you love her." He hesitated. The phrase was not part of his vocabulary. The words gagged him, getting caught in his throat like a swallowed knife. She sat on his lap wrapping her legs around him. "You love Lila don't you?" He looked in to her eyes wanting her, to fill her in ways he was still learning to enjoy. He closed his eyes tightly listening to her pleading voice. "Tell Lila you love her?" He felt like he was losing control. He said the words without any heartfelt emotion.

He felt he had betrayed himself. She felt his emptiness and embraced him; when they were done she pulled on her clothing without looking at him. He sat with his clothing around his ankles, staring up at her exhausted. She lit another cigarette and held it up to the night sky, admiring the glowing amber.

It was a ritual that had nothing to do with love. It was a desperate act filled with a longing they were not capable of sharing. Tommy wanted to say something meaningful. He watched as she neared the steps exiting the park. With his clothing in disarray he stood up yelling, "It's not easy to love yourself!"

He watched her hesitate on the top step. She looked back at him with her head tilted in a way that almost represented innocence. Tommy stood looking at her waiting for a response. She sat down on a bench near the steps. They looked at one another across the parks garden. He saw her wipe something from her eyes; he did not believe she was capable of crying. It felt like hours had passed while they stared at one another in silence. Slowly, she rubbed her face on her sleeve and walked toward him.

She sat down next to him. They sat listening to the cars passing on the highway behind them. Lila finally turned to him saying, "I don't like ice cream." Tommy felt her hand touch his. They sat holding hands. Tommy looked at her smiling, "Not even chocolate?"

She turned to look in to his eyes, "Especially chocolate. It leaves stains when you miss your mouth." Tommy nodded; aware he had never had a real conversation with a girl. Looking at her he realized he had never had a real conversation with anyone.

He whispered, "You're sitting on my bed." She smiled softly in a way that made him feel comfortable. He looked away from her and continued speaking in a low voice, "I sleep on the bench after you leave. I don't like to go home."

She nodded with understanding, "Are you afraid?"

He could feel his eyes damp with tears, a sensation he vowed to never let anyone witness. "I have my reasons." She reached out and wiped tears from his cheeks. She whispered, "I have my reasons too." They sat closer than Tommy knew he would ever let anyone get.

He said, "If I tell you my reasons, will you tell me yours?"

She nodded, yes.

He took a deep breath, a sigh he was certain felt almost religious. She reached out with her hands to hold both of his in her lap. He gasped for air and started, "I'm not someone who opens up easily. I feel safe when no one is around. Things happen at home I don't talk about. I would rather no one look at me. When anyone does, I want to hurt them."

He looked at her knowing things would never be the same after he told her what he kept bottled up inside him. She was the most beautiful girl in the world, he thought, for listening to him. He continued, "My mother does things when she thinks I look at her the wrong way. She taught me how to hurt others without caring who it is. My father works at night. I have seen him sleeping more times than awake. At night, while he is working, she drinks. The drinking makes her angry. Some nights the drinking is so bad she hurts herself. The ways she cannot control herself can make you wish you were dead. Have you ever felt a fist hitting you in the stomach while you wanted to vomit, but you knew if you made such a mess it would prolong the hitting?"

Lila felt tears rolling down her cheeks. The taste of salt formed on her open lips.

She whispered, "I know."

It was how she said, "I know" that made Tommy pull away. He doubled over clutching his stomach with his head between his knees. She touched the back of his head with her fingers. She looked out at the park in the early morning light. Her fears were similar and it frightened her to realize she was no longer alone. Being alone made her feel special; it allowed her to act any way she pleased. Loneliness gave her strength to be who ever she wanted to be without caring for herself. It was a shield she knew was mightier than any knife or leather strap. Tommy, with his head down and sensing he had confessed too much stood up and screamed, "I want you out of here now!" She was afraid of him for reasons she knew too well. They both crossed a fine line by betraying their own strengths. He knew letting someone see him so vulnerable made things worse. He stood up and ran to a small garden behind the bench. He punched a tree and fell to the ground holding his hand. He began to vomit with a sound so wretched it filled the park with sounds of absolute surrender. He was surrendering to himself with each bout of uncontrollable coughing. When it was done he fell back against the trunk of a tree staring out in to the darkness. He could see her walking away. She was not coming back. They had shared a darkness no one wants to see. The battle inside them would one day require a sense of forgiveness, but first they had to learn to forgive themselves. For some it takes a lifetime.

Chapter Nineteen

Dear Moron,

You would not believe the weather here this time of year. I live in my bob-house with endless lake front property. A bob-house is what they call the shacks perched out on the lake year round. I have a kerosene heater on at all times and it actually is quite comfortable. I only have to wear one layer of clothes when I am listening to my radio. There's something to be said about Alaskan Radio. On clear nights you can pick up Radio Moscow. You would not believe what they say about us Americans! One night I swear some deejay claimed that Russia invented classical music. Do you think that's possible? Sure they have like a thousand years on us in history – but to actually say they invented an entire genre of music? I plan to look in to this as soon as I can figure out whom I need to send a letter to! I know, you and Kidd are probably wondering the obvious question about how does he live in a shack all year round and not get tired of eating fish and moose steak. Not only that, you're probably wondering where he goes to go. Well, first of all I like fish and moose steaks are very tasty. As for where I go to the bathroom – I will have you know the phrase “does a bear shit in the woods” is an Alaskan phrase. This is a state held secret so please do not go blabbing all over town about it. I could get evicted for letting anyone know these things. Since moving here and attending the state university I have learned many things that make me proud to call Alaska my home. For example the whole thing about Eskimos being the friendliest original natives of America is true. Just the other night I was invited in Zhaghu Mostonvitch’s igloo. You wouldn’t believe how huge his igloo is once you crawl through the main entrance. The guy has a duplex igloo! Bet you never heard of anything like that before! It’s amazing, and to beat all it has a two snow mobile garage connected to the side of the igloo! There are so many things people who don’t live here don’t know. I’ll bet you didn’t know that people can have penguins for pets? Well they do. Zhaghu Mostonvitch and his wife Izuzu have two penguins and six Siberian huskies. The penguins do not get along very well with the dogs but that’s to be expected since penguins are practical jokers. The other day I was visiting and the penguins were sliding on their bellies past the dogs. One of the dogs leaped and ended up atop the penguin! It was quite a sight to see a dog riding a penguin down a hill. The dog would have drowned for sure if it didn’t fall off at the last second when the penguin dove in to the lake. You know they say, “A dog is man’s best friend.” I agree to some extent because they’re only as smart as men. Penguins are smart, I’m telling you – what other animal do you know can trick another to jump on its back and then dive in to sub-freezing water knowing damn well only they could survive such a thing! That’s what it’s like here in Anchorage everyday. It’s a great place to live. Of course, I have learned to stick to myself. There’s not much fraternizing in sub-zero weather. You have your circle of friends and you pretty much keep to yourself. It's not so bad once you get used to it. I met a woman. Yes I know, it's not very gentlemanly of me to be telling you these things – but who else can I tell if not you and Kidd, my oldest friends! Her name is Natasha Puskinov. She's half American Eskimo and half Russian Eskimo. I don't know what side is which since she's very shy about sharing intimate details of her upbringing. Her father may be the Russian half with a name like Puskinov – but does it really matter? I know I must sound like a silly schoolboy, but it's how I feel and I'm not embarrassed to say so. One night Natasha stayed in my bob-house. I did not need kerosene heat that night if you know what I mean? As a matter of fact, it was the first time since moving here I did not wear my long johns! Ok, I don't want you to get a picture about Natasha in your head that she's that kind of Eskimo – because she's not. If you need to know the truth – nothing happened! We just lay naked together and it was better than sex! You would know what I mean if you had the opportunity to see a naked Eskimo. She's beautiful. I think I may become a painter so I can paint her picture. You can laugh all you want, but years from now when I am the world's prominent naked woman Eskimo painter – you're going to be jealous as hell! I will write more soon, today Natasha and I are attending Penguin Behavior courses together. At school the professor told us; Penguins are natural lovers. I will report back on everything I learn.

Keep Warm and Chill Out
Bob Googenblatt

The letters became a form of entertainment for Billy and me. They would arrive when least expected filled with some of the most off the wall commentaries about life that it wasn't possible to have a conversation about them. Often the letters would cross in the mail and the zaniness of having just completed one letter made it impossible to talk about it when we saw one another. Billy's Mom enjoyed them so much she had a special drawer in her china closet for the letters. She actually sent Bob Googenblatt a Christmas card one year! It would definitely have blown our cover if it wasn't for Billy's Dad. He had finished writing a letter of his own to the Mayor of New York City; he handed the Christmas cards and his letter to Billy saying – there's something in here you may want to mail for yourself.

We knew he was more than suspicious about Googenblatt letters – but to his credit he never let on to Billy's Mom. I believe once in a while Billy's Dad had some fun penning a Googenblatt letter or two. It was right after the Christmas card was sent – and secured – that a reply came back. I never actually spoke about it with Billy – but I do believe something was definitely strange about the response since it was so brilliantly written to Billy's mother; it has to be one of the classic letters of all time! Here's what it said:

Dear Mrs. Moran,

You touched me with your kind words in your Christmas card. Billy is so lucky to have a Mom like you. My Mom and Dad never married. I never told this to anyone before – but my mother was an Egyptian princess. I think my father was a sand sweeper, I never knew him. You can imagine what it was like growing up wondering who your father was all the time. I think I moved to Alaska because I really miss all those brown and tan hills of sand. I enjoy knowing they are still outside on the open plains; only here they are all white. It's not very different when you think about it. As a child I rode Jake, who was my camel. Here, I ride on a sled with a lead dog named Jack. As a child I went to school by walking up hill both ways sinking in the sand. Here I walk to school up hill both ways sinking in the snow. It's a good life.

My mother moved to New York when I started High School. I still lose sleep thinking about my poor father sweeping sand all day. Those hills you see in pictures, the wind isn't the only thing that makes them look so inviting! Sand sweepers are out night and day making them look just right. My mother never told me, but I think my Dad got lost one night. My mother only said; "all those hills and no sign of your father."

I thank you for the card and hope to visit if I ever come back to New York. Up here we sing traditional Christmas songs and a few of our own. The most popular Christmas song this year is called "Voodoo Igloo." Here are some lyrics from the song:

Who left the light on Christmas Eve?
Santa must have a new pair of boots
'Cos there's a glow in the north
And momma wants to dance
At the Voodoo Igloo
It must be something only mother's can do
Waiting for the light to shine
While drinking wine
Down at the Voodoo Igloo

It's a great song, and you wouldn't believe how many times it gets played everyday! I will try to get a copy for you! Thanks again.

Keep warm and chill out
Bob Googenblatt

Like I said, it got so Billy and I couldn't keep track of the letters coming and going. I saved my letters from "Googenblatt" in an old mayonnaise jar. I saw *Carnac the Magnificent* on the Johnny Carson Show and that's what he kept his secret envelopes in so if it was good enough for a famous soothsayer, than it was good enough for me.

Chapter Twenty

It was inevitable that the girls would start to create changes no one could predict. I watched the guys fall victim to the take over. Mind you it was not a hostile take over, but more like a kidnapping in which each member of our crew began to talk and act differently. Billy and I were witnesses to this change and in retrospect it was a necessary rite of passage for each of us. As each of the guys became "enchanted" we watched them become complete fools on the ball field. In the past they would not hesitate to dive for a fly ball, now they would return to the dugout and worry if their clothes were dirty. I had a conversation after a game with my brother that went something like this:

Jono – Can I borrow your comb?

Hank – What for?

This exchange of dialogue summed up perfectly the level of intelligence we were dealing with and losing on a daily basis. My brother, I learned and was told by the adoring crowds of girls – was a looker. My brother had the grace of a ball player. As I mentioned he was a natural born athlete. He played third base. I played left field right behind him. It got so I needed to help him keep his mind on the game. The girls would line up behind the backstop and swoon – yelling his name like he was some kind of movie star. I hated the attention he got. I needed to do something about it. I told him during one game if I had to catch a ground ball that I thought he should have caught I would come in from the outfield and kick his ass. Each time it happened I would run in from left field and proceed to pummel him in front of his adoring fans. It got so even when he did lean down to catch a routine ground ball he would sneak a peak over his shoulder to make certain I saw him doing it. It became a classic move over time, forcing runners on the bases to hesitate before running. It even forced the batters who hit the ball to hesitate moving out of the batters box. He never thanked me for perfecting this move, even if it happened unintentionally and due to the promise of violence.

The summer of 1972 proved to be the changing season in many ways for everyone. Every neighborhood has a year that defines its past with its future. In Real, New York – 1972 proved to be that season. Hank became the talk of the town when his name appeared in the local papers as a promising athlete to watch. His picture was printed along with the article in the newspaper. I wanted to toss every copy of the stupid paper in puddles when I tossed them off the back of my father's truck. My father was very proud and hysterical about my reaction. My mother had copies of the paper to give to anyone who might have missed it. His damn picture was on our refrigerator for the next three years! Billy thought it was funny as well when one of the girls actually brought a copy of the stupid photo to the ball field in a frame; asking my brother to sign it. It was disgusting! Why couldn't he just play ball and leave all this Hollywood stuff some place else?

Years later, I do not know if I was jealous or envious – I was stupid enough to believe he was good enough to be the best and this ridiculous local fame crap was the worst that could happen. I told him one night; "You do realize you're good enough to play third base for the Yankees?" He looked at me and started laughing. I did not appreciate being laughed at when I was being sincere. He told me, "I play baseball in Real, New York. The scouts are out in the Midwest or the West Coast." I did not fully understand his point.

Was it possible he doubted his own talent? He told me I was delusional. That's the word he used: Delusional.

"Besides" he said, as we lay in our room in the last space we would share before things all changed; "I only play that well because I know you're backing me up." I was silenced beyond words. The room had no windows. It was pitch black in the middle of what was called a "railroad room apartment." I left it that way. I thought it was a nice way to end a day. It was a nice way to start a dream.

I do not have precise dates, so you will need to forgive me about that. I think after a while life happens in stages, not in years. Then it happens in eras and finally so I hear, everything is translated in to "the good old days." I think that night marked the end of an era. My brother and I would never be as close.

We played the final game of the summer against a team of college aged guys from Colombia University. They all had matching uniforms and leather jackets with C O L U M B I A, printed in nice shiny letters on the back. The uniforms were ok, but those jackets were the coolest things I had ever seen. They had a group of college-aged girlfriends who sat behind the outfield fence smoking cigarettes and throwing back bottles of beer. Being so close to the outfield fence as I played left field they were carrying on all day when I was out there. "Stay focused", our coach yelled at all the outfielders, "Especially you Kidd! Don't let those gals rattle ya!"

It had rained the day we were supposed to play this team during the season, so we had to have a double header. The league standings depended on the outcome of these two games. Not only were they the best-dressed team in the league; they were one of the best on the field and in hitting. The girls forming our fan club stood on the sidelines behind the dugout silenced by the appearance of the college girls who were in many ways unrelenting in their style of applauding and cheering.

They said things like:

SHOW US YOUR BUTT BUSTER!

Buster as it turned out was the Colombia team left fielder and he was a good ball player. Twice he had sent me in to the fence diving to catch fly balls. When I came down with them he shook his bat at me and the college girls winced and carried on. My brother turned and looked over his shoulder that day making plays that would have made any scout leave the fields of Oklahoma and rush home to Real, New York. Billy was pitching one hell of a game. By the ninth inning it was tied 4-4. My brother had two home runs. Each time he hit one I was on base with a hit when he landed the ball behind Buster and in to the laps of his private fan club. One time one of the girls tossed the ball on to the parkway where it careened off a passing car and ended up back on the field. Everyone cheered like she was some kind of magician. The thing about playing a game is anything can happen – even balls ricocheting off a passing car and landing back on the field. It happened everyday, so I did not see what all the cheering was about. In the top of the 9th the strangest inning of ball I ever played or saw, clouds rolled in fast and furious. It started raining sleet the size of small cats and dogs. Everyone ran from the field looking for cover. There was a tunnel that separated the ball field from the golf course. Inside two teams of ballplayers – the coaching staff and the fans waited out the storm. It was like being in a bar waiting to hear the greatest damn band that ever played in New York City. It was loud and as the lightning hit and the thunder cracked the girls would screech so loud it just about made me wish I was dead.

"We got to call the game!" the Colombia team yelled. They all had cars and wanted to make a run for it so they could go home. The two umpires were standing and looking at the sky wondering what to do. "It will pass", I yelled as loud as I could. Everyone looked at me. I shrugged my shoulders and said, "It's New York, not Iowa! A storm like this will pass." The umpires contemplated making a run for their cars, as the sun appeared out of the western sky. The way it shined silenced everyone in the tunnel and slowly everyone was staring at the sky like they were waiting for it to fall. The umpires walked out of the tunnel taking off their caps and holding out their hands. They started shaking their heads in agreement announcing the game would continue. Everyone cheered. The field was slick from the rain. The umpires did the best they could, trying to clean the field by kicking water out of the puddles with their feet. Both teams helped by using bats to swipe at the puddles thinking we could distribute the water evenly. The umpires took one last look at the field and decided it was time to PLAY BALL!

Out on to the field we went, standing in puddles of mud and debris. The college girls stayed in the tunnel with the girls from our crew. After a storm the worst place to be is on the field. There is no telling what could happen to a ball once it leaves the bat. The worst place for a ball to be hit on a wet field is the ground. The Colombia boys knew it. They started slapping at Billy's pitches sending the ball in to spins and strange hops. Before anyone could say "what the huck!" the bases were loaded. They batted for what felt like an entire day. When we finally got the third out, those bastards were winning 10-4. The last game we would play as a team was ending horribly.

The strange thing about the game of baseball is this: the other team gets up with the same conditions. Once in the dugout, Mike the giant owner and coach of the team started yelling like some kind of mad Fuehrer. He called us in to a small huddle and asked us each to remember who were are! He took out a bottle of Jagermeister and held it in the air high above his head. He screamed: "Zig-a-zagger – Zig-a-zagger"

At first we stood dumbfounded and afraid and then we yelled in reply: "OY! OY! OY!"

He screamed louder then we ever heard him yell before: "Zig-a-zagger – Zig-a-zagger"

The team looked at each other and as if out of the skies like another storm we hollered at the top of our lungs: "OY! OY! OY!"

The girls in the tunnel screamed the chant again and again as we prepared for our final at bat. Mike stood at first base holding the bottle over his head taunting everyone. Each time he chanted the girls answered louder – and with each chant Mike took a swig of Jagermeister. We began the inning with the same strategy used by the Colombia boys. We slapped, bunted and rounded the bases like we were on some kind of wild carousel ride. The Colombia boys had lost all levels of decorum. They were cursing at each other and at one point time had to be called because the outfielders were beating the hell out of each other for missing easy fly balls. When the inning was over, the score was again tied 10-10 and the sun was slowly fading in the distance.

The umpires informed us, there was no need to play a second game since only one game would decide who would win our division. The umpires also told us the game would not be called on a kind of darkness. This meant we would be in complete darkness on a wet field, trying to win a game that anywhere else on earth would have been called at least a dozen times.

In to the 15th inning we went, the 21st and finally under a moonless sky, it was official everyone on the field was blind. The infield had the advantage, if any was to be had – because the cars passing on the parkway would occasionally throw a beam of light on the ground. A fly ball was a different story. At best, sound was the only means of tracking the flight of the ball. "In the air!" screamed the Colombia coach. "They can't see shit out there!" The first batter came up and smashed a ball high in the sky. The entire infield started chasing the flight of the ball to the outfield. *"IT'S RIGHT THERE! OVER HERE! JUST STAND AND HOLD UP YOUR GLOVE!"* Roland Gunner in right field listened and at the warning track felt the ball land in the webbing of his glove. The entire team started cheering like we had won the World Series. The next batter came up and he too smacked the ball high in the air. The ball this time was headed straight for Crazy Al, the former axe murder and now a running sideways drunk blinded by darkness. Crazy Al finally came to a stop and yelled – *"EVERYBODY BACK OFF!"* The entire team froze in their tracks looking up at the sky and then back down at Crazy

Al. He was standing there looking up at the sky the way someone might look at a bird about to drop a surprise on your head. He stood there moving his head one way, then another with his hands at his sides. Then as casual as anything, like it was broad daylight he said calmly "I got it."

He lifted his hand with the glove and "Plop!" Unlike a few moments earlier when Roland Gunner in right caught the ball, everyone was silent. The umpire ran out past second base and raised his thumb signaling an out. It was amazing. "Two Out!" screamed the umpire and everyone went back to their positions awestruck by what we had just witnessed.

The next batter was Buster – the left fielder for Colombia who played one of the best games that day I'd ever seen. He took a few practice swings then raised his arm pointing to the left field fence. I couldn't see him. My brother's voice came out of the darkness of the infield yelling, *"HE'S COMING AT YOU KIDD!"* I stood for a second with my hands on my knees down in a crouching position. I was waiting to hear the crack of the bat. I yelled back *"TIME OUT!"* Billy nearly broke his arm holding on to the pitch. I came running in from the outfield and stood at third base with my brother. I had a plan.

Soon the entire team was on the mound with Billy and he was staring at me like I had lost my mind. The fact that my brother did not think it sounded crazy was perhaps one of the greatest moments in my life. Just as I had said, the night before we would never again share the same room, here we were on our field of dreams and he believed in what I wanted to do. The umpires came on to the mound to break up our meeting. We all headed back to our positions.

Billy looked around the infield, shaking his head and in a strange way laughing inside at the crazy idea. He went in to his motion and just before releasing the pitch – right before the ball left his hand – the entire infield charged the plate screaming like a bunch of mad dogs. Buster standing at the plate was so startled he took a step back in horror. The ball glanced off the front of the bat and sailed straight up in the air. Billy stood under the ball visible only by the passing headlights of cars on the parkway. He caught the ball and we celebrated again like we had won the greatest game ever played.

In the bottom of the inning, Mike took us aside, having put away three bottles of Jagermeister; he confessed he was in no condition to provide us with any strategy. He then went to the far end of the dugout and passed out. I looked at the team, this bunch of guys who had sweat, struggled and entertained each other for an entire year. I felt a strange affection for what we had accomplished. It was a feeling that would never come over me again as long as I lived. My brother suggested something that night which proved to be the most brilliant idea of his young life. He said, "Hit it where they ain't."

At first we all wanted to say "Duh!" in harmony. But then he followed it with the logic of a real baseball thinker. He said, "On the ground, soft and slow."

The first three batters reached base quickly. Again the Colombia boys were their own worse enemies. My brother came to bat with no outs, 10-10 in the bottom of the 21st knowing a fly ball deep to any field was the game. To this day, I am not certain if the crack of the bat made the sound, or if it was the ball landing on top of a police car screaming by on the parkway. We never found that ball. It went up and never came down. To this day it's referred to as home run that defied the laws of physics. In short when we would talk about it at all, we would just call it "the hit."

Chapter Twenty One

"*Chinese Checkers*", Billy said staring from the park bench in to the distance.

I looked at him sitting there not knowing if he was in one of his intellectual moods or feeling something else. Again with out hesitation he said, "Chinese Checkers."

"Ok Billy, what the huck?"

A look came over him I had not witnessed before. "I'm thinking every thing in life looks like a board game. The only board that looks remotely like I feel is Chinese Checkers."

"I lost you pal. You're going to need to be a little more specific?"

He was not himself; he was as close to miserable as anyone I ever seen. We sat there on the park bench in silence for a better part of the morning. Usually we would be engrossed in any number of conversations before the rest of the guys would show up. On this morning Billy wasn't talking. His usual optimistic take on every thing was missing. "Listen", I said after the second hour of silence, "We can sit here and wait for you to come around, or we can take a walk and talk about it. The guys will be here soon and unless you want to hear about conquest and midnight masturbation stories, we better move on." Billy got up and began walking past the basketball courts, out on to the service road for the parkway. I tried to keep up with him but he was deep in thought. He got on to Myrtle Avenue, walked past his block beside the cemetery and kept on going. "Do we have a destination in mind Billy, or are we just getting lost?"

"Why don't you shut the huck up and walk Kidd?"

We walked along the cemetery's edge with the grey tombstones glistening in the morning sun. We walked past the Real Library, past Bob's Diner and continued with the cemetery stones now casting shadows in the afternoon sun.

It had to be bad for Billy to be quiet for so long. I knew him too well and it was starting to make me feel depressed to see him this way. We walked across the service road to the parkway on a small pathway that required us to walk single file behind one another. Since he was the one with the sense of direction I followed behind trying to keep pace. He reached a fence for the cemetery and walked inside without hesitation. I knew where we were but could not guess why coming here was going to give him solace. He walked right up to the tombstone and sat down next to the stone sculpture of a woman in waiting. We were at Harry Houdini's grave. There were birds chirping further inside the cemetery and as I sat next to Billy, I felt a tinge of fear emanating from the granite around us. It did not take long for Billy to open up once we were seated and he stood looking at the stone sculpture of the woman, who was looking up at the name on the grave weeping.

"I thought she liked me."

I knew to keep my mouth shut. There are times when people want to vent and not hear advice or have their thoughts judged.

"She's the one who said I should meet her in the park last night. I never told anyone, not even you now how I felt about her. All summer long she kept me awake in my dreams. Her long blonde hair and those shorts she wore. I wanted to be with her, but did not know how to ask. You think I'm some kind of wimp, I know. It hurts too much to argue about it out loud. That bitch!"

I had no idea of knowing that Billy was experiencing a broken heart. It's the hardest thing to witness anyone go through no less your best friend. The fact was that we were sitting surrounded by tombstones, but most of all sitting on one of the most famous of all. I managed to keep quiet about how I was feeling and let Billy get it out of his system.

He choked back tears, and managed to hide any if they did appear. "That bitch shows up last night and we start talking. She grabs my hand ok? My hands were numb like they were run over by a bus. She's holding my hand and saying – "I think you're nice." What does **nice** mean anyway? Next thing I know she puts her head on my shoulder. I am thinking that this is what it must feel like to have someone really like you. If you tell anyone about this – I will personally kill you with my Uncle's souvenir German Luger!

So she's snuggling up to me and I can smell the shampoo on her hair. My hands, like I said are numb and she's holding them so tight I'm starting to think I'm paralyzed. How stupid is that? I finally get the girl I've been dreaming about all summer and I'm a damn paraplegic! Then it happened. She leaned up and kissed me. Not just like a peck you give your Aunt or mother. I mean like a kiss. Suddenly, I'm numb all over and I can't breathe! I start to feel like I am going to hyperventilate. I start heaving – the dry heaves you know – and she's like into the kiss so much she's sitting on my lap and holding the back of my neck with both hands and her tongue is half way down my throat! She doesn't know it, but I'm like having a near death experience! She starts grinding her hips in to my pelvis. Jesus Christ if I don't start to turn blue! The bitch was killing me! Why didn't anyone ever explain this shit to us! It was humiliating."

I cleared my throat, winced against the granite sticking in to my back and said, "If that's humiliation, then I want all I can get!"

He looked at me with anger in his eyes – "You don't get it. I was supposed to be the one all over her. She stopped kissing me and my eyes are bugging out of my head! I puked all over her!"

I couldn't help myself, I screamed, "You did what?"

He stood up and staring at the stone sculpture he started yelling like a mad man. "Screw you Kidd! I had no damn idea what I was supposed to be doing! I wanted to go home and tell my mother and father that they had abused me by not giving me the slightest clue what to do in a situation like that!"

I yelled at him, "Parents don't have a clue what to do in a situation like that! No one would! Not even Houdini!"

He sat down shaking his head. "At night in bed, under the covers, in the dark I knew exactly what to do and say. Once it was there in front of me – I freaked."

I did not know to feel sorry for my friend Billy or laugh. Feeling sorry for a friend when you're 17 years old is not an easy thing to do. I began to laugh. Then I fell off the bench in front of Houdini's grave and started howling like a damn idiot. I lay there rolling around laughing until Billy jumped on me and started pummeling my head with his fists. I started hitting back and we rolled away into the sitting woman where Billy's head hit her feet. He grabbed the back of his head and pulled his hands out to display blood. "Jesus Christ!" I screamed, "Houdini's bride is trying to kill you!"

He reached back behind his head, looked at his hands covered in blood and started laughing. "What the hell is so funny?" I yelled, "You're bleeding to death!"

"Don't be an idiot." He said in the Billy voice I knew. He took off his t-shirt and rubbed the back of his head with it. He dabbed at it several times, laughing harder and harder.

"I better get you to a hospital Billy", I was starting to think the blood would seep through the granite and Harry Houdini would rise up to kill us both for disturbing his wife.

Slowly, Billy stood up and with his hand covering his head with the bloody t-shirt; he tied it around his head looking like Lawrence of Arabia after a huge battle in the desert. "Come on Kidd, we're done here." He walked back out on to the service road of the parkway. I stood looking at the massive pools of blood seeping through the concrete and on the feet of the weeping widow statue. I got out of there as fast as I could run.

We walked back through the cemetery on the other side of the parkway. Billy said he had a headache and I told him again we should get to a doctor. He shook his head telling me it was just a small cut. He said, "When things like that happen, it always looks worse than it is." I told him he should still get it looked at, but he refused to listen. We walked past the mausoleums and large praying mantis saint statues in the cemetery. Billy stopped and looked at me with the sun now fading in the western sky, "Listen, I don't want to talk about this ever again." I understood but felt there had to be more to the story than his throwing up all over some girl. I waited until we were in the middle of the cemetery where the oldest graves from a hundred years ago were located; covered in a murky grey color no artist could every truly paint. "Billy? It happens you know." He turned and we stood there silent. I stood back on one leg planting myself in case he became enraged again at my lack of fully understanding him. He shook his head slowly, the blood soaked t-shirt shaking on his head like a surrendered flag. "It wasn't just how I reacted to feeling so unready. It was what she said and did after it happened. It wasn't enough that I felt humiliated and embarrassed. She showed her true colors and that's what makes her a bitch." I looked at him and could feel the intensity coming off his body like steam. "I was embarrassed and angry at myself. I was terrified in a way. She stands up and says, "Look what you did to me!" What I did to her? Like puking is voluntary!

"She could not see what I was going through? It was all about her! I was so humiliated and afraid – still choking my brains up and she's standing there screaming, "Why would you do something like that!" What did she think; I had a plan in mind when she started shoving her tongue down my throat?" Billy stood there shaking with his fists clenched as the last shadows of the day filtered through the evening sky. We had been at it all day, sitting, walking, talking, fighting, more walking, talking and finally lost.

We had wondered so far in to the damn cemetery we had gotten lost. Darkness was coming and we had no idea where we were. "Billy", I said looking around at the tombstones that seemed to be glowing in the dark; 'Do you have any idea where we are?"

He took a step back, removing the blood soaked t-shirt from his head, looked around and said in a quiet voice, “Not a clue.”

“What do you mean NOT A CLUE?” I screamed at the top of my lungs.

It was early September and the night air had hints of autumn. Billy stood with his blood covered t-shirt in one hand, with droplets of blood still falling on his neck, matted in his hair and we were lost in the damn cemetery.

“Don’t panic”, he said straining his neck and covering his one ear with his blood covered free hand. “Listen”, he said – “all we have to do is follow that sound.”

“What sound Billy?” I said furious for having been stupid enough to have him lead me in to the cemetery. He looked at me and again started laughing. “Watch Out!” he screamed as I ran past him looking everywhere around me. “Bats!” he said in a high-pitched voice. We began running with Billy swinging his t-shirt over his head splashing wet blood over everything including me. We were swatting at bats we could not see. We heard their loud shrill voices and kept running with no idea where we were going. Billy came to a stop attempting to catch his breath. I stopped next to him thinking we were going to be eaten alive by bats. The same bats we had heard people talk about and never believed were real. We sat down under a tree breathing heavily and unable to speak in coherent sentences. Every curse word ever dreamed of was used in the space of the ten minutes we stood idle under that tree. Billy stood up and said, “Come on, I know where we are.”

I couldn’t believe it. I looked at him angrier than ever before, “What do you mean you know where we are?” He started walking casually in the darkness towards a known direction. He laid the t-shirt down, patting it a few times watching the blood soak down over the tombstone. He said, "You can hear the ocean."

"The Ocean?" I said in a voice that must have sounded like someone drowning. We were at least 15 miles from the nearest ocean. Rockaway Beach was so far away there was no way it could be heard in a cemetery. Billy kept walking like someone who knew exactly where he was going. He talked over his shoulder as I followed, looking at his hair matted with blood from his wound. "Not the real ocean", he said walking faster; "It's the cars on the highway. The rubber wheels sound like waves crashing on the shore." His steps were determined and sure of themselves as I tried to hear what he was talking about. He was right. There was a distinct powerful sound in the distance that sounded like waves coming to shore. Sure enough, after several minutes of walking in the moonlit cemetery we could see the headlights of cars crossing over the parkway near our hometown. We traveled that day in more ways than we would understand until years later. It was an adventure. A journey. It was another rite of passage for two friends growing up in the neighborhood of Real.

Chapter Twenty Two

Dear Billy,

What in God's name were you thinking? Here in Anchorage, we have a name for people who do what you do – we call them stiffs. You can go to the lake and see them lying all over the place. When Kidd told me what happened I couldn't believe it. I'm thinking that girl you puked on was some kind of evil spirit. Yeah, and her smell caused you to vomit. It's a good thing you did because if you keep that smell in your system for too long – I hear you turn in to a ghoul. I don't think you wanted to be a ghoul, so thank God you had the good sense to throw up the way you did! Here in Anchorage, the annual ice-fishing contest is underway. Last year, I placed second behind some foreigner from England. That bastard cheated big time. He had all kinds of gadgets and a fishing device that looked like a damn lamppost. I swear it wasn't fishing; it was some form of probing.

You know those rich bastards come in here with their scientifically proven ideas and equipment, destroying the sport. I wanted to launch an investigation but the officials all welcomed the idea of someone besides an American winning as an opportunity to make the contest an international event. It already was an international event – I mean do you think every Eskimo in Alaska thinks they're from the United States? It's hard being disconnected from the rest of the world here. I guess we should protest that come the next election. A few months back President Nixon visited Anchorage saying, "He needed to cool off." I don't think many of us appreciated that kind of humor until we saw the President igloo hunting. Can you imagine having a President of the United States as a neighbor? The thing is there's little need for secret service and worries about anything harmful happening here in Alaska. The only thing he's going to need to worry about is frostbite. People have no idea what cold is until they spend a few nights trying to remember how to wiggle their toes. I will keep you posted on the Nixon Campaign. I hope you and Kidd can maybe visit me some day? It gets lonely up here despite all the events and daily get-rich quick schemes. A few days ago I thought of a way to make a lot of money. Imagine if some how I could bottle the ice and sell it? I would call it something like the Alaskan Cold. I'm willing to bet some day this will become popular. Every state will have its own water products to sell. I know it sounds crazy – but you wait and see.

Stay Warm and Keep Cool

Bob Googenblatt

Billy received the letter and left it for his mother to read. She was annoyed Billy had not told her about his flu symptoms. He advised her it was nothing to worry about and left it at that. Billy's Dad walked around the house smirking and placing his fingers down his throat. Billy wasn't amused. He was preparing for his last year of High School aware that some things would never change while other things would always be in constant motion.

Chapter Twenty Three

Despite everything that happened in the summer of 1972, Billy and I entered our final year of High School with a sense of having accomplished something we could not define. Eras in life are like that, you reach an end to something you worked for and it feels anti-climatic or celebratory in a way that makes it seem surreal. The thing about time and passing from one era to the next is you never know what can happen. Billy and I did not see one another as much as we had in the past during the final year of High School. It wasn't like we went in separate directions, life gets in the way and there's nothing you can do about it. We both met at the bus stop each morning. We both nodded our heads in recognition of each other's friendship; but it was different. We were growing up and growing apart. The radio was filled with music that makes some people argue 1972 was a pinnacle year in the history of rock music. FM radio was in full bloom after AM radio had owned the airwaves for the better part of the past 40 years. On FM Radio, the deejays it seemed had no rules to govern their play lists. Songs rolled from one artist in to the next with a vengeance for telling a story the deejay was trying to convey. The music became a deejays way of expressing his emotions. It was a way to reach out to the listener and share new ideas along with the growing list of bands and musical taste. Artists like John Lennon, who released his album "Imagine" in 1971, began to see big time airplay. Artists like Elton John, Eric Clapton, Neil Young, and bands like The Rolling Stones, The Hollies and the Moody Blues began to make a serious climb into the psyche of all people interested in good music. While the Stones had been around since the dawn of time, they seemed to be growing in popularity with the release of their album "Exile On Main Street." The album wasn't pretty. The album had a rawness to it that made people sit up and listen. When the songs from the album were heard on the radio, people immediately knew what it was. From September 1972 through June 1973, there was a new language being learned by every one under 30 years of age, it was called Rock and Roll. Every generation has its musical revolution. I started studying the liner notes on the back and inside album sleeves. I became a recluse, choosing to stay in my room and listen to music than bother with the outside world. That was how it was until Easter Sunday, 1973. On that day, my Mom insisted we all go to church as a family. We went to church but it was not a central part of our upbringing. My brother and I attended Catholic School up to the eighth grade. We had been anointed, appointed, saved, blessed, and had the fear of God beaten in to us. Church was the last connection to a life long quest that had no end and a million questions. At church that morning, I saw an angel. She stood on the altar with long blonde hair, wearing a grey dress with a guitar strapped to her waist. It was like seeing an apparition appear in your room singing. I was mesmerized. The Catholic Church had come up with a new way to keep things fresh and appealing to the younger generation, it was called Folk Mass. The small group of musicians played along with the mass singing songs that reached out and grabbed the attention of the younger audience. The older crowd either embraced it or hated it. The band on this morning was playing along with the mass in a new style, which included an electric guitar and a tambourine. They went in to the song "My Sweet Lord" by George Harrison with such abandonment people started clapping along and practically dancing in the aisles. This was not something the Catholic Church condoned as far as I knew and it felt in many ways like the youth of America was rising up to introduce their hopes and dreams to the world. I watched the angel swaying with her guitar and could not help but whisper in to my brother's ear – "Who's the babe with the guitar?" He looked at me with a sense of disgust at first. It was Easter morning, in church to celebrate the risen Lord and I wanted to know who the chick was with the guitar. It was a natural reaction to how my brain was working in those days. He replied, "That's Gayle Cooper." The name "Gayle Cooper" resonated in my brain the same way one might say Joni Mitchell, Carole King, Melanie or Cher. She was a goddess in a church saving my heart and soul.

My brother knew Gayle Cooper. He invited her to the park one night to watch us play ball. With the autumn chill in the air, she arrived wearing white corduroy pants, a Godspell t-shirt and sandals. When she appeared at the top of the steps to the ball field I was dumbstruck. I blamed the ball hitting me in the face on the sun being in my eyes. It was instead the appearance of the rest of my life.

A guy knows when he sees his destiny in the smile of another person. The same way he can sense the kind of people to avoid.

Gayle Cooper was too smart for me. She got a scholarship to go to a big name college. Her friends were from another walk of life. I was out of her league. These are the things everyone said when they knew I was interested in her. I never believed it. I did not know it right away, but there was a connection to Gayle Cooper that not even she would know until I met her parents. Her parents went to Bingo every Saturday night. They went to the Bingo Hall above my Uncle's candy store where I inserted parts of the N.Y. Times and Daily News. When you see the same people every week for a period of time they become special. I started giving Mr. Cooper; Gayle's father the paper for free. This was long before I knew he was her father. Walking past her house one night I saw her sitting on her front steps with friends. I stopped by to talk. Before I knew it, her friends had gone home and we were talking about music, movies, television and books we liked. It was obvious we had little in common in these categories but it was interesting to listen to someone passionate about the same things. Her father and mother came home. I was sitting next to her on the steps. Mr. Cooper walked up and before I could say a thing he started smiling from ear to ear. I recognized him as well and we both greeted one another like old friends. Gayle had a look on her face of complete shock. Her mother came by asking why she was talking to their paperboy. Her mother did not know any other way to describe me. It was amusing and I welcomed the opportunity to skip over any awkward introductions. I was invited inside for cake and coffee. Gayle was amazed to hear me talking with her Dad. It wasn't a date, it was something far better; it was acceptance without pretense. After that night we began to see each other often. She liked to take walks and show me poems she had written. I had never been with a girl before and she was easy to talk to and I felt myself falling in love. My senior year went by faster than any other period of time in my life. It was sad and beautiful at the same time in so many ways. My father was diagnosed with cancer. I was confused about the future and uncertain of my responsibilities as a son, a brother and a friend. In the summer of 1973, I needed to make a decision. Go to college or join the military. I opted for school, feeling there would be an opportunity to stay near home and help my mother cope. Two weeks in to college I sat in a friend's car in the pouring rain. I watched him run inside a building on campus. I sat looking out the window aware I needed to make a change. I got out of the car, walked to the corner and dropped my schoolbooks in to a trash basket. I walked several miles to an Army recruiting station. I asked the Sergeant if there were openings in Journalism. He told me to take a test. I sat in a small room in the back of the office and took a test. He looked it over and advised me I had what it took to be a journalist in the Army. He asked me when I wanted to start. I told him I needed to start as soon as possible. I told no one. It was a Tuesday afternoon in October. I left on Saturday.

Chapter Twenty Four

The decisions made in life do not always require plans. I did not have a plan when I joined the Army. On the day I was inducted in to the military at Fort Hamilton, New York my mother and brother arrived with Billy and several other friends. They did not have much to say because to them it was too fresh in their minds to fully understand. I could make up stories about how I knew what I was doing but that would be lying. I could tell you how I knew the war in Vietnam was still happening, but that too would be lying. In truth, I needed to make a change in my life. I needed to find myself which sounds like some kind of profound cop-out, but inevitably was the most important reason of all. I had no idea what to expect. I asked my brother to take care of himself and to help my mother cope with the pressures of my father's health. I promised to send home money to help pay the mounting medical bills.

I had never been on a plane before. The first day of my military experience seems surreal now when I think about it. We left from JFK and landed in Columbia, South Carolina. I was to start my military career in a place called Fort Jackson. A yellow school bus met us at the airport. There were 36 other recruits joining the Army that day. I do not remember talking with any one. I was too busy holding on to the seat on the plane to talk. Once at Fort Jackson we were told to line up in size order. With the sun already fading in the South Carolina sky, the process of lining up took longer than the Drill Sergeant anticipated. He started initiating us in to the Army's idea of decorum and discipline.

"YOU STUPID BUNCH OF YORKSHIRE PUPPIES!" This was the best he could come up with on such short notice. In retrospect it was rather an inspired statement. He knew we were all from New York and we were in a way dogs waiting to be trained. While standing in formation the Drill Sergeant stood in front of the platoon. We were now, a platoon according to him and soon we would be a Company. Getting used to the military structure was either understood quickly or you were reminded again of your heritage – which in our case was "YORKSHIRE PUPPIES!" He stood in front of us advising everyone we were now the SOLE PROPERTY OF THE U.S. ARMY! WE WERE NO LONGER MEMBERS OF ANY OTHER FAMILY! IT WAS OUR DUTY TO SHUT UP AND LISTEN! He took a step back and was handed an envelope by another Drill Sergeant. He looked at the envelope and said, "WE HAVE A RULE IN THIS PLATOON! THE FIRST RULE IS NO ONE GETS SOMETHING UNLESS WE ALL GET SOMETHING! This sounded reasonable to everyone. The Drill Sergeant looked closer at the envelope and said, "DO WE HAVE A PRIVATE JONATHAN KIDDRANE HERE?" I could not imagine why I was being singled out after being in the Army all of 10 minutes in any official capacity. I raised my hand like any good student should – "HERE!" I said hoping to sound respectful. He looked at me and screamed louder than he had yelled before, "FRONT AND CENTER SOLDIER!" I ran up and stood shaking not knowing what to expect. He looked me up and down waving the envelope in my face and said, "WE HAVE A FIRST HERE PEOPLE – IT SEEMS THIS ASSHOLE HAS A LETTER FROM HOME WAITING FOR HIS ARRIVAL! THIS GIVES US AN OPPORTUNITY TO DISPLAY TO YOU WHAT HAPPENS WHEN ONE OF US GETS SOMETHING NO ONE ELSE HAS! PRIVATE KIDDRANE HERE WILL NOW DROP AND GIVE ME TWENTY PUSH-UPS!" I fell in to a prone position and knocked out the best twenty push-ups I could muster under the circumstances. I finished the push-ups and stood back up. The Drill Sergeant looked at me grinning. He put his nose against mine and said loudly, "I DID NOT HEAR YOU COUNTING OFF THOSE PUSH-UPS PRIVATE! NOW DROP AND SOUND OFF SO EVERYONE CAN APPRECIATE HOW YOU EARN YOUR LETTER FROM HOME!" I dropped again to the prone position and counted off the twenty push-ups. When I was done I stood back up breathing heavily and sweating in the night air. Again he put his nose to my face and said, I DID NOT HEAR YOU SAYING WHO YOU WERE DOING THE PUSH-UPS FOR PRIVATE! I NEED TO HEAR YOU SAYING "ONE DRILL SERGEANT – TWO DRILL SERGEANT AND SO ON UNTIL EVERY ONE UNDERSTANDS OUR FIRST LESSON!" For the third time I went down in to a prone position and counted off each push-up announcing each one as instructed. I stood up and could feel my shirt sticking to my back and my face blushing red with humiliation. The Drill Sergeant put his nose to my face a fourth time and advised me, "YOU CAN NOW OPEN THIS LETTER

AND READ IT OUT LOUD TO US!" I had no idea who would send me a letter, only hours after being in the Army. I opened the envelope with my hands shaking and a feeling of being made a fool. The Drill Sergeant brought over a milk crate and sat down with his hand on his chin smiling. He looked up at me and said, NOW READ IT NICE AND LOUD SO EVERYONE CAN FEEL ALL WARM AND CUDDLY KNOWING SOMEONE AT HOME MISSES US!" I pulled out the letter and was immediately mortified recognizing for the first time it was a Googenblatt letter. I tried to tell the Drill Sergeant there had been a mistake. I explained to him how the letter was a joke.

"READ IT NOW!" He said with a look of growing impatience.

Dear Kidd,

What the hell is wrong with you? Don't you realize there is no longer a draft? When Billy gave me the news I just about had to shit. No one joins the Army on purpose anymore! Here in Anchorage we have names for people like you – we call them frozen meatheads! Talking about frozen meatheads, I shot a moose the other night. The damn thing came out of nowhere and it was unbelievable! I heard something crunching on the ice outside my shack. I opened the door and I'm staring at a moose! At first it was like something out of some damn movie, so I just stood there looking at it and it at me! I started to shoo it away like you would any other animal. But a moose is a moose you know what I mean? It starts grinding its front leg in to the ice getting ready to charge. So I leaned back in to my shack and I took out the nearest thing I own to a gun. You know the thing about shooting a wild moose with a harpoon gun is not a good idea. I hope you can learn something from my story because the damn harpoon hit the moose and he took off like a wounded buffalo. You know harpoon guns have ropes attached to the arrow thing-ma-gig and the next thing I knew I'm behind the damn moose like I was on skis. I must have made one hell of sight flying over the damn lake being pulled by a moose! The moose ran onto land and as soon as it hit the trees the harpoon came lose and I crashed ashore like a damn torpedo! I thought you would need to know what could happen when you least expect it. Now that you're in the Army I'll write more often so I can keep you up to date about what's going on. For God sake watch out for the moose! Keep Warm and Stay Cool

Bob Googenblatt

I folded the letter and started putting it back in to the envelope. The Drill Sergeant licked his lips, removed his hat and ran his fingers on his scalp. He stood up and looked around at the platoons that were in all states of smirking and uncontrollable laughter. He managed to wipe a smirk from his own face; walk over to me and advise: "EVERY DAMN PLATOON HAS A COMEDIAN! IT APPEARS YOU HAVE FOUND A NEW WAY TO AMUSE ME PRIVATE KIDD! I WILL BE WATCHING YOU!

He told me to get back to my position. He turned away from the platoon for a moment looking at the other Drill Sergeant who was doubled over on the ground laughing. His body was trembling for a while before he composed himself enough to turn around and advise everyone – WE WIL MEET BACK HERE AT 0600 HOURS! AT THAT TIME YOU WILL BE GIVEN A PROPER HAIR CUT WHICH YOU WILL PAY UNCLE SAM FOR GIVING YOU! YOU WILL BE ISSUED YOUR UNIFORMS, WHICH YOU WILL PROMPTLY PUT ON! THIS IS THE LAST TIME I WANT TO SEE ANY OF YOU

WEARING THESE CIVILIAN CLOWN SUITS! NOW GET OUT OF MY SIGHT!

We were escorted to a barracks where everyone immediately started taking beds on bunks lined up as far as the eye could see. It was my first day in the Army. I had made a name for myself and could not wait to tell everyone not to write.

Chapter Twenty Five

The first night in a barracks with a hundred different people around you that you never met before is scary. Some of the guys could not stop talking. There were whimpers from around the long hallway of some guys crying. Mostly, there were guys making noises of what they assumed were "moose calls." There was laughter in some parts of the room and in the distance there was a radio playing "Midnight Train to Georgia" by Gladys Knight and The Pips. It was an odd song to hear on your first day in the Army. There was a chorus of voices singing along with the Pips as the lights went out and a voice came over a loud speaker, "ALRIGHT YOU MAGGOTS GET SOME SLEEP – YOU'RE GONNA NEED IT!" There were a few giggles and few "Oh Shits!" heard as the song faded to silence. The silence in a room filled with others can be the most quiet you can imagine, as slowly voices turned to whispers into snoring dreams.

Just as the Drill Sergeant had predicted we were all ushered to the barbershop where no matter how short your hair already was Uncle Sam required his 5 dollars for a haircut. We were then issued our uniforms and told to stand in formation for our first inspection. The Drill Sergeant referred to everyone as "Ladies" or "Maggots" each word representing what he considered a compliment. The first day came and went with drills showing us how to march up one side of the parade ground to the other. An entire day disappeared before our eyes with no one even speaking a word. Every face looked afraid but determined to listen to what needed to be done next. We were becoming a unit according to the Drill Sergeant. We were, "A unified weapon of war." He marched us in and around the same field for hours yelling, "You get to be the first assholes shipped home in a nice pine box! Thank you for serving your country!"

If we had doubts about joining the Army before we marched that first day, they were confirmed multiple times. If there was fear, it had multiplied in different ways for each of us. As the sun drifted out of the sky, the Drill Sergeant had us standing in the middle of the parade field covered in sweat and thirsty. His final speech to us on our first day went something like this: "Each of you is thinking you had a bad day! Let me be the first to assure you, this was easy compared to what happens tomorrow and the day after that. For the next several months Ladies, your asses belong to me! It is my job to turn you in to soldiers of the United States Army. To earn this privilege, it is my duty as your Drill Sergeant to weed out the shit! Uncle Sam does not like shit! Uncle Sam has his own version of the shit and your shit is not worth smelling until I say so! IS THAT CLEAR?

Every one screamed loudly, "YES DRILL SERGEANT!"

"Now I am going to dismiss your sorry asses today, so you can eat in our four star restaurant known as The Mess Hall! If any of you YORKSHIRE ASSHOLES do not feel the meal is up to your taste – too bad! Get out of my sight!"

Drill Sergeant Pelfry was not really a bad person. He had good intentions. It was the way he went about those intentions that had everyone scratching our heads. We ate in silence covered in the same sweat and mud we accumulated during our first day. It was reminiscent of the days to follow, each one a lesson in tolerance, perseverance and acceptance. My first letter home to Billy tried to encapsulate how I was feeling.

Dear Moron,

That damn Googenblatt got me in trouble! What the hell could he be thinking?

I know I told people to write. He sends a damn telegram, making me look like an idiot!

He owes me 60 pushups! This is the first time I have been able to write a letter in over a week. Let me tell you what it's like. The first night was a nightmare because of that stupid letter. On the first full day, which was a Sunday we were given haircuts and our uniforms. I have to wear boots day and night. It's like being reminded snow is on the way at all times. Breakfast is in a Mess Hall. It's nothing like our cafeteria in High School. There are tables lined up as far as you can see and filled with other soldiers eating in silence. Drill Sergeants, who are a lot like prison guards walk around making sure no one talks. If you look at them the wrong way, watch out! There were people counting off more pushups than our entire class did in four years of gym. That first Sunday, which was last week, went by quietly. Little did any of us realize it was the calm before any storm?

On Monday morning we were lined up in formation and ushered on to these trucks called "cattle cars." We were stuffed in to these trucks standing up with our duffle bags like sardines. The trucks managed to find every pothole possible. Tempers flared as every one of us were tossed around inside the truck. Fists were flying and everyone was yelling like we were on that damn Cyclone rollercoaster at Coney Island. Then the trucks stopped and it seemed like it took forever before they opened the doors. We baked in the morning sun inside that damn truck which had no windows and felt like they were going to let us die a horrible death. Suddenly, the doors flung open and everyone fell out of the truck on to sand. We had arrived at our destination. Boot Camp had officially begun.

This bastard Drill Sergeant who has my name imbedded in his brain because of that damn Googenblatt letter started dragging me through the sand. He told me to do pushups while he stood on my back! It felt like we were being tortured instead of trained. The next thing I knew we were sitting in a room while a bunch of Officers and other Drill Sergeants welcomed us. This is what they said:

WELCOME TO YOUR NEW HOME! WELCOME TO THE LAST DAYS OF YOUR LIFE! THE UNITED STATES WANTS TO THANK YOU FOR PREPARING TO DIE!

The first week is over now. Tell everyone I loved them. Have a good life.

Kidd

Chapter Twenty Six

Back home people in the 1970s were removed from the war in many ways. Despite how movies depict a country on edge, in Real, New York – it was life as usual. Gayle Cooper found comfort in hanging out with her friends. Billy Moran discovered the challenges of college, spending his nights studying or going out for an occasional beer. Things were normal, quiet and civilized. Gayle and her parents argued as she prepared for college. There was a part of her that wanted to be married and settle down. They told her she was too young. As the days turned in to weeks, months in to a year, it became necessary for people to find things to do. Television was a boring distraction as there was very little that catered to the teenage mind. Unlike today, where it would seem everything is catered to the youth, young people stayed close to home and the local religious establishments or they careened out of control with hidden addictions and assorted attractions to keep them amused. Gayle continued singing at the local church, each Sunday strumming along with the hymns, breaking more hearts than she knew. She wrote letters every night. She wrote more letters than my forearms or back could tolerate with pushups and continued hazing tactics. One letter included a cassette tape with songs she sang. I played the tape and needed to make copies for everyone including Drill Sergeant Pelfry. There was something special about a voice and a guitar that made tolerating the coming changes worthwhile. Billy Moran was quietly becoming a scholar studying things like Philosophy and Sociology. He began sending me quotes from authors like Arthur Schopenhauer, Sigmund Freud and Carl Jung. These were inspired comments about the struggle of understanding the human mind. I did not know I was struggling until I read about it in letters from Billy Moran.

At night in the barracks, with Gayle singing low on a tape player, reading her letters and Billy's observations about mankind, I was getting an education no one could fully understand. It was an education that future generations would dismiss as wasted time. The only education worthy of recognition in the future would be a certified degree declaring someone graduated from a college of their choice. A Bachelors Degree would outweigh the value of an Honorable Discharge in the free world. Soldiers who dedicated three years of their life willing to die for maintaining freedom would be considered fools. It's important you understand this before I can continue with what happened through the following years. In so many ways history was being re-written before our eyes by individuals who had no idea what it took to keep them in their free-minded pursuits. In Real, storeowners began to get too old to maintain their responsibilities. Things were changing and few were capable of seeing it because they were too busy chasing dreams. It must be true of "Every Place", America; but in Real the changes were happening at a pace only those who left for a while could see. I did not ask for any powers of observation, but they came never the less when I returned for Christmas in 1973.

On the plane ride home from South Carolina, the experiences of being away-created thoughts and ideas different from those who stayed. The youthful mind takes on information at a higher speed than a complacent middle-aged brain. I had forgotten about the concept of snow, cold weather and the seasonal changes. The pilot announced we would need to wait for landing instructions, as there was a snowstorm at LaGuardia Airport. We circled the airport as the crew celebrated our arrival with free drinks. After my fifth gin and tonic I fell asleep.

I did not anticipate the dream. The most unlikely visitors come to us in our sleep.

At first I was confused to see Louis Armstrong sitting on his steps at his home in Queens. I was a young boy again walking down his street listening to the sound of his trumpet playing. I was mesmerized by the sincerity of its tone and slowly approached his door.

Louis: Why if it isn't Frankie's boy?

Jono: Hello Louis. I missed you.

Louis: Of course you did, everyone misses Louis Armstrong.

The way he laughed with a cackle and a snort, wiping his brow with his handkerchief put me at ease. I was fighting with myself to stay in the comfort of his smile.

Louis: Lucille was saying just the other day, what happened to Frankie and his boy?

Jono: I grew up Louis. I went away.

Louis: You're here now and all is well.

Jono: I am scared Louis. My mom says my Dad is not doing well.

Louis: Not doing well? What's the matter with Frankie?

Jono: He's been sick. I went away and he's been to the doctor. They say it's bad.

Louis: Doctor's always say it's bad. How they going to keep you coming back?

Jono: Not this time Louis, it sounds like he's not going to get better.

Louis: Everyone gets better son. It's either that or die smiling in your sleep.

Jono: I don't want my Dad to die smiling in his sleep.

Louis: Louis hears you son. I'm trying to put you at ease. Why don't you come inside and have Lucille cook you up something to eat?

Jono: I was hoping to catch my Dad delivering the papers.

Louis: Come to think of it, Frankie has not been by in almost three months.

Jono: I joined the Army.

Louis: A youngster like you in the Army! Gosh-darn what's the world coming to?

Jono: It's a crazy world Louis.

Louis: No it's a wonderful world, like I sing in my song.

Jono: Louis, I don't think we're supposed to be seeing one another.

Louis: Who put something like that in your young mind?

Jono: It's just how it is. Ghosts and spirits and things like that don't exist.

Louis: What are you going on about now? Ghosts? Spirits?

You been visiting your father's liquor cabinet?

Jono: You mean you don't know?

Louis: I know I ain't ever felt better in my life and Lucille is here to prove it.

Jono: Maybe it's me. I'm confused and not myself these days.

Louis: Not yourself is an under statement. You need to rest easy and not worry so much.

Jono: How do you stop from doing that? Worrying and stuff?

Louis: Son, you gots to believe. In the higher spirit. Now if you're talking about the higher spirit, well I am here to tell you you're in good hands.

Jono: It's not easy being young Louis, not anymore.

Louis: When was it fun to be young? You got to have something to lift you up. Look at this horn; someone who believed in me, and after that it was up to me to believe in myself. What do you have that makes you feel complete?

Jono: I have Gayle Cooper and I'm still searching for the next thing.

Louis: Well then you let Gayle Cooper be your light. She will show you what you were meant to be.

Jono: You mean love?

Louis: Love? That's a mighty word for a young boy. If you found love – I better tell Lucille to cook us up her best meal. You gots that, then you found it all.

Jono: And my Dad?

Louis: Your Dad will be along just fine when he gets good and ready.

Jono: You mean to be with you?

Louis: No my boy, to be with you.

Jono: But I don't…

The pilot came on the speakers announcing we were making our final approach in to New York. "I HOPE YOU BOYS ARE DRESSED WARM – IT'S TEN DEGREES AND SNOWING HEAVILY IN NEW YORK! MERRY CHRISTMAS AND THANK YOU FOR FLYING WITH DELTA AIRLINES!

I watched as the other soldiers continued to celebrate with their glasses held high and singing Christmas songs at the top of their lungs. I was going back to my home. I had no idea what to expect. I had relied on letters to tell me what was happening. I read each one, earning each one with feats of strength and determination. The plane was landing and I was relieved to be home but afraid of what I might find.

Chapter Twenty-Seven

"What's with the red bandana?" I asked Billy when I met him in the park after saying hello to my parents and brother. The one comment unanimous with everyone was, "nice head." The concept of a crew cut was considered to be more in keeping with becoming a member of Hare Krishna than being in the military. Billy, in only a few short months had hair to his shoulders complimented with a red bandana that he wore around his head looking like an Indian refugee in an old John Wayne film. We sat in the park, on the bench where we had met for years in silence for longer than I thought possible. He had questions for me and I had questions for him. Our appearance made us think we were different. The silence was necessary to erase the cobwebs surrounding an absence. The snow was deeper than anticipated and the bench was half in ice as we sat mulling over what to say. The first thing I thought to ask was about was his hair. His first thought was to comment my lack of hair. We had seemingly become interested in our appearances like strangers opening a door on Halloween to discover masked trick-or-treaters with their bags open screaming TRICK-OR-TREAT!

Billy ran his hands through his hair saying, "I think its laziness or maybe something to do with conformity." I brushed my hand over my baldhead replying, "I didn't have a choice." Again the silence echoed through the park as children rushed through the snow with sleds in tow on their way in to the Golf Course behind the ball field. A ritual we had done a hundred times in our younger days and now looked upon them with a mixture of envy and sadness. Billy sat shaking his head before filling me in on everything I missed and not mentioned in letters. He began by laughing out loud, "I guess you heard about Dickie Blues?" I had not heard anything about anyone since leaving. The main topic of most letters being "taking care of myself" and the one constant comment being "There's not much happening here." I looked at Billy waiting to hear the Dickie Blues story. Billy adjusted himself on the cold bench before telling me what had happened to our first baseman who was responsible in many ways for us playing ball in a bar league.

"We were sitting over there on the overhang to the entrance of the park one night." Billy started reflecting on his conversation with Dickie. "He was in one of those talkative moods and it was awkward. His Dad died a month after you joined up, right before Thanksgiving. It seems his entire family fell apart in a matter of days. His Mom sold their house and moved in with some insurance salesman. Dickie's brother Max, he went off on his own without graduating from High School or anything. Can you imagine an entire family exploding because the father died? So, we're sitting there and he starts telling me about a lifelong passion to steal a fire truck. I don't know why it was so important for him, but he emphasized that it had to be a fire truck. The thing is he wanted to drive the fire truck straight down the block in to the wall where we were sitting. He meant it too. Every night since then when I hear a fire engine I think Dickie Blues is out there making his dream come true. I lay awake anticipating a loud crashing noise. The sirens pass and the silence some nights are worse than the anticipation of the crash. It's weird I know, but that's what Dickie Blues is up to these days. He drives around and he blasts Led Zeppelin's album Physical Graffiti like it was the best damn record ever made. People have gone a bit crazy." I waited to see if Billy was done sharing his news. I looked at him and asked, "Is it a particular side of the album he likes more than the rest?"

Billy started chuckling; "I didn't ask him about the album. It's typical that you would catch that as being a central piece of the story."

"I was trying to see if there was a lyric in a particular song that has him thinking about crashing in to a wall."

"I'll have to listen to the record again and get back to you."

"Why that wall, with a fire truck?"

"I never thought about it as being something he actually wanted to do Kidd. He's distraught about losing his Dad, his mother and brother going off the way they did – maybe he just wanted to tell me how much everything around him feels like it's falling apart."

"That would make a lot of sense, except that Dickie's Dad did not raise his children to steal anything, no less a fire truck."

"You see, this is why I did not mention it in my letters. You over think things. It's just one of a million stories you missed by going away."

"I joined the Army Billy. I didn't just go away."

"Hey, I know that. But you can't expect me to sit around waiting for you to come back home so I can play news reporter or something."

"I'm just talking here Billy. What are you so upset about?"

"I'm not upset; I just don't enjoy rehashing things that happened. They're over with as far as I care."

"Ok, so we can maybe talk about the weather? It looks like we're going to have a White Christmas."

"Hey, drop dead!"

"What? What did I say?"

Billy stood up and started walking towards the stairs that led out of the park.

He turned with his gloved fingers pointing at me. "I don't need you mocking me! I'm happy with my red bandana and you're an asshole!" He slid down the stairs holding on to the railing like someone going down a ski lift in the wrong direction. I sat in the darkness contemplating what I wanted to do next. I knew I needed to let Gayle know I was home. I wanted to call her so I did not have to hear any more comments from people who looked at soldiers like we were alien invaders. There was a phone booth right outside the park and I started making my way to call her. I watched as Billy Moran trudged across Myrtle Avenue on his way home, his hair flowing in the wind beneath a red bandana.

Chapter Twenty-Eight

I dropped the dime in to the phone waiting for the dial tone. From the phone booth I could see the window of my room. I dialed Gayle Cooper praying she would be the one to answer. An unanswered phone can be like a whisper said out loud no one hears. I hung up the phone while standing in the phone booth. Snow had begun falling and I thought about how much I longed to be home, and how desperate it felt to get away. The windows of the phone booth fogged up fast. I felt for a moment like a guy at a tollbooth on a highway. I put my hand outside the door watching the flakes accumulate in my palm. I looked down at the wall where Billy told me he spoke with Dickie Blues who had in a short span of time lost everything he deemed worthy of calling his own. He lost his father. His mother up and married some stranger. His brother took off without a trace. I left the phone booth walking towards the wall Dickie Blues wanted to crash a fire engine. At that particular moment in time, more than anyone else alive, I understood Dickie Blues. I knew where to find him. It was the most obvious place on earth for him. He was at Mike's Tavern drinking and singing along with Led Zeppelin and Sinatra songs on the jukebox. I looked down the Avenue seeing no bus or car in sight. I started walking towards Mike's Tavern and my meeting with Dickie, whom I knew couldn't wait to see me.

The snow was coming down harder. I could have easily walked across the street and went up to my room. The window seemed to be shimmering in the night air. I ignored everything and headed straight down the middle of Myrtle Avenue. I tucked my head in to my snorkel coat pulling it down over my eyes. My Army boots were my greatest weapon against the storm and I was happy I chose to put them on. I walked past Woodhaven Boulevard dodging only a few cars out on the road. I walked past the track and field at Victory Park and down past Freedom Road where Billy and I had first discussed Bob Googenblatt. I thought about Bob as being the only one who could understand what was really happening in the world. As I walked down the middle of the Avenue I began a conversation with good ole Bob in my head.

Kidd: Bob! What's happening?

Bob: Good to see you pal. Did I mention about my ice fishing tournament?

Kidd: Got all your letters Bob, quite a story you winning all those fishing awards.

Bob: Damn straight. You see these New Yorkers getting all bent out of shape over a little snow? Makes you want to fall down and laugh yourself to death!

Kidd: Well, there are a lot of spoiled people in New York Bob.

Bob: Spoiled? These people need something to come along that will shake them up beyond belief! It's the only way they would all come out of their cocoons and realize everyone's in the same damn race. That's the problem with most places you know today. They got the white race, the black race, the yellow race, this race – that race and what do you know? We're all part of the same damn thing! The RAT RACE!

Kidd: No one's ready for that ole buddy. Besides people want to be left alone. They enjoy being a part of their little groups and it's always been that way.

Bob: Always Spalways! Some day a real pain is going to wake them up.

Kidd: I think you're right Bob. But you know what would happen after they were all shown the truth about being on the same side? They would retreat back in to their holes like animals in a forest.

Bob: You might be right Kidd. During a fire it's every one for themselves. Every one of them running every which way and falling down but someone will pick you up to keep the escape in motion. Fascinating to think about really. But when the fire's over – the animals will mill about on the outskirts of the damage. They will stare in wonder at what was and is no longer there and then, quite by habit, they will return to their own ways. The squirrel searching for nuts. The damn hawks swooping down to grab whatever they damn well please. The rats waiting to capitalize on the debris. Yeah, you might be right Kidd. People only accept things they can't have. You know if there was a cure of cancer found tomorrow – it would put like a million people out of work. You ever think about that?

Kidd: It's a wonder anything gets done huh Bob?

Bob: A damn wonder. Makes your head spin around.

I had reached the end of the Avenue and made my turn towards Mike's Tavern. As usual Bob Googenblatt had helped me find my way. I turned on to Jamaica Avenue and stood frozen for a moment. There was Dickie Blues. He was standing on the hood of his car trying to kick in the front windshield. His voice was echoing through the snow-covered streets. "DAMN! STUPID! SON OF A STUPID…..!"

Dickie Blues always had a way with words. I walked up to the car covered in snow and said in the calmest voice I could muster. "Dickie? Why are you trying to destroy your car?" He stopped to look at me. I had forgotten for a moment that I was wearing a hooded coat; covered in snow and no way of looking like anyone he would know. Dickie looked down at me from the hood of his red Mustang and said, "What's it to you?" I realized he did not know who I was and it was an awkward moment before I announced who I was.

"Dickie!" I removed my hood, "Jonathan Kiddrane"

He stepped down from his car hood and stood at my side. "Kidd? Where have you been man?"

"I joined the Army Dickie. I am home on Christmas leave."

"It's Christmas Eve already?"

"No, not yet Dickie, I said I am home on Christmas leave."

"How can you be home on Christmas Eve, if it didn't happen yet?"

It was obvious Dickie had been drinking. His drinking was legendary. I was present after a game once when he cleared the bar yelling out obscenities that would curl anyone's hair. "The prodigal Kidd has returned", he said nearly falling down in to a pile of snow at the side of the road.

"Dickie?" Is there something I could do to help?

"You want to help me?"

"You're the only one standing here?"

"You want to help me?"

"Yes Dickie, I came here to talk to you tonight."

"I don't want to be in the Army Kidd."

"No, no Dickie, I don't want you to join the Army."

"You don't think I would make a good soldier?"

"You would be a fine soldier Dickie, it's just that I needed someone to talk to. Someone like you. I think we have a lot in common."

"We do?"

"Yes, I don't know what exactly – but you told Billy Moran something that makes me think you'd understand how I feel."

"Billy Moran is an asshole!"

"No Billy's a good guy; he's going through some life changes now. He will come around."

"Life changes? You mean he's getting his period?"

"No Dickie, Billy is just growing up and moving away from a lot of things."

"Is he joining the damn Army too?"

"No, nothing like that. I mean he's going through some things he has to figure out on his own. It happens to everyone sooner or later."

"My damn car is busted."

"Maybe we can get a tow truck and get you some help."

"The kind of help I need doesn't come on a tow truck."

"There you see I understand what you mean. You speak in metaphors. I speak metaphor too."

"Metaphors? What the hell are they teaching you in that Army Kidd?"

"You told Billy you wanted to steal a fire engine? You said you wanted to crash the fire engine in to the wall near the park. It's a metaphor for what's really bothering you?"

"I have no idea what language you are speaking Kidd. You didn't become a spy or something did you?"

"Look at your car Dickie. It's fire red! You wanted to be standing here smashing in your car window in the snow!"

"I did?"

"Well yeah its obvious isn't it?"

"It is?"

"You're not crazy are you?"

"I don't think so."

"Then it has to be a set plan. A sign or something?"

"You mean from God?"

"God, or someone like that."

"My father hated this car."

"Well there you go Dickie. It's a sign from your Dad!"

"Holy Shit! My Dad's telling me to trash my car? How cool is that Kidd?"

"I'd say it's very cool? As cool as it gets Dickie!"

"Wow, who would have thought it? A sign from heaven."

"I knew you'd understand Dickie. Now why don't we get you a tow truck?"

"Damn straight. There's a phone inside Mike's Tavern. I'll buy!"

And so it was that I walked the final blocks to the bar arm in arm, in a blizzard singing Christmas carols with Dickie Blues thinking it was good to be home.

Chapter Twenty-Nine

"You're home and entire day and I don't hear from you", Gayle said standing at the foot of my bed. I opened my eyes staring at her with hands on her hips. I adjusted my eyes trying to find some semblance of balance from the night before. "I'm sorry Gayle, I was in no condition to see you", slurring my words unable to fully lift my head from the pillow. I had left the radio on. The deejay was spinning "My Favorite Things" by John Coltrane. Gayle looked at me as I lay with one eye opened trying not to vomit. "Listen Gayle, I had every intention of seeing you and only you, but things got a little out of hand with Dickie Blues last night. Did you hear his father died?"

She was looking at me and the radio with a quizzical look in her eyes. "Why are you listening to show tunes?" I lifted my head trying to grasp the music before sitting upright and advising her, "That's not a show tune! That's John Coltrane!" She backed up towards the doorway and started laughing. "It's from a musical Jonathan. It's My Favorite Things from The Sound of Music. I should know it's one of my favorite movies."

"Well then they ripped Coltrane off."

"No my dear, he's merely playing homage to the music."

"Homage?"

"Don't make fun of me Jonathan Kiddrane. You may be the big music fan, but when I know a song I will say so."

We sat there listening to the song, the thriving saxophone over the monotone piano and marching drum beat. The deejay waited for the song to fully end before advising, "That was John Coltrane's homage to the musical The Sound of Music with My Favorite Things." I looked at her and we both started laughing. I reached out to her and we hugged one another. It was the hug that made me realize how comfortable I felt in her arms. The day seemed to disappear as we stayed for hours listening to music on the radio and watching the sun fade from the sky across the tree lines in the park. I was home and more than ever I realized it was where I belonged. Gayle broke the silence of the music induced trance by telling me she needed to go to her Aunt Ro's for Christmas Eve.

"What's an Aunt Ro?" I said half asleep and enjoying the music.

"She's my Aunt and it's her birthday on Christmas Eve."

"I thought only Jesus was born on Christmas Eve?"

"He gets top billing, but I assure you in my family, he shares it with my Aunt Ro."

"We don't do much of anything on Christmas Eve. When we were kids it was all the rage, now it's hardly a part of the holiday until Christmas morning."

"Well, you should get back to some traditions in your family and celebrate Christmas Eve." "You're probably right. Only it's hard to celebrate anything with my father being as sick as he has been."

"I didn't know he was sick. Your brother doesn't say much."

"I don't think he knows how bad it is, my mother writes me letters that would break your heart."

"Do my letters break your heart Jonathan Kiddrane?"

"If they stopped, that would break my heart, but I'm serious; feel these muscles! I think I owe this physique to your letters and Billy's."

"Let's not forget Bob Googenblatt!"

"Who could forget good ole Bob? Are you in on the latest thing? I get 20 letters from Googenblatt last week! No way he was in on that alone?"

Gayle started laughing as she stood up. "Billy told everyone we know to send letters using an Alaska address. You got them all?"

"Yeah and more push-ups than any human should have to do in a single day!"

"I think your brother was in on it big time. You probably got letters from people you never heard of before!"

"A regular riot, wait till I get my hands on Billy. You know I saw Billy, he was the first one I called, I don't know why. We sat in the park and he told me about Dickie. It was odd really, I never thought about the letters until now. I can't explain it actually, it turns out Dickie needed a friend and I needed to be a friend."

"Maybe that's what I find attractive about you."

"You mean you don't know if you're attracted to me yet?"

"Shut up!"

Gayle gave me a kiss, whispering Merry Christmas as she left waving.

"When can I see you?"

"I have family commitments through the week."

"We can't take in a movie? A walk in the park?"

"Give me a holler after Christmas."

"Come on! I can't wait that long to see you?"

"I'll count the minutes, you count the days."

"No really, come on – I'll drop by Christmas Eve?"

"It's really only for family."

"Then count me in!"

"I don't know."

"Come on, whom do I need to ask?"

"You're silly."

"I'm in love."

She stood motionless and then returned hugging me, holding me tighter and for the first time in many months I felt secure.

She kissed my cheek and said she needed to run.

"I'll be there at 9pm. I'll bring something for you."

"I don't know."

"Don't think about it, just mention to your folks that The Kidd is Back!"

"I don't know."

"See you later Gayle!"

My father was home for Christmas. My mother had arranged to have a hospital bed brought in. It was in the corner of her bedroom next to her bed. My father did not talk much as pride is an emotion that affects people in different ways. He lay in the bed looking out the window in to the park. Our dog had become a constant companion choosing to lie at my father's feet night and day. We had given the dog a unique name, which everyone in the family was proud of for different reasons. The dog was a beagle and answered to any one of his names: Tiger Wolfgang Steppenwolf III.

Originally the name was just plain old Tiger because of the markings on him that were not conventional brown and white but more like the stripes of a tiger. Wolfgang came in to play when I played loudly one day something from Mozart and the dog started howling like a banshee. Steppenwolf was the name of a rock band that had one of the classic songs of the day "Born to Be Wild." Tiger was the third dog we had as a family.

When my father was still driving his truck, he would come home and complain about Tiger when he was a puppy. Tiger would gnaw at the legs of furniture and tear at the linoleum causing damage that could not be repaired. One night my father took Tiger in his truck and dumped him out on the side of the highway. He came home the next morning after delivering his newspapers and there was Tiger sitting on the front steps with its tail wagging. From that moment on Tiger Wolfgang Steppenwolf III and my father were friends for life. A lot of people do not understand having a dog as a friend. The thing is dogs look at you in ways that make you feel like whatever you're saying is important. Tiger had a way of listening to my father's voice that made everyone in the room almost feel as if you were intruding on a friendship. If someone new came to visit Tiger would bark and try to bite their ankles. It was not until my father approved of them that Tiger would back down and calmly lay at his feet. I think in some ways there should be a dog hall of fame. I am certain Tiger would be nominated and forever enshrined in brass. Being home after being away has its own way of causing problems. There's this saying that must be like a million years old, "You Can't Go Home Again."

The thing about Going Home Again for me had differences that I did not fully understand. I arranged to be home more often because my father's health was not improving.

Chapter Thirty

The Army stationed me at Fort Dix, New Jersey. I worked at the USAREUR AGLO, which was an acronym for the United States Army Recruiting for Europe as part of the Adjutant Generals Liaison Office. I just told people I was a recruiter. It was like any other job people had working 9-5 had in America. I would sit at a desk and take phone calls from around the world. All the recruiters would call and ask if there was a position open for someone wanting to join the Army. They would have to put the name of the person who approved the position on the inducting paperwork. This is how I had to spell my name **K**ilo, **I**ndia, **D**elta, **D**elta, **R**omeo, **A**lpha, **N**ovember, **E**cho. The recruiters hated getting anyone with names other than "Smith" or "Jones."

The guys with short names seemed to get the most calls. Promotions were based on activities and I was getting less and less calls because no one wanted to spell my name out on their forms. One day I told a recruiter he was talking to the Sundance Kidd. In the month that followed I received more calls than any one else. Everyone would sit around holding their phone in the air saying "Kidd, Line Two – its Hawaii!" or "Line Five – its

Montana!" and so on and so on. It got to be a big joke. Everyone started calling himself or herself "The Hole in the Wall Gang." Captain Ponder was the Company Commander and he had been passed over for promotion three times already. In the military when you do not get promoted to the next rank as an officer, you tend to find yourself sitting in limbo. Being in charge of a bunch of recruiters sitting in a wooden barracks at the back of Fort Dix was about as far away from promotion one could get. He was a good man despite his not being considered a part of the War Machine. He saw to it that we were respected and every day we would play games like volleyball, football, and baseball on the grounds behind the barracks. Most of the soldiers at Fort Dix stayed in huge three story brick buildings. AGLO was like a hidden unit no one knew anything about unless they needed to. After the first month of my decision to call myself officially The Sundance Kidd, Captain Ponder called me in to his office. I honestly thought he was going to pin a medal on me for taking so many calls. At least I figured I was due a promotion. Instead, good ole Captain Ponder, with his round belly sticking out over his belt buckle, his hair almost completely gone, told me to sit down. I sat there while he went through a pile of papers on his desk. He had taken to calling me "Kidd" as well.

"Kidd", he said shaking his head and grinning, "We have a problem."

I was not expecting bad news and his statement made me sit up straighter in the chair.

He looked at the papers continuing to shake his head and at one point needing to cover his mouth to stop himself from laughing out loud. "Kidd, I got a call today from Headquarters. It has to do with you." Headquarters was The Pentagon where the most powerful people on the planet worked and pretty much controlled the universe. "Kidd, it seems people are getting out of the Army on a technicality. The technicality has to do with the official names on their papers the day they agreed to join the Army." I was still at a loss as to what Captain Ponder was implying. "Kidd, it's a problem because this little loophole some are discovering has to do with the fact there is no Sundance Kidd in the military." He looked at me and could not help but crack a smile. It was uncomfortable to be told I was in trouble while Captain Ponder smiled at me. "Kidd, what we decided to do is remove you from our recruiting team. I made a few calls and it appears we have an opening right here for our Overnight Attaché Position. Are you interested?"

I had no idea what an Overnight Attaché did. I liked working with the other recruiters. I felt we made a good team. "Kidd, what you're going to be is the person in charge of picking up dignitaries at McGuire Air Force base, as well as getting the manifest of all soldiers coming and going around the world. It's the best I can do and I think you'll enjoy working alone and handling these tasks." I felt like I did not have a choice. I was confused sensing I was being demoted for doing a good job. "Kidd, do you like music?" It was the first question I felt I could answer. "Yes Sir!"

Captain Ponder looked at me smiling an even broader smile, "Kidd, you will also be in charge of WDIX, the radio station from midnight until 8am! Hell son, you can play whatever you want and have a good time doing it! Everyone has had a bit of laugh over the Sundance incident and I told them I would reassign you as soon as possible."

I left Captain Ponder's office confused about what had happened. There were two other soldiers in the unit who were

Overnight Attaché's. They were both married and lived off base. I was told I would work three overnights and have four days off. Captain Ponder had somehow made a deal for me that would give me more free time and open my options up for the future. The OA's as we were called were considered Military Royalty as it turned out. Because of the hours we worked we did not have to be seen by anyone. We picked up important people and shuttled them to where they had to go. OA's were like secret agents and they had a license to broadcast music over the airwaves. It took me a few days to fully appreciate what had happened to me. I was going to learn how to work on something called the Internet. I was introduced to Teletype machines, which lined the wall of a room in the main office of AGLO. I learned from the other OA's what my duties would be. They could not wait for me to come on board as they had been sharing the duties by themselves for quite some time. It took me all of one week to learn what my duties were going to be. I was shown the Broadcast room where WDIX went out over the airways in New Jersey. "Be careful what you say", Sammy Winthrop told me the first night, "Because the damn civilians can pick us up." I could not fathom being a deejay although Sammy, who was one of the other OA's told me, "You're not really a deejay, it's more like you're a voice in the darkness." I did not know what he meant but learned as fast as possible so I could be on my own. Raymond Guy was the other OA. Ray was quiet and went about his work diligently and seriously. He told me, "You may have to pick up some big-wig so it's important that you keep a clean uniform around. Otherwise you could walk around in anything you want." I appreciated Sammy and Ray teaching me the ropes and after a week of working every night with them – I was ready to be alone. The first night I drove up to relieve the night shift I passed the barracks before turning in to the parking lot thinking this was going to be the coolest thing I ever did. When the night shift staff left I stood looking around the office. I realized any office, in the world, after midnight is the strangest place on earth.

I looked on the wall to see the flight schedule at McGuire Air Force Base. There were two flights, one coming and one going, an hour apart. I wanted to make certain my first night went perfectly. I wore my best khaki uniform and left to pick up the manifest. Going through the gates at McGuire made me feel official and important. A Military Policeman waved me through as soon as he recognized the sedan I was driving.

I got to the terminal and reported to the main desk where I would get the paperwork to be typed and sent to The Pentagon. As I stood there, all I could think about was how I wanted to call Gayle. I wanted to call Billy and tell him too! It was so cool.

"SERGEANT KIDDRANE! PAGING KIDDRANE!" Hearing my name on the loud speakers scared me half out of my shoes. I walked over to the Main Desk.

The Officer in Charge looked at me and told me to follow him in to an office.

"Listen Kiddrane, we got a major league player coming through here in another 15 minutes! It needs to be on the down low so you can't say a word to anyone!"

I looked at the Officer who seemed more nervous than if he were told the base was under attack. "Excuse me Sir", I said hoping to put him at ease, "I'm here to pick up a few manifests and return back to Dix to get the information to The Pentagon."

"Change of orders Sergeant Kiddrane! We got ourselves a BOO-KOO name coming in and he wants to be IN-COG-

NITO! That means you're driving him from here to the Officers Quarters!"

I told him I needed to ask for permission from my Commanding officer. I called Captain Ponder and it being 2am in the morning, I woke up his entire family.

"I'm sorry Sir for the lateness of this call, but I'm being told by the CO on duty here at McGuire that I have to drive a major player to the Officer's Quarters."

It must be the late hour because Captain Ponder could not understand why I had to drive a Major Player anywhere.

"No sir, there is no Major Player – the guy who's coming in is a major player."

I gave the phone to the CO in charge and told him to explain it to Captain Ponder.

He walked around the office and in a whispered voice said "The Major Player is Henry Kissinger." I think my eyes started to bug out of my head. He handed me back the phone with a stern look on his face. Captain Ponder was suddenly more awake then I had ever heard him. "Kidd! Don't mess this up! You understand me?"

Of course I understood him. I was the one needing to drive the Secretary of State. Henry Kissinger was my commander and chief's Chief advisor. He was bigger than big! Here I was my first night on the job and I'm entrusted with driving possibly the second most powerful man on earth! Everyone was bugging out in the terminal. Word spread like wildfire and for the first time it became apparent that I was the only one not at all worried or concerned about the arrival of Henry Kissinger. I stood off to the side awaiting the arrival of the plane. I asked myself questions as I stood there wondering why would the Secretary of

State need car service? Why was one of the most powerful men on earth flying in to New Jersey? A plane could be seen on the runway and I watched the CO fussing with everyone. He was yelling demands that were so ridiculous I almost had to laugh. As a matter of fact I did laugh. So loud that my cackling voice echoed through the silenced terminal as Henry Kissinger's plane drew near. The CO was screaming now: "WHO THE HELL IS LAUGHING? THIS IS SERIOUSER THAN SHIT!"

"SOMEONE HIDE THAT TRASH CAN! WE DON'T HAVE ANY GARBAGE HERE!" "SOMEONE PICK UP THAT CANDY WRAPPER! HIDE IT QUICK!"

"EVERYONE TUCK IN YOUR STOMACHS – NO FATTIES ALLOWED!"

His ranting became so ridiculous that Henry Kissinger's attaché walked right past the CO when he came in to check if everything was ready for the Secretary's arrival. It all seemed surreal as the CO did everything but kneel down and kiss the attaché's shoes. The CO pointed at me and I walked over nonchalantly and introduced myself.

The Secretary's attaché handed me a briefcase and shook my hand. He asked where my car was parked. I told him I would bring it around to the main entrance. He thanked me and walked back outside to the plane. I calmly looked around at the terminal while the CO was again barking orders like a raving lunatic: "DON'T FORGET TO STAND UP STRAIGHT AND PROUD! I DO NOT WANT TO HEAR A SNEEZE FROM ANYONE! NO ONE SNEEZE!" I caught the eye of a few people as I walked to get my car. They were afraid to give themselves away but before I left the building I whispered to two guards, "Assholes come in every shape, size and color in America." They almost burst out laughing but managed to stand straight without losing it.

Henry Kissinger was ushered to my waiting car. I held the back door open for him and nodded my head to the attaché from the plane.

With the entire commotion-taking place I had forgotten to ask where the Officer's Quarters were located. I sat in the front seat and calmly picked up the microphone connected to the CB radio on the dashboard. "This is Sergeant Kiddrane with Major Player; can someone tell me where the Officer's Quarters are located?" There was a static sound on the radio that almost sent the Secretary and me scurrying from the car. The CO got on the line "YOU'RE CARRYING MAJOR PLAYER AND DON'T KNOW WHERE YOU'RE GOING!" I looked through the rear view mirror smiling at the Secretary. He did not seem the least bit concerned about what I was doing or saying. I spoke quietly in to the microphone, "Just some simple directions will do Sir. Thank you." Again the static was followed by the CO's voice "YOU'LL BE DRIVING GOLF CARTS IN THE DESERT KIDDRANE!" There was a knock on my window and I rolled it down. The attaché from the plane was standing there smiling. "I apologize", he said "You can take the Secretary to the General's office, they are waiting for his arrival. Just make a left at the turn up ahead and you'll see the building. Thanks for keeping your head." I rolled down the window and switched off the screaming CO's voice. I looked in my rearview mirror and told the Secretary, "I apologize for the delay." He nodded his head and looked out the window.

I drove to the turn in the road and immediately saw the building with its lights on. The drive took all of ten minutes. I got out of the car and opened the door for the Secretary. He nodded his head and met the General at the door. I was 19 years old. I realized at 19 years of age that power is sometimes recognized in ways that makes the weakest people on earth in to bumbling idiots. I drove away making certain I had my manifest in the front seat. I smiled. I was not a bumbling idiot.

Chapter Thirty-One

Louis: Hey Kidd, it's me Louis?

Kidd: Who's that with you Mr. Armstrong?

Louis: Kidd, I want you to meet a friend of mine – Jack Kerouac. He's a writer.

Kidd: Hello Mr. Kerouac.

Jack: Louis tells me you're a jazz fan?

Kidd: I learned all I know from Mr. Armstrong. He's a friend of my Dad's.

Louis: We have been discussing jazz music and writing.

Kidd: What did you find out?

Louis: Well, Jack has come up with an interesting definition for jazz.

Kidd: Which is?

Louis: He says it is the music that translates rain drops.

Kidd: I don't understand.

Louis: My friend Jack tends to translate things in between the beats.

Kidd: I guess I have a lot to learn.

Louis: It never gets old Kidd no matter how old you get.

Kidd: I wonder when it starts to make sense. Can you tell me?

Jack: Louis told me all about it. I've been here for a while now and it's not bad.

Kidd: Here?

Louis: I wanted to be the one to tell you son. Your Dad and I are going to be reunited.

Kidd: Reunited?

Louis: Now son, it's a part of living, like when I played those old songs years ago.

Kidd: I do not understand you?

Jack: It's not so bad once you get used to it. The water actually tastes like wine.

Kidd: Are you saying?

Louis: Now son, you know you can always call on me and I'll be there. As soon as your Dad gets adjusted, he'll be around for you to talk to as well.

Kidd: How long does it take to get adjusted?

Jack: This is a smart boy just like you said Louis.

Louis: His Dad and I go way back. His father was a newspaperman.

Kidd: You make it sound like he was a writer.

Louis: You don't have to write the words out on paper to be a writer.

Jack: If I knew that when I was out there – it would have saved me a lifetime of pain.

Louis: You and Jackson spent your whole lives worrying too much.

Kidd: Jackson?

Louis: Ah son, it's a crazy place up here. This guy Jackson

Pollack was a painter. A real crazy dude with a vision like sounds coming out of a saxophone after midnight.

Kidd: Do you have a lot of friends?

Louis: Jono my boy, everyone is your friend in a perfect place.

Kidd: And my Dad?

Jack: He's our friend and we never met him yet.

Kidd: How long do I have Mr. Armstrong?

Louis: Call home and tell your mother you're on your way.

Kidd: Now?

Jack: Time to wake up son. These visions only last a short while.

I came out of the sleep that I would remember for the rest of my life like I was lightly touching down after parachuting through the night sky. I did not feel anguish, regret or sadness. I trusted the visions in my dream. I called home. My mother's voice was filled with the despair I should have been feeling. I tried to calm her. I left for home.

On the bus, moving down the New Jersey Turnpike I stared out the window at the blackness along the highway's edge. I knew at the journeys end, I would see my father alive for the last time. I savored the moment as the miles brought me closer to New York.

At the hospital, my brother sat with my mother in the waiting room. They told me my father was dying. I entered the hospital room not knowing what to expect. The tubes, blinking lights and beeping machines are never as real until they are connected to someone you love. I sat at the bedside looking at the monitors and then at my father. I could not separate the two and was at a loss for words. My father's eyes opened up briefly and they had that twinkle I saw a hundred times looking at me through the rearview mirror as I readied another bundle of papers to be tossed off his truck.

"Dad, I'm here. I got a message from Louis. He say's to tell you there's a lot of people looking forward to meeting you."

My father opened his eyes slowly and smiled.

"Dad, there's these people waiting; Writers and painters, and Louis has been telling them all about you for years. It's like they know you better than anyone here."

He shook his head acknowledging he could hear me.

"Louis says, after you get adjusted you can visit with anyone you want down here. Dad, maybe you can give me a sign that lets me know you're alright?"

He squeezed my hand. He winced for a moment. Then he was gone.

I stayed in the room for a few minutes listening to the beeping machines. One machine started to deliver a loud squelch. It displayed for a moment a blinking light and then it fell in to silence. I closed my eyes sensing I would never again feel a need to say the prayer I whispered. I said, "Thank you Father."

Chapter Thirty-Two

The thing about time is it's not always real. Before I knew it, I was back shuffling papers and thinking myself lost in some kind of surreal dream. One day flowed in to the next and before I knew it my time had come to be shipped overseas. There were several choices for someone in my position, Germany, Korea or Vietnam. The choice was not of my choosing. It was not like your name was put in a hat and suddenly you won some kind of lottery. I often think it was more like some kind of alphabetical curse. Another thing people always get confused about when they see these big Hollywood movies is people having time to say goodbye to family and friends. You get your orders and you're on the next plane out. I did have time to call Gayle. I told her I was going to the show. That's what we called NAM in my unit. Hell, it was on television enough times a day that it might as well be a damn show. The trouble was the slant the media started to put on the war that made it all so damn unpopular. I don't want to sound like a know-it-all or some kind of party-pooper, but all that damn protesting did was light a fire under networks. Some mastermind sitting in a big office somewhere said one day "If we could get all these people who are against the war to watch our network, we'd be ten times bigger than we are now!" In my mind that's what happened, not the nonsense you read about in history books and how the protestors rallied around one another to stop the war. The only way to stop a war is to stop sending soldiers. I was on my way to the show and my only hope of coming back alive was maybe more people would start watching CBS over NBC or ABC. That's all there was to watch back then. Hell you had local stations but all they were good for was sports and reruns of I Love Lucy and The Honeymooners. For whatever reason, this stuff got lost in translation over time.

Gayle told me to be careful. She was on her way to college and I was about to be one of those damn slobs who didn't have enough money to pay my way out of the show. A show we all prayed would be cancelled. The thing was it was a long way from being stopped.

I do not remember now if I landed or was dropped in to the shit. All the guys you thought you would know forever seemed to either find ways to escape going or they ended up somewhere else. By the time I got to the show, there were only fragments of dumb slobs left to clean up the mess that was everywhere you looked. My damn experience had put me in the middle of a place called Saigon. At first glance it appeared to be a paradise. A crowded paradise but one filled with amazing scenery and some kind of hidden undercurrent of excitement. I worked in the Headquarters Building. Learning how to type can open doors or have them shut so tightly you wished you remained an ignorant student who couldn't spell. I hated dictation which is what officers of every rank loved to do standing over your shoulder and barking the day's events as you scrambled to keep pace with their maddening interpretation of what was happening. There were fights taking place closer and closer everyday. Sleeping was almost impossible. It got so thinking about being a reporter was more like being a typist in a foxhole on fire. It didn't take long before I realized I would never be a journalist in the Army or anywhere else. I had a problem with eliminating the truth from stories. The officers would get a report of a night fight advising 15 dead and 4 wounded. When I typed it, the report was changed to 5 dead, 10 missing and 1 wounded. I always wondered after a long day of shuffling facts back to the states what those dead soldiers must have been thinking. Lying there dead and news sent back that they were missing in action. There are always a lot of problems with statistics in war. No one wants to share bad news. I would lie in my bunk at night and want to write Gayle letters telling her what it was like to be in the show. The problem was no one in Headquarters was permitted to send letters home. Everything we said and done was labeled "CONFIDENTIAL", making it impossible to share any version of the truth.

It got so no one knew whether they were coming or going. Through it all, no matter what, I still doubted that our Commander and Chief was as stupid as the press made him out to be. Propaganda is a bigger weapon in war than any bomb. I thought about sending a letter directly to my buddy Henry Kissinger. Hell, I personally knew the man and did not see him as the war monger the papers and television were painting him as. In Headquarters, there was an actual "red phone" like the kind on the show Batman. The Commanding Officer would pick up the phone and presto-chango – the White House was on the other end. I had a good mind to make use of that phone!

"Hello Henry! It's me Private Kiddrane! We met when I drove you from McGuire Air Force Base to that General's house! Listen, you got to do something about this situation over here! There's all kinds of stuff that doesn't exactly add up to what you're being told. I think because of this miscommunication you and the President are being fed a load of crap!" I wondered if it was ok to say "a load of crap" to Henry Kissinger. I would lie in bed thinking I had to find a better way to articulate the crap I was witnessing. The thing is once you're not considered a part of the solution; you're labeled a part of the problem. It's like that in any bureaucratic nightmare. I was told my services were needed on a secret mission. Secret mission at this time in history meant only one thing, I was being sent off the reservation. The Headquarters Building in Saigon was not a very big facility. It was certainly well guarded and there was ample enough security immediately surrounding the streets near it; but once you went past the zone, all bets were off. I was made part of a small platoon led by Sgt Charlie Dancer. Everyone who knew Sgt Dancer agreed he made a pact with the devil to live so long. He would return from these secret missions after leading 10 men in to the jungle, returning with five men missing or carrying the wounded who probably wished they were dead. He had a scowl when you looked him in the eye that made you aware to never talk to him unless spoken to first. The reason I was added to the next "secret mission" and I was convinced of it was I had been found out. Military people and those individuals who get so powerful in any corporation somehow can tell when you're not willing to play by their rules. I was told differently. The Commanding Officer called me in to his office one morning. "Son?" he said while looking out the window that looked out on to an airstrip behind the building, "I don't have to remind you how delicate information is during war. We need you to accompany Sgt. Dancer here on a special mission." I looked at Sgt. Dancer and I needed to turn away from his glare for fear I would be turned in to stone or worse, glass and find myself shattered into little fragments. "Son! What we need is a statistical report from the jungle of how many of our men are involved in what we pray will be our final stand. Sgt. Dancer here does not have the time to be counting such things. You go with him and when you come back we'll have a better idea of what we're dealing with here!"

I was dismissed and advised we would be leaving at dusk. I had no idea what my orders meant. I was given a counting device, a clicker that I was to use to tabulate how many soldiers were either holed up in foxholes, dead, wounded or missing. I was advised that radio transmissions had been compromised and my clicker was to represent the precise number needed to report what was happening. It was a load of crap and everyone knew it! Never the less, at 7pm, Sgt. Dancer stood at the main gate with 8 other sorry-assed soldiers waiting for me to join their ranks. I packed a toothbrush, my clicker, pen and paper and for the first time picked up my M-16 rifle having never used it since Basic Training nearly two years since getting myself caught up in this mess. I slung it over my shoulder and met up with the others at the gate. The gates swung open and we left in single file down the crowded streets. There were people on bicycles and it seemed like hundreds of people just standing around and waiting for something to happen, staring off in to the distant skies. We started to double-time through the streets until we were near a bunch of abandoned buildings with nothing but the jungle beyond. I had heard stories of the jungle. Stories that were always followed with a single request, "Don't tell anyone I ever told you this?"

The thing is I always shook my head in agreement when I would hear some of what was experienced out there. I knew deep down that fear made anyone embellish the truth, but when it came to war, the truth was as pure as anything ever said. Time somehow had a way of making it worse in some people's minds. I believed every word I heard the first time I heard it. If the same person stopped me and told me again what happened, I noticed there was an added sense of trepidation. It was not like a "fish story" but something I called a "fear story." After the same experience is gone over in your mind so many times I think you can't believe you survived the damn thing so you need to do one of two things, you make it sound like the greatest story ever told or you never talk about it again for the rest of your life. There are a lot more stories never told when it comes to war than anything else.

Sgt. Dancer made a signal with his hand and we all followed him. I don't know if it's been proven, but I think buildings have hearts and souls like people. As we passed through the abandoned and bombed out buildings I could swear I heard whispering. As we moved out behind the buildings and closer to the jungles edge I swore I heard the buildings saying "Don't go in there." My heart was racing and I could not believe how dry my throat felt. We followed Sgt. Dancer into the jungle and as the forest closed in around us the buildings seemed to be calling out to us, "This is your last chance! Come back!"

I wanted to ask one of the other guys if they could hear it, but I didn't want to spook anyone. Working in administration of any Headquarters, whether it was the military or a large corporation, has its benefits. I was aware of something about Sgt. Dancer that no one else in our unit knew. On days when I was not sitting at a damn Teletype machine sending messages I was detailed to the Mail Room. A mailroom clerk has more knowledge about things than anyone else, before anyone else. Sgt Charlie Dancer had to be the most avid reader on earth. On a daily basis he received every known magazine published in America. By weeks end he had received the equivalent of every magazine any one could find on the largest newspaper stand in Manhattan. Having worked with my Dad and sometimes helping out at my Uncle's candy store I knew about such things. I wanted to ask him what he did with all those subscriptions. I was afraid to look him in the eye no less ask him about his mail. We got to a clearing in the jungle and again Sgt. Dancer gave us a signal that immediately had us all lying in a prone position. He looked out over the field in front of us and seemed to be trying to smell like a dog does when hunting for something.

He pointed two fingers at his eyes advising us to keep our eyes open and focused on a ridge on the other side of the field. He looked directly at me and I knew instinctively I was being summoned with my counting clicker. On the ridge suddenly there was a group of our guys with their hands over their heads being lead by a small group of enemy soldiers. Sgt Charlie Dancer did not like it when the enemy was referred to as "Charley." He seemingly took it as a personal affront that someone with his namesake was labeled as the enemy. I imagine it was something that troubled him long after we were all someplace else in our lives. He smacked me in the back of my head, which was his way of telling me "Start counting you dick brain!"

I started pushing the clicker and keeping my eyes peeled to the ridge. When they had passed I took out my notebook and tabulated my findings. I was still confused why this mattered to anyone except of course feeling it was ridiculous to watch our guys being lead somewhere and the mission did not include our helping them.

The sun had completely disappeared from the sky when we began to move through the open field. On the other side of the field there was something more to count.

The guys on the ridge appeared now to be the lucky ones. There were bodies of our guys in different positions, all dead and looking as if they never knew what hit them. I had carried body bags off planes sensing a part of what death means to a soldier. I had seen it up close. There was a pleading look in the eyes of every dead soldier. A question they all yearned to ask before dying. "Why?"

Again, Sgt. Dancer slapped me in the back of my head and I began to click away. My thumb felt numb as I crawled through the massacre praying I did not miss accounting for everyone. In the darkness I am certain I may have clicked counting shadows more than once. I took out my notebook and tabulated my numbers. I looked directly in to Sgt. Dancer's eyes for the first time and no longer felt any fear. I was angry and he was the bastard who was responsible for what I was seeing. Being baptized by such visions can make you cold inside. I no longer felt my heart beating. I was no longer aware if I was breathing or holding my breath waiting to wake up from the nightmare around me. This was not what I wanted to remember. Sgt. Charlie Dancer, all 175 pounds of rock solid demeanor and professional soldier, sensed my despair. He reached out and this time it was not a slap that registered on my helmet but a sort of patting. He spoke in a voice that sounded far away, like it was somehow coming out of the trees. "You never get used to it, so don't try." I could sense the other men in our unit let out a soft sigh. Our heads bowed like we were being blessed. Sgt. Dancer sat down and cradled his rifle. He looked at us and said, "Listen, this is as far as we go tonight. If anyone asks we humped our asses all over the map of Asia! You make up numbers from now on! Forget the bull. Keep your eyes open and let's stay alive out here. I don't want to be a goddamn statistic on the evening news!"

I was uncertain if what Sgt. Dancer said was in direct violation of orders or if he was deciding to spare us anything worse than what we already saw. Everyone found a place to bear down for the night. There were foxholes dug out by the troops who lay dead around us, and Sgt. Dancer calmly disappeared into one. I lay in a prone position for a while smelling death, convinced again I could hear whispering; this time coming down from out of the trees. The whispers seemed to turn into some kind of unified singing.

I started to hum the song, Daydream by a band called The Lovin' Spoonful. It was like some kind of gospel hymn and I could hear others in the unit start to sing along with my humming. There was a loud crashing noise and a tree close to us fell in an explosion. Everyone gathered close and we were all looking at the darkness wondering what would happen next. I whispered loudly over to the foxhole I saw Sgt. Dancer disappear into; "Sgt. Dancer! What was that?" A voice as calm as could be said out loud, "Maybe they don't like your singing." The way he delivered the line made us all chuckle to ourselves. The chuckles erupted in to laughter and we suddenly found ourselves hysterical beyond words. We could not see Sgt. Dancer but again his voice rang out, saving us from the worried feeling of fear, he said, "Strike

One! Low and outside. There's got to be a reason why ole Mickey doesn't swing at a pitch like that!" I immediately recognized the banter being delivered by Sgt. Dancer. I chimed in with a response, "There's no way he gets that pitch again and doesn't put the ball out of here!" There was brief silence and then Sgt. Dancer's voice replied, "Oh look at that ball go! What a ride! Off the upper deck!" A few voices around me echoed with appraisal "Way to go Mick!" Then the silence came back falling on us like a wave hitting a shoreline. I crawled to the foxhole where Sgt, Dancer lay down resting his arms at the back of head like he was laying in a hammock in his backyard. I felt we had something in common that was more powerful than many things.

"Hey Sarge? Where did you grow up?"

He was staring up at the stars and for the first time I saw a smile.

"Brooklyn."

"And you're a Yankee fan?"

"You inherit things from your parents without asking questions."

"I know what you mean."

"My ole man saw Ruth play."

"My Dad too. He told me all about it when we delivered newspapers around Yankee Stadium."

"Best damn job on earth."

"He didn't think so at the time. I lost him a few months ago."

"Rough break. You'll always have Mickey."

"That's for damn sure. Let me ask you something?"

"We're fans not friends."

"I know that Sarge, it's about all those magazines you get. Do you read them all?"

"You were looking at my mail?"

"You can't help but notice a shit load of magazines and they all come to the same guy."

"A gift from my old high school. I get every magazine ever published."

"It's a very impressive gift."

"It helps me escape. You know what I like the best?"

"National Geographic?"

"Hell no. Good Housekeeping."

"Come on! You're shitting me right?"

"Nope, I think every day about what I'm doing and it's the damn slogan that goes through my head. I like knowing I can give the Good Housekeeping seal of approval to all the crap I witness."

"They would be pleased to know that."

"I doubt that. They would probably sue me for using their slogan to win a war."

"Do you really think we have a chance of winning this war?"

"Of course not, but it makes me happy to think it's possible."

"What do you think is going to happen?"

"Some sort of cat and mouse game followed by something that will look like we're abandoning everything we tried to accomplish."

"What are we trying to accomplish?"

"Damn if I know. It's a game. We're all a bunch of chess pieces being moved around on a board by some huge hand that has no idea what to do next."

"A bunch of pawns capable of being sacrificed at a moments notice."

"Like lambs being led to the slaughter."

"Sarge, shouldn't we try to help those guys we saw being taken prisoner?"

Silence. He reached up out of the foxhole and grabbed me by my shoulders dragging me in to the mud inside. "Listen, you dickwad, our mission is to count. Do you know how many times I tried to save prisoners? Do you have any idea why I return from those damn missions with wounded and dead men? I don't want to spoil your heroism dreams, but this time we're all walking back to that shit hole they call paradise with everyone alive and well! Now press that damn counting machine and make as much shit up as you can possibly dream!"

I had pressed a wrong button. Sgt. Charlie Dancer hated failure. More than anything in the world he wanted to chase after the enemy and save as many people that he could. After years of chasing shadows in the jungle Sgt. Dancer was content to return with the nine men he left with. Sgt. Dancer was cutting his losses. He was saving the ones he could. The last thing Sgt Dancer said in the jungle was, "The people in charge of the numbers control the truth."

We returned to Headquarters the next morning. I turned in my report. I counted shadows more times than I ever would again in life. Some lived. Some learned to use their missing arms and legs in new ways. Some I never saw again.

Too many died.

Chapter Thirty-Three

Dear Kidd,

What the hell is happening? The way I hear it you have not been heard from in so long there's rumor you might be dead! If I don't hear from you I can only assume the rumor is correct. Things are scary here and I'm not sure which side of the fence I belong on. I used to endorse a lot of things associated with this country; now I'm not so sure. Living where I do, it is amazing to see so many things frozen and standing still. Do you remember how we destroyed copies of The Beatles White Album? Do you really think we heard what was on those records or did we hear it because that's what we were told we were supposed to be hearing? Remember the way we listened to the last side of the album? How many times did we use the code words from the song Revolution to let on we did not agree with something someone said?

What Is The Situation?

They Are Standing Still.

I don't think we ever heard better lyrics in our lives. A phrase so simplistic and now I must use them to express how I feel about the way things look and sound about this crazy war. I know it's not proper to be telling you these things while you're over there – but damn it Kidd, it sounds like everyone's gone completely renegade! It's like a bunch of crazies supporting Kurtz in the jungles of Africa. You mark my words; some one is going to make this distinction some day! Joseph Conrad and his Heart of Darkness vision are being played out right before our eyes. You got to save yourself man! Try to find a way out! I'm not kidding man; the campuses are going insane with rage. If you want to, I highly recommend you hide out here in Alaska for a while. Going home now would be madness. No one gives a damn about the crap-taking place over there anymore. You might as well have joined the Hole In the Wall gang! I'm telling you because you're my friend. We're still friends right? Run like hell! The shit is about to hit the fan!

I'm not kidding! Keep Warm and Chill Out.

Googenblatt

Chapter Thirty-Four

Gayle Cooper hated going to college when things got so crazy no one knew where they stood. At college, where she was one day proud to tell everyone her boyfriend was in Vietnam; had somehow overnight made her think about how foolish everyone acted. Comments echoed through the campus like wildfire. "How's that baby killer of a boyfriend of yours?" I can't say I blamed her for no longer writing. I can't say I blamed even Bob Googenblatt for saying the things he said in letters. Being in a position where things need to be interpreted to make sense every hour of the day hardly put me in a position to be a judge. I honestly did not have time to worry about anything except what was going on right outside the gates of Headquarters in Saigon.

I got a rare letter from my brother advising me what was really happening at home.

Dear Jono,

Mom and I are worried. The newspapers and the television are making it sound like you guys have lost any chance of winning the war. I just hope you are all right.

Listen, I don't know what you hear from others, but Gayle's

been seeing this new guy. I've seen him around the neighborhood and you should feel good knowing he gives her a ride to and from college every day. I guess some things were never meant to be. A few days ago I saw her holding hands with the guy and she looked happy. It must be hard for her to let on that she had a boyfriend in the Army. On my campus the other night they were burning American Flags and effigies of Nixon. That guy really screwed things up big time for everyone. I don't pretend to know anything about politics but his stepping down the way he did on national television was really an embarrassment. You guys must feel like the bottom fell out of any chance you had of getting out of this stupid war with some dignity. I hope you're not sore with me for telling you these things, but I know you'll understand. I saw Billy Moran the other day and he says he was feeling the same way and advised he would be sending you a letter soon. Gayle was at a dance held at the local church and she looked good. She cut her hair. Did you know she was going to do that? It makes her look older for some strange reason. She was with that same guy. I talked to her for a little while and she told me the guy wants to marry her. I never talked to someone our age that was talking about marriage already. She told me her mother and father was thrilled because they already know the family of the guy. Life is strange isn't it? Listen, there's a chance, it's not certain yet that we might be moving. Mom's mentioned it a few times and I don't know but it sounds ok to me. She's been working at this bakery on Long Island out near Aunt Millie's house. I think she's getting serious with one of the bakers. At first I was pissed about her not leaving any time for grieving, but then I thought about it and maybe it's for the best. I think ever since Dad was sick she was feeling his loss. I don't know what to think anymore. I'm seeing this girl named Sandy. She's a nice girl. I met her at college. You would like her. Gayle told me she might go on a double date with Sandy and I some time. Hey, I hope I'm not brining you down with all this news, but you told me to always keep it real. Do you mind if I sell your baseball glove to this guy named Andy? We play ball together and I've been letting him use it anyway. Since Mom's talking about us moving and all she asked me to start cleaning out your room. I found all those boxes of baseball cards in the closet and sold them already. I figure since all we did with those cards was put them in the spokes of our bikes there's no need for them anymore. I don't think we'll be riding bikes any way. I bought a car. It's a second hand 1968 Mustang. It has a great stereo. Do you get to hear music over there? I also sold those comic books you had piled under the bed. Mom says they attracted bugs. I hope you're ok, and I hope you come home real soon.

Your brother, Huck You!

Hank

Chapter Thirty-Five

I was confused. I was not sure from one day to the next if I was suicidal or homicidal. I was not certain anymore if there was an actual difference. Losing the support of loved ones is one thing, but hearing and seeing how the entire country had lost interest in what we were trying to do was making everyone's job very difficult. There was no longer any need for counting anything. As the days passed we were doing more things that made everything insane. There are periods in your life marked by events that can never make sense. Between August 1974 and April 1975, I saw things happen that made me question everything I would ever see or hear again for the rest of my life. The first thing I decided was to stop opening any mail. It was obvious the media machine had turned everyone against what was happening around me. I liked to touch the envelopes at night as they piled up in a shoebox. I would pretend what each one said. I wrote home to anyone who sent me letters. I did not need to know what they were telling me in their letters. Googenblatt had taught me how to write. He was the best damn writer who ever lived. I made carbon copies on a typewriter and when I needed to read anything, I would read the

Googenblatt letters. A letter to Gayle was a classic!

Dear Gayle,

You wouldn't believe how warm it gets here. One day last week I needed to melt some rubber for the soles of my boots and I put them out on the sidewalk in front of the building. It only took about five minutes for me to scoop up that melted rubber and apply them to my boots. Good as new! I hope you miss me as much as I miss you. Hell, I think about you all the time. I close my eyes real tight and I picture your long hair flowing the way it does and it's like we're on the beach at Rockaway. It must be really difficult for you to be going to college, holding down a job and worrying about me all the time. Well, don't worry about me! I'm going to be fine! You wait and see – when I come home it will be like none of this ever happened. A few nights ago we had to investigate this noise out behind the building and there was this entire family of people begging us for something to eat. I don't know how anyone can think its easy seeing things like that. We gathered up as much food as we could carry and they were so appreciative. I pretty much stopped reading the newspapers because there doesn't seem to be anyone telling the truth anymore. If you want to know the truth about it I could care less about whether President Nixon knew about Watergate. It's hard enough trying to win a war when you have a strong leader. We all know he sounded like a crazy man. Maybe that's what we liked about him. I don't really know. God Gayle, it sure is good to hold your picture close to my heart late at night. I'll bet you can't wait for me to get home! What's the first thing we should do? I just want to hold your hand and walk in the moonlight in the park. I'll bet you haven't been in the park since I was home. Remember that night we sat on the bench at Christmas time when I was home? You told me the names you had picked out for children. Just the thought of that made me so warm I started sweating. It was freezing and your smile made me think the entire world was ours to control anyway we wanted to. Listen, I better go. Keep those cards and letters coming!

Love ya, Jono

P.S. I hope you're keeping your dancing shoes polished. I know how you love to dance. I promise we'll go dancing every night of the week when I get home!

Chapter Thirty-Six

Interpretation is an amazing attribute. Everyone can see the same thing and gather in their minds thoughts brought about by the vision. After sending letters home dismissing anything remotely negative, I started to concentrate on the little things in life. In the mailroom there was a basket filled to overflowing with postcards. Each postcard depicted a different photo, painting, message from back home. One night while on duty walking the hallways of the Headquarters Building I sat down and went through the postcards. Each postcard was for a soldier who could not be found. They were collected and sorted for return. Letters were easily forwarded back to America because the return addresses were immediately visible on the envelope. Postcards required time. Each postcard was addressed and required tracing. In most cases the postcards would be sent back to the soldiers' home address. I sat going through the basket, holding each postcard in my hand, studying the photos, turning them over and reading out loud the messages on back of each one. It was a solace I had not anticipated finding in a place about to fall.

On one postcard, there was a black and white photo of a

woman. Below the photo was a name: Lillian Russell – "Rotograph Series No. B 518"

I studied the postcard for a lone time before turning it over in my hands. The woman was from another era. Her hair was short and her features were captured in a way only photographers can use shadows. I did not know whom Lillian Russell was or why someone chose to send the postcard instead of a more modern one. I turned the postcard over seeing it addressed to a Pvt. Stanley Morse of the 108th Air Calvary. The message was printed in the most delicate handwriting obviously belonging to a woman. Maybe the letter was from Lillian Russell herself I thought.

I did not know Pvt. Charlie Morse, but after reading his mail I envied him more than he could ever know.

Dear Charlie,

I miss you. It's been quite some time since your last letter. I found this old postcard in an antique store. Doesn't she look like my Aunt Shana? Charlie, please write and let me know you're ok. Your sister had a recital last week. She plays the piano so beautifully. Your father sends his love. Please write soon. Love, Mom

I put the postcard aside resting it on my lap; I promised to never forget Lillian Russell and Pvt. Charlie Morse.

The next postcard depicted a train roaring down tracks with steam pouring from the locomotive. Looking closely I made out the small words defining the train as the Empire State Express between New York and Buffalo. I longed to be on that train. Turning it over, I could hardly make out the scribbled script.

Dear Danny,

How are you? The baby looks at a photo of you in our H.S. yearbook and smiles. I swear she recognizes her father's eyes. I know we did not have time for a honeymoon so I thought we could all hop on a train to Niagara Falls. You always said that you wanted to see them. There's a boat that goes under the falls. I hope they have a raincoat to fit Lizzie. We miss you. Love Sissy

On another postcard there was a street in Montreal called the St-Louis Square. It showed a line of Victorian homes each painted in a different color. I studied the photo and could sense it was autumn because there were no leaves on the trees.

Dear Billy,

I'm waiting for you. Enough is enough. We'll make ends meet somehow. More and more each day seem to be coming here to survive. It's scary being here without you. I'm living with a family who loves cats. The cats purr all day long sounding like a crazy orchestra. Hurry home. Do not pass go, do not collect 200 dollars! Love ya, Steph

I read through the postcards, each one beautiful and filled with love. I stacked them in to a pile next to me on the floor. When they reached eye level, morning had broken and the final day was upon us.

Chapter Thirty-Seven

There was a mad shuffling of feet everywhere. Outside, for the past week the marines guarding the gates had gone through more emotional stress than thought humanly possible. The villagers were passing their babies over the fence begging that they be kept inside the Embassy for safe keeping. What were we doing about this madness? The officials were busy looting their own offices. Garbage cans burning fires were spread through out the first floor. Papers were being tossed inside the burning cans as we prepared for what we were told was an all out evacuation. It did not feel like an evacuation. It felt like surrender. Something more on the order of having our stripes torn off and our flag burned. Looking out at the melee on the street in front of the Embassy I could tell as the sun slowly creased the morning sky something was about to happen.

A marine, with his face stricken with concern for his men and the poor people struggling to get inside, started shouting orders. He was a Master Sergeant who had seen more war than one man needs to see in his lifetime. He lost two of his oldest friends to a gun battle only a few days earlier. It was April 30th, 1975. There was a whisper in the air above us representing a sound that could mean only one of two things, rescue or attack. The helicopters were coming. We were told if we heard thirty seconds of "White Christmas" sung by Bing Crosby that the evacuation would be taking place as planned. I picked up as many postcards as I could, stuffing them inside my uniform. "What are you doing there soldier?" demanded the Master Sergeant. "Someone's got to save the mail Sarge!" I screamed above the now deafening sound of the helicopters coming in overhead. He looked at me shaking his head in disgust, "Get your stupid mud-filled ass up those stairs and help us get these people out of here!" I did not notice behind him was a group of people holding on to objects, clutching photos and other belongings to their bodies. "WELL GET YOUR ASS IN GEAR SOLDIER! THIS IS IT!"

"White Christmas" echoed in my ears as I started toward the group of people. Several marines were manning the stairwell and I climbed up past the people to the rooftop. Once on the roof I could not hear myself thinking. The roar of the helicopters, the screaming in the streets and in the distance the awareness of the worst yet to come for so many people who had suffered for so long. The first helicopter touched down and I began ushering Embassy personnel on board followed by frightened Vietnamese men, women and children. The Master Sergeant could be heard above the roar of everything. He was waving his hands in one direction and shouting out what to do without once blinking in to the rising sun. It was mass mayhem and confusion wherever I looked. "SOLDIER! TOSS THAT SUITCASE OVER THE SIDE!" I heard the Master Sergeant shouting and I took the suitcase from a woman who was boarding the helicopter about to take off. She screamed loudly with terror in her voice. I watched as the suitcase sailed off the rooftop to the ground below. I had stolen her only belongings in the world, discarding them in a quest to make room for more people running for their lives. The suitcase seemingly sailed in slow motion and fell with a thud on the ground. The woman lifted off clutching to a man's arm screaming at me with a look of horror in her eyes. I turned to look at the suitcase and was suddenly struck with a feeling of immense pain and heartache. There was blood on the ground around the suitcase. The Master Sergeant started yelling louder than before as another helicopter landed. "GET THESE PEOPLE OUT OF HERE NOW!" I could not move. I was frozen to the rooftop as the madness swirled around me.

The Master Sergeant grabbed me and shook me in his strong arms. "IF YOU'RE NOT GOING TO BE OF ANY HELP GET YOUR ASS ON THAT HUEY NOW!"

I was tossed on to the helicopter. I looked out the window as people huddled against me. My face was smashed against the window as screaming people holding one another with more intensity than I thought imaginable kept getting onboard. I looked in to the eyes of the Master Sergeant who had caught a glimpse of the suitcase on the ground. His eyes would be one of the last things I remember about Saigon. They wanted to say something beyond words. He turned and glanced down at the confusion around him. He started shouting loudly again – "GET IT OUT OF HERE NOW!"

The helicopter lifted off the rooftop. There were thousands of people running towards the Embassy in the streets. The marines were assembling themselves firing their weapons in the air and trying to create order out of complete chaos. I closed my eyes. I felt the surge of bodies around me as the helicopter sailed toward the ocean. All of Saigon was outside my window and I had been responsible for the death of innocence.

Chapter Thirty-Eight

I stood on the top deck of the USS Okinawa watching the fall of Saigon. From a safe distance it looked like any 4th of July in any big American city. I watched as a helicopter was pushed off the deck to make room for more people. I did not speak. I did not hear any one else speaking. I saw many heads bowed in reverence for things we did not yet fully understand. I watched the last helicopter land with the Master Sergeant on board. He made certain to be the last one off the helicopter looking back inside and over his shoulder a few times before slowly walking away. He reminded me of an actor I saw once on Broadway who said what he had to say in low whispers. They were whispers that forced the audience to pay attention to every word and movement until he gracefully stood alone in the spotlight, his head bowed as if sharing a prayer. I felt in many ways as if I could never share what happened to me. I had seen things and in the end did things I could not tell anyone. I know deep down I need to let someone know. Holding such things inside is not healthy. I sat down on the top deck of the USS Okinawa grabbed a pen and I wrote.

Dear Moron,

You're not going to believe this one. I'm on a boat leaving Nam. It's the biggest damn boat you ever saw. There are more people on this boat than in all of Real, New York. There are so many people only a handful knows each other. Do you remember how you once told me that you know there are a lot of people when only a few know you're alive? Well at this moment no one knows I'm alive. How about that? I'll bet anything you never found yourself in a place with that many people? Ok maybe once or twice but ballgames don't count and besides everyone in the stands knows somebody on the field. Listen, there's a good chance I'll be home soon. Do you think we could maybe just once sit on that old bench and talk things out? The way I see it, I'm not caring what side of the fence you were on about the war. I mean who cares whether we won or lost; it's over, right?

The thing is I've been thinking about going in to business for myself. Well not all by myself, I figure we could do something special. Maybe we could start by selling stuff no one wants? Yeah I know that sounds crazy but I have a feeling people will want to own a lot of stuff they don't even know they need someday. My brother sold my comic books and baseball cards and he made a killing. Imagine if we could go door-to-door and ask people if we could clean out their basements or attics? Instead of throwing that stuff away we open a store and sell it. Crazy huh? I really believe this might work. And another thing, I'm thinking we could maybe take some time to settle down. Did you ever think about settling down? If I learned anything while in Nam it was to never take anything for granted. Did you know you can't take for granted that a postcard you mail will reach the person you sent it to? I have hundreds of them to prove it. The first thing I plan on doing when I get home is sit down and get these postcards to their rightful owners. I have no idea how I'm going to go about it. I wish there was some kind of way to sit down in one place and type in a name and up would pop the information you need. Do you suppose that might ever happen in our lifetime? If it does we could maybe find everything we ever dreamed or talked about since we were kids. You know I'm willing to bet that if something like that ever does get invented, people will take it for granted. I'll bet anything that if it ever came to be people would sit around and yell at the damn thing like it was a person. That's what it all comes down to any way isn't it? We all need someone to yell at, to blame and curse and complain about. Why do you think that is Billy?

Remember how your Dad and your Uncle Tom were so proud of what they did as soldiers in World War II? We would sit for hours listening to their stories. Yeah, most of the stories were not really about war. That kind of stuff God-willing gets left on the battlefield. Of course, Hollywood always finds a way to exploit even the worst tragedies of time. Maybe there's truth to the old saying, "misery loves company." I don't know Billy, there's a few things I'd rather not talk about having seen and did while over here. I think that's why people learn how to whisper. As little kids you do it so you can sneak up and scare someone. That's always fun. But scaring someone isn't very nice is it? It's still funny no matter what I guess. I've been hearing a lot of whispering the past few days. Mostly it's when I look around to see others as scared as I am about the future. I think it's like praying only people whisper because they're afraid to let on they're afraid. Does that make sense Billy? Of course with everything happening in the world today I don't think anyone's listening to those prayers. All those unanswered whispers are falling on deaf ears. But it makes people feel good, so what's the fault of trying? I got snippets of things happening at home from other guys here. I've read some of the articles in the newspapers. I heard some of the music by the biggest names in the music business. It's all rather depressing if you want to know the truth of it. I mean whatever happened to not knowing what it's like to know someone until you walked a mile in his or her shoes? That's just another saying isn't it? Of course there are a lot of people who love to play both ends against the middle. They say things like they were against the war but support the troops. How many oxymorons does it take to describe the justification of war? I wanted to be a journalist Billy. I wanted to write stories that would make people see the world in a whole new light. I never thought the light would be so dim. The sun is fading from the sky now as I finish this letter to you. I look back over my shoulder and cannot make sense of the time I spent here. I mean it was supposed to mean something right? In the end I'll bet it sold a lot of music. The music industry will probably turn in to some kind of giant super power industry. I'll bet you anything that one day there will be TV channels devoted to music all day and night. Not only that there will be so much music that no one will know what they really enjoy anymore. You know even too much of a good thing can bore you to death sometimes.

I remember Louis telling me one night how music can save the world. He really believed it. Only thing was, he said, "No two people hear a song the same way." I acted like I understood what he meant because I was afraid to ask for an explanation. It was always best to let Louie ramble on sometimes. Stopping him when he was talking the talk was insulting. I thought so anyway. The thing is it took me all this time to fully understand what he said about music and how people hear a song. It has to do with being emotionally open to what you hear. That can be the hardest lesson anyone ever learns in life.

One night, not so long ago when this experience of war was at its worst, I put on a pair of headphones and listened to a record. There are not many albums made that you can listen to in one sitting and feel that it's a good use of your time. It was this record by a group called Pink Floyd, "Dark Side of the Moon." If you have not heard it I highly recommend it. I think this album may have helped me make sense of what I was experiencing. I cannot explain it in words really. Although I am certain one day when we sit down and listen together we will find the right words. Then again, I don't think that will work. Like Louis said, I doubt you will hear the album the same way I do. It has to do with your surroundings. It gets lost in translation. While listening to Pink Floyd it reminded me of a record Louis gave me years ago by Miles Davis. It was called "Bitches Brew." Now that record will scare you if you're not up to learning the power of music. There are notes Miles Davis plays on Bitches Brew that have not been invented yet. Can you believe that? Of course it took listening to Louis to know what to listen for, and even then, now years later, I am not sure anyone knows what Miles was trying to say. Still, albums like Bitches Brew and Dark Side of the Moon made sense to me in a confusing place. Maybe it's best if you and I agree to never listen to records in their entirety? I think that is what will happen in the future anyway – people will hear a song and they will own it like immediately. It will be like Osmosis music. You think of a song and it will be playing almost instantly on this hand held device that will hold like a million songs! OK, not a million, but it might as well be a million because people will choose to listen to the same song over and over again anyway.

I think time changes for the better in a lot of ways and yet, things get more confusing. I could make a list of my favorite albums that in a lot of ways were my only real friends here, but we would probably argue about the list. The last thing I need is to argue with anyone about music. It would be like arguing about a sunny day.

I don't know how long this will take to reach you. Maybe you will never get it, and just like these postcards I'm carrying around the words will get lost in the wind. You know like that song by that singer Bob Dylan, Blowing in the Wind? He has a lot of different ways of making us think twice about things doesn't he? It's probably a good thing he learned how to play a guitar instead of shooting a rifle. Nothing good comes of shooting a rifle. It's like you're holding life and death in your hands and you never know which way it's going to turn out. If I close my eyes I think about where I've been and where I hope to be someday. My here and now feels like I'm in some kind of cage and I have no idea who has the key to letting me out. I think about Gayle Cooper. My brother wrote me a letter saying she's been seen around town with some guy who wants to be a doctor. I mean she's an intelligent girl, what chance do I have? I don't know Billy, there will be a lot of stuff to figure out but I guess that never ends. What's that story your Mom told us about people and their problems? If you go to a party and drop all of your problems in a basket most people when they go home will pick up their own problems when they leave. Do you think that's true? Maybe we should ask her to tell us the story again.

I'll let you go Billy. I'll call you when I get home. I don't know how long that will take. Right now it feels like I'm on a slow boat to China. Hey, you don't think they'd trick us and drop us off in China do you? That could happen someday. I hate when I think about this stuff, it could come true or something close to it!

Your buddy

Kidd

Chapter Thirty-Nine

Dear Kidd,

Hurry home! There are so many things changing there that you won't recognize the neighborhood anymore. They're knocking down restaurants to make room for condoms. A few months back someone drove a fire truck in to the wall that leads up to the ball field. Would you know anything about that? I hear that the police questioned Billy Moran but he said he did not know anyone crazy enough to do something like that. The police have been asking everyone and strangely enough Dickie Blues has not been seen nor heard from since it happened. The police arrested Tommy Hargrove. For some unknown reason he is believed to be the one behind the fire truck incident. Billy Moran when he heard this said, "I guess you need to learn not to cry over spilled milk." I do not quite understand his response. Maybe it makes sense to you? Billy Moran has himself a girlfriend. Can you believe that any woman on the planet earth would find him the least bit attractive? The word on the street is that he's either lying or there really are UFOs and he's fallen in love with an alien. Here in Anchorage there's no time for such things. I have ice-fishing tournaments to win! Last week I caught a whopper. They had to expand the size of the newspaper to fit the picture of me holding it on the front page. Somebody wrote in to the paper advising that some guy named Herman Melville wrote a book about the fish I caught. The war being over is a big relief but it's probably going to cost me a fortune! Someone told me that the rubber alone from the fish I caught could have bought me a huge condom. Condoms are all the rage now; every Tom, Dick and Harry wants one! You should see them; they're popping up everywhere you look. Here in Anchorage there's talk of people building them right on the lake. You know even here the lakes do not stay frozen year round. But, that's not stopping the real estate people. They would sell the ground out from underneath you if you walked too slowly. Back home in Real, that girl you said you missed, what's her name, Gayle Cooper? You have it all wrong. She wants to be a nurse. I can understand how you got it ass backwards; your brother had no idea she was asking the guy about how she can get in to nursing. The way I hear it she talks about you so much it makes most people sick. Maybe that's why she wants to become a nurse. Life sure is strange, from one day to the next you might as well throw everything up in the air and you get to keep only what comes back down. The thing is some people forget what they throw up so a lot gets lost. Anyway, I have a tournament to prepare for tomorrow. I'm planning on catching an even bigger fish this time out. I always do.

Keep Warm and Chill Out,

Googenblatt

Chapter Forty

On the jet plane home from Nam I could not wait to get back home. Knowing you spent a part of life that you could never fully explain was difficult enough. Still, I wanted to start making sense again and could not wait to begin. I sat on the plane thinking about all the things I wanted to do when I got home. The very first thing I wanted to do was lay on my own bed listening to the cars going by on the highway. The sound of tires on asphalt sounded like waves crossing on the shore at Rockaway. I longed to hear that simple sound. The next thing I wanted to do was take Gayle for a walk in the sand at the beach. I wanted her to close her eyes and listen so she could hear what I heard and missed. I did not want to waste any more time. I wanted her to marry me as soon as possible. I wanted to have children and name each one after a song. I was crazy with the sense of freedom in my life. I thought to myself how freedom lies if not celebrated. I wanted to celebrate being home and try if possible to leave everything bad behind me. On the plane there were guys who could not stop singing. They sang everything with a feeling of pure joy. Just like me they had survived something that would take a hundred years to be fully understood. As the plane slowly descended towards the New York skyline I marveled at the tall buildings. A few buildings had been built while I was away. The skyline looked as beautiful as it ever did but was made more so by the majestic monuments of two new buildings called the World Trade Center that stood on the tip of Manhattan like beacons of light. Everyone onboard seemed to stop speaking at the same time as we took in the view. Some one yelled out, "Can you go all the way to the top?" We were transfixed by these buildings that seemed to reach out of the clouds like two fingers pointing us home. A stewardess started to give out statistics proud of the building's majestic beauty. She stood in the aisle watching as we looked out the windows: "Each building is 110 stories high. Yes, you can go to the top. Inside, you take elevators to a floor called the "sky lobby" where you change for another elevator that takes you all the way to the top. There is a restaurant at the top called Windows On The World. Inside, you can sit and view the Manhattan skyline like no where else. It opened in April of 1973." As she spoke we watched in reverence turning to look at the stewardess who said each word as if she were sharing every fact for the first time. A few guys whistled after she mentioned each statistic. The Twin Towers seemed to move in a majestic dance with the autumn breeze. They were like the peace signal extended out from the hands of so many Americans praying for an end to war. A war that like so many went on for too long. Changes caused by war are always felt hardest by families who would never again see a loved one alive.

As we passed over the towers memories clouded my vision. I looked around at the other soldiers and they too seemed to be reflecting on things they witnessed and things that could not be explained. A few of us caught up in the reveries of singing only moments before, bowed our heads in silent prayer. The towers standing in their all their glory for a moment seemed to whisper out loud the names of ghosts we had seen come and go. Ghosts, that lingered in the clouds over Manhattan as a reminder how war never truly ends. The stewardess was sharing her wisdom of the towers in a voice that was filled with respect and appreciation. Every one applauded when she got up from her kneeling stance telling us, "Welcome Home."

At the airport I was not expecting anyone to be waiting. I did not have time to call and let anyone know exactly what flight I would be on. As the plane made its final approach I closed my eyes listening for whispers that I prayed were answered prayers.

Louis: Welcome home Kidd.

Jono: Louis? Thanks man I appreciate that.

Louis: You're not going to be hearing that from many people.

Jono: What do you mean?

Jack: He means it takes time for people to forget enough to remember.

Jono: Hello Jack. How are you doing?

Jack: It takes getting used to, but things work out if you let them.

Dad: You're going to be ok son.

Jono: Dad! Wow, I miss you.

Dad: Back at ya Kiddo, now get off this plane and get on with your life.

Jono: Will I know where to begin?

Dad: Don't worry about it. Just tell her you love her.

Jono: Who?

Dad: Trust me.

Jack: Stay off the road and settle down.

Jono: Are you feeling ok Jack?

Jack: It doesn't work for everyone. Hell it can kill you.

Louis: It's a wonderful world Kidd.

The wheels hit the pavement at John F. Kennedy airport. I was jolted out of my short nap and could feel the edges of my mouth smiling. A feeling I had not felt in many months. I promised myself I would learn to do it more often. I picked up my duffle bag and slung it over my shoulder and began to walk through the terminal. A song called "Hello It's Me" by Todd Rundgren was playing on the sound system. I looked up to see Gayle Cooper standing with her hands on her hips. She pointed at her watch and pursed her lips and smiled. She said, "What took you so long Kidd?"

PART TWO

There's No Place like Home
Or is there?

Chapter One

You can lie around thinking about the past and dreaming of the future for just so long.

After a while it begins to feel like a foxhole on any battlefield. The worst kind of enemy is the one you find inside yourself. You cannot run very far from yourself. More than anything I wanted to start fresh. I wanted to believe that you could still make dreams come true. I did not have any clue what that meant but everyone kept saying to me "You have your whole life ahead of you." I felt in many ways I had already lived an entire lifetime. I seen things no one could forget. My mother and brother moved the day I got home from the Army. I showed up at the last place I knew I lived and rang the bell. No one answered the door. I went to landlord and asked if he knew where my Mom might be. He informed me she had left that morning. She left a forwarding address for someplace on Long Island. The landlord misplaced the address but promised he would find it so I could know where I lived.

It was a strange feeling to be back on the street where you grew up not recognizing anyone. The landlord welcomed me home by saying, "What are you going to do now?" I tried to smile as I nodded my head in acknowledgement of his greeting. I walked in to the park with my duffle bag slung over my shoulder. A thousand memories ran through my mind. It was already late afternoon and I sat on a bench trying to figure out what to do next.

I fell asleep on the bench and did not wake up until after dark. I was home and still I felt in many ways like it was a foreign place. Things had changed in the neighborhood of my youth. I knew exactly where I was but felt more lost than I could comprehend. It is hard to explain that giving time for something you believe in can erase years from your life that you never get back. It was 9'o'clock when I emerged from the park and started walking down the Avenue. From a phone booth I called Gayle Cooper. I told her my mother had moved and I had no place to go. I showed up at her doorstep and her parents welcomed me home. I wanted to get out of my uniform. I needed to put something on that made me feel free. As I took off my uniform for the last time in the downstairs bathroom of Gayle Cooper's house I felt like I was stripping away a part of my past that no one would ever know anything about. It would never make sense to people who took freedom for granted. It would not make a bit of sense to so many people wanting to believe everything they owned was deserved. I folded the uniform and tucked in to the bottom of my duffle bag. I had poured everything I owned on the floor of Gayle Cooper's basement. I picked up a pair of blue jeans and a t-shirt. I held a pair of old sneakers in my hands sensing they had magic inside them. For a moment as I slipped them on my feet I felt my body change. I tossed the shoes I was wearing in to the duffle bag and managed to get everything else inside as well. There wasn't much left; just a bunch of belongings that meant so much for too long in a place far away. It was time to move on.

Chapter Two

I lay in the basement of Gayle Cooper's house looking at the ceiling. There was an old radio on a table. I turned it on. I was not expecting to hear anything that would matter. I was looking for something to take my mind off thinking about what to do next. A male voice was in the middle of what could only be called an epiphany. I sat up and turned the radio louder. It was past midnight and this voice was sharing something I had never heard another person share. I recognized the voice but for a moment could not place it. I remembered hearing the voice when I was younger than I would ever be again. It was the same deejay who had played music with a passion only Louis could fully appreciate. His name was Ben Kelsa and hearing his voice still alive on the radio after all the things I saw and experienced made me feel there was still hope for the world. That night he spoke in a voice that yearned for understanding. It was exactly the sentiment I needed.

"Listen to me? It matters that I know you are out there listening. Not just with one ear waiting for the next song – but both ears and look at me when I am talking to you. Yes You! Ok, now here's the deal, I am asking for your undivided attention on this one.

I am not here to amuse you or myself for that matter. This is personal. I realize people do not open up this way. I am not like anyone you know. I am a voice without a face on your radio. I have to be honest with someone or I am going to explode inside.

I am looking for some understanding. Don't call me – I do not take phone calls. I'm funny that way. If you are still out there; I will try to share what I want to say.

I will talk, you listen.

I found out today that a friend of mine died. I know I should have stayed home but I needed to play music and the more people I thought I could share this with, the better. I did not know until today how I felt about this person. We were not close in the same way I might be with people I see everyday. Friendship is like that. You meet someone and you do not know you have a connection with him or her until you meet years later when you least expect. Ok, listen he did not die a natural death. I need you to know that I am not condoning his decision to do what he did. Quite frankly, if he was alive sitting next to me right now – I would smack him and say. "What the hell were you thinking?" Ok, let me say this, I feel responsible in a way! Not for what he did but how long he did it and I did nothing about it. Does that make sense? Of course not, how can you make sense of someone killing themselves? I watched him do it. Not the actual final scene but damn it I should have said something. Lay off that stuff, it's going to kill you! He would not have listened to me but at least I would not feel so guilty now for not saying something. In the end was it really the drugs that did him in? Maybe he knew it was it was too much to take in one dose? Who knows what goes in to a decision like that? Hey! I am no saint here – let me get that assumption right out of the way now. I did my share too. I wanted to be cool too. I wanted to think I could live forever. I wanted to escape from time to time just for the hell of it. I guess I am angry with him for not saying something. Hey! I have a problem here! There are no saints in the city. It is one damn nightmare for people searching for answers they cannot find. I wanted you to know I am not myself tonight. I wanted you to know that there are songs you might hear the remainder of the night that I need to play. I need to play them because these songs are my way of dealing with losing a friend. Are you still there? I cannot get through this night alone. I have the music and I pray you're out there sharing it with me. It's just us now. I don't know how many of you are out there. I don't want to know. I just need to know you care. This is for my friend. More than that, it's for me and for you."

There was a silence before the first chords of a song filled the air. It was a sound I had not heard before. Something new. It was a voice angry and poetic like Bob Dylan from the early 1960s. He was singing about how hard it was to be a saint in the city. There was a driving beat behind the music that sounded like a band of gypsies lost in the mountains. The lyrics were astounding. I turned the radio higher. The song ended and it immediately flowed in to another song, just as intense and new sounding. I recognized the second voice as being Van Morrison. He was waxing poetic and singing "Oh Domino!" My feet started to shuffle on the cold basement floor. I was no longer thinking about yesterday or tomorrow. I was dancing around the basement with my eyes closed. "Oh Domino!"

I did not hear Gayle Cooper open the basement door. She was standing on the stairs watching me. I did not feel the least bit embarrassed. I raised my hands and asked her to join me. She came off the stairs hesitating at first with a smile that whispered a thousand words. "What are you doing, Jonathan? I told her I was celebrating life and death at the same time. She took my hand and we bounced around her basement with the radio blaring in the background, played by a mad wizard deejay asking us to take a trip with him and music was our drug. Van Morrison stopped singing and there was brief silence before a slow jazz riff filled the room. I held Gayle close and we swayed to the music. I could feel her heart beating against mine. I could feel her breathing in my ear. The music played on and on for hours. Gayle Cooper never asked what we were listening to. It was a night of bliss. We held hands and during the playing of a few songs we closed our eyes or maybe even cried a little. We were being transformed; without realizing it, it would unite us for all eternity. We were exhausted from listening to music. I looked in to her eyes as the final song of this extended set of music played. We fell to the couch and we listened to the deejay reel off every song and the artist who sang it. His voice was no longer pleading or distraught. He had played the sadness out of his heart. He had shared a moment in time special to those who heard it. In an almost whisper, the deejay said "that first song I played way back at the beginning of our journey was "It's Hard To Be A Saint In The City" by Bruce Springsteen off his first album "Greetings From Asbury Park. Thanks for staying with me tonight. I needed a friend and you were there to help me make it through the night. I have one last song before leaving you tonight. He played "Help Me Make It Through The Night" by Kris Kristofferson. Gayle and I held hands, falling asleep in one another's arms

Chapter Three

Sometimes things that are sentimental in nature get misunderstood. Gayle's parents were not pleased to discover their daughter had stayed in the basement with me. I woke to hear her trying to explain to them that nothing had happened. She was pleading with them to have faith in her judgment. I heard her say to her mother "Don't you think you can trust me?" I quietly made my way to a backdoor that led in to the yard. I walked slowly down the driveway and made my way to the Avenue. I stood at the top of Gayle's block like a child looking at traffic coming in both directions waiting to cross the street. We had experienced something simple and pure but we never realized her parents might see it differently. I started to walk to the last place I knew I lived. The landlord had not yet opened his store. He was a shoe repairman. I respected people who could repair things with their hands, it was a dying art form that fewer and fewer people bothered to appreciate. His store had been part of the community for three generations. He inherited the store from his father who had worked side by side with his father learning the craft. I sat on the stoop in front of my old house and waited for the businesses to open up around me starting a new day. At one time or another, my brother or I had delivered for each store on the block. Next to the shoe store was a Chinese Laundry. The man inside the store, Mr. Wong lived in the back of the store. He saved my family's life one night when a gas heater exploded on the first floor. He banged on the pipes and screamed in broken English up the stairs until everyone in my family was awake and running out in to a cold November night. I sat there on the stoop reminiscing about growing up in a room I would never see again. I though about my old room that looked out over the park like a turret on a castle. I could hear my father's voice imitating Jackie Gleason from an old television show, "This is my castle Alice!" and my brother and I would laugh along with my Mom who loved him so much when he was happy and carefree about life. I imagined every family if they took the time could find something special only to them. I thought about the other people who once lived on the block. A girl named "Dee" who loved the football player Joe Namath. She went on and on about "Broadway Joe", as he was known, so much that it made every one crazy. I delivered papers to her family. During one game a linebacker from the Oakland Raiders, Big Ben Davidson, tackled Joe Namath. The back page of the Daily News showed Ben Davidson's forearm crushing Joe Namath's chin. I saved copies of that paper and delivered it to Dee's house every Sunday for 52 weeks. I sat on the small stoop of my house as the sun began to peak through the trees in the park across the street. I was laughing out loud at how Dee had caught up with me in one of the most unlikely of places. I was attending an Army-Navy game at West Point thrilled to find some solace before going overseas. I was on the sidelines when someone slapped me in the back of my head, knocking off my cap. I turned to see Dee with her hands on her hips pointing her finger at me. "That's for being an asshole Kiddrane!" she said before leaping in to my arms and giving me a hug. She told me she secretly looked forward to my bringing the paper everyday. It was a standing joke in her family that I was madly in love with her because I was jealous of Joe Namath. I had never thought about it that way. When you're young you sometimes do stupid things because in your mind they strike you as being funny. For an entire year delivering that newspaper, I was funny. Dee had joined the Army to be a nurse. I sat on the stoop wondering what happened to her. The grocery store opened and I watched Heinz, the owner carrying in his boxes of milk left in his doorway earlier. I got up to help him. He was happy to see me and in his rough Jewish accent he said, "My boy, I was sad to hear about your father. He was a good man." With those words in the air I shook hands with Heinz. It occurred to me that my mother and my brother were leaving so much history behind on this street. Store owners who knew my brother and me since when we were young boys. I thought how each storeowner was special. I never cared when I was a kid what nationality some one was or where they came from. As I helped Heinz bring in the cases of milk I immediately set to taking the cartons and placing them in the bins where they belonged. "Hey, you remember what to do! Always a smart boy!" I chatted a few moments with Heinz telling him how I had gotten out of the Army only the day before. He told me how proud my father was when he was still up and around. "Your father would come in here with a letter you wrote and would not leave anyone alone until they heard what you had to say. He was proud of his soldier boy!" I thanked Heinz for his kind remarks and went back outside on to the street. Mr. Jampol was opening up the pharmacy on the corner. I waved to him and he too was thrilled to see me. He came over to shake my hand yelling "Hey Heinz, look who's here? It's Frank's boy!" I enjoyed the attention from people who in many ways were a part of everyone's family in the community. They knew more people by their first names than even the priest at the local church. I walked back toward my old home and I could see Mr. C opening the Dry Cleaners. Mr. C, like Heinz and Mr. Jampol welcomed me home. I thought it was a very special place to live and I again wondered why my mother would choose to leave. Mr. C immediately began checking the day's list of things to do. He walked over to the Chinese Laundry knocking on the door. "Mr. Wong! Wake up! My horses won yesterday now pay up!" Mr. Wong was sort of the bookie for the neighborhood. When my father was alive they had a sweet business going. People in the neighborhood would bet on the horses that ran all year round at Belmont Racetrack on Long Island and Aqueduct Park in Queens. On days my father did not work Mr. Wong would give the day's bets to him and my Dad would go over to the track and place the bets. It was illegal for some reason and my father would leave the Chinese Laundry with money wrapped in brown paper bags. To any one passing by he was a regular customer picking up his shirts. I wanted to ask Mr. C who had taken over the job of going to the track but opted to let it go. Mr. Wong opened up his door and he started hollering at

Mr. C in Chinese who in turn yelled back in Italian. It was a daily dose of hysterical interplay between the both of them. To someone not in the know it would look like a war was about to break out between China and Italy. In reality, it was a pure friendship that did not require a language but had instead a love of banter and the speed of racehorses. I waved at Mr. Wong and he, like the others, was genuinely happy to see me. His grace and elegance had inherited a form of etiquette. He bowed his head and clasped his hands together in a prayerful sign of respect. I offered my best bow in return, knowing it was something he had tried to teach me since I was a young boy. He looked at me and I could see tears forming in the corners of his eyes. I could not understand what Mr. Wong could say with words, but I knew how much he treasured my father's friendship. I knew how much he missed my father's visits. I realized that in life sometimes the least unlikely group of people can represent a place called home. I pointed at the shoe store and then at my watch asking when Mr. Astor would open for business. Mr. Wong shrugged his shoulders and smiled. He walked back in to his shop and I sat down on my stoop for the last time waiting to find out where I lived.

I could feel an energy sitting on that stoop that represented years of growing up and taking for granted everything around me. Mr. Astor turned the corner and I watched him wave Good Morning to Mr. Jampol, Heinz, and Mr. C before stopping in his doorway and looking at me. "Did you sleep there all night?" he said with a worried smile on his face. I assured him I did not and was waiting for the forwarding address my Mom had left with him. "Yes, yes, I remembered where I put it." He opened the front door of his shop and turned on the lights. I thought how he must have done the same thing for 50 years and yet he still had a spark in his step and a glee about starting a new day. I wondered as I watched him adjust shoes behind the counter, if I would ever be as thrilled to be anywhere for so long. "Can you believe it? I put the address in your mother's boots!" he said reaching in to a pair of my mother's boots. "She said to me before leaving yesterday, "Tony, fix my boots. Look inside for my new paradise!

You believe that, your Mom has found paradise?" I laughed as I watched him open a folded piece of paper. "Ah here she lives now, in Belmont, Long Island."

I could not believe my ears. My mother had moved to Belmont. Belmont was a special place for my family. We had a second life during summers spent at my Aunt Millie and Uncle Pete's house. I knew why my Mom had moved to Belmont. It was a place where my father was always happy. He and my Uncle Pete played a card game called Pinochle. They did not just play it; there were times when my brother and I were convinced they lived it. There were card games that would start on a Friday night and not end until Sunday evening. They did not sleep during these marathon games. Members of my Aunt Millie and Uncle Pete's family would gather on weekends in the summer. There might be close to 80 to 100 people camped out at their Belmont home on weekends when I was a kid. There was food being cooked 24 hours a day. Coffee was brewed on the stove constantly; one pot after another. My cousins and I were free to run wild in the streets without restrictions or rules. The only rule was that we had to stay "on the block." This meant that any of the neighbor's yards were fair game, since they were probably inside playing cards with the others. As I stood there waiting for Mr. Astor to hand me the paper, Belmont seemed to me a place where time stood still. "Here! You give these boots to your mother! No charge!" I thanked Mr. Astor and carried my mother's boots, along with the slip of paper telling me where I lived.

I walked to the corner and looked back at the storefronts. I felt in so many ways like I was losing a part of myself forever. I crossed the street and stood in front of the restaurant, Durows. That corner had held a restaurant or saloon since the early 1900s.

It was painted aqua-blue; the color made people question if the owners wished they were from Bermuda or some Caribbean island. I was going to miss my neighborhood by moving out to paradise. I thought as I walked past the parking lot of Durows that there was so much of what was paradise to me growing up in Real. I stood at the parking lot looking across the street in to the ball field. It was the field where I learned to love the game of baseball. I made my way back to Gayle's house. I walked back down the driveway and went in through the unlocked basement door. I listened for voices coming from upstairs and heard none. I slowly climbed the stairs and opened the door in to the kitchen. Gayle's sister Lynn was sitting and reading the paper at the kitchen table. She looked up startled for a moment and in between bites of her toast muttered the words, "Oh it's only you."

"Is it safe?" I said peeking out from the door through the rest of the house.

"Is what safe?" She said without looking up from reading the paper.

"Are your parents' home?"

"Why would they be home? They work for a living like normal people."

"Thank you." I said as I stepped out of the basement.

"What are you thanking me for?"

"I don't know. I guess for letting me know it was safe to come out of the basement."

"Is there something dangerous I don't know anything about?"

"It's a long story. I will let your sister explain it to you. Where is she?"

"She's normal in some ways, too. She went to work."

It never occurred to me that Gayle had a job. I stood smiling as I thought how I had kept her awake dancing around the basement and carrying on about songs and she had to get up to go to work. At that moment I was never more convinced that something called love happens when you least expect it.

"Where does she work?"

"If she wanted you to know where she worked, she would have told you herself."

I took a deep breath, attempting to weigh her response before responding.

I walked back to the basement door. Before going downstairs I said, "We're going to have a wonderful life together."

She yelled from the kitchen table as I made my way downstairs; "What about a wonderful life?"

I screamed up the stairs, "It's a wonderful life! Wonderful world! Louis Armstrong! Do you know him? I did! You and I are going to grow old together!"

She was at the top of the stairs, calling down, "What about growing old?"

From the bottom of the stairs I looked up at her, smiling, "You're sister and I are getting married. You're the first to know."

"She didn't say anything to me about marriage!"

"I just told you! You're the first to know."

"You mean first as in you didn't tell my sister about this yet?"

"I mean first as in I just thought about it this second!"

"She's too young to get married! She's still in college for the next three years!"

"I think she may wait for college. Love has come to town!"

"I'm telling my mother!"

She stormed off back to the kitchen and I could hear her dialing the rotary phone.

I ran up the stairs and took the phone from her hands.

"Hey!"

"I'm sorry – but I need you to keep this a secret for awhile."

"I don't like to keep secrets!"

"I apologize for that, but I just know everything is going to work out OK. Are you going to help me keep this a secret?"

"I can't make a promise like that."

"Can we agree that you say nothing until I let your sister decide whether she can make a promise?"

"I don't know. I don't like this."

I put my hands on her shoulders. "I appreciate your honesty. Just think about it but for now I have to go. I need to run. I just found out where I live."

She looked at me with the same strange expression as when I first startled her.

"It's a long story", I said as I turned away, heading downstairs. "When your sister is ready she will clue you in on everything you need to know."

"I'm not sure I want to know anything."

"Good. Then we never had this discussion and you're off the hook."

"What hook?"

"The 'secret' hook."

"There's a 'secret' hook? First I've ever heard about it."

I banged my head against the basement door. "Listen, it will all make sense soon. I can't say when, but just give everything a little time to work out."

She turned back to the kitchen table, pulled out a chair and sat down. She picked up a piece of toast. She said, "I hate cold toast."

Chapter Four

I placed my duffle bag in a closet beneath the basement stairs. There was no need to lug that all the way to Long Island. I knew the way to Belmont in my sleep. I could walk there if I had to. Instead I mapped out in my head the buses I had to take. I left through the basement door and again for the second time that morning made my way to Myrtle Avenue where I would wait for the Jamaica bound bus.

As I stood on the corner waiting for the bus I thought about a friend I had in high school named Terrence Trans. He was an interesting guy. We went to Richmond Hill High School. It was a public high school, but this did not stop Terrence from wearing a white shirt and tie each morning to school. I would meet him at the bus stop each morning and every day I was amused and fascinated by his appearance. Terrance Trans, dressed in an inspired way. While the majority of students at Richmond Hill wore the traditional jeans and t-shirts uniform of public high school students, Terrance stood out in a special way. What was most impressive was that Terrance had a secret. He was an avid fan of the late night talk show host, Johnny Carson. He dressed just like him. It was fascinating and impressive that somehow, Terrance Trans managed to wear the exact same kind of tie Johnny Carson wore the night before on his show each day to school. It was awe-inspiring. I would watch The Tonight Show hosted by Johnny Carson from 11:30pm until 1am in the morning, and was never disappointed the next day when Terrance Trans would show up at the bus stop sporting the same outfit. I mentioned to him one morning that I saw Johnny Carson wearing the same tie last night. Terrance would look at his tie and say in a low voice, "Interesting. Very interesting."

I stood now waiting for the bus, wondering what had happened to Terrence, the best- dressed kid to ever attend Richmond Hill High School. We spent four years together taking the same bus each morning, and we waited for each other at the end of the day if one of us did not stay late for some reason. And here I was less than five years later not knowing where he was or what happened to him. I thought of this as I saw the bus coming down the avenue.

It occurred to me as I boarded the bus how small the world. As we pulled out on to the avenue, I looked at the expanse of Forest Park to my right and the interlocking tree lined streets of the community I once called home. I had a plan in mind that included marrying Gayle Cooper and somehow finding a way to stay right where I belonged in Real. The bus went past Woodhaven Boulevard and Victory Field where I ran track for the high school team. I watched out the window as the bus rolled past Freedom Drive where Billy Moran and I discovered our deepest roots as friends so many years earlier. In to the heart of the darkness the bus rolled as trees surrounded both sides of the Avenue for the last time with Forest Park spread out as far as the eye could see.

Down past the final streets to the last stop, now in Richmond Hill and the sight of some of the oldest buildings in New York. Old Victorian homes with huge attics and porches that wrap around the first floors like reminders of something long since faded into history. What had occurred to me about how small the world was my finding out that Jack Kerouac had once lived in Richmond Hill. I did not know that the author who would write a life's work dedicated to his exploits on the road once lived nearby.

I looked over at two empty seats on the bus and closed my eyes. Immediately those seats were taken.

Jack – You see this here Louis? My stomping grounds as a young man!

Louis – Do tell, Jack!

Jack – My folks fell on hard times at home back in Lowell. Back in the day people went where the work was. There was no question or hesitation about uprooting an entire family to go where the work was. I found my voice here, Louis. Do you remember where you found your voice?

Louis – In the heart of man, Jack. I found my voice in the heart of man. If people believe in you, there's no stopping you!

Jack – Yeah well, writing is a little different than finding a way to get in to people's hearts with a song. If a writer could find a way to make a pen sing, well, there you would have something special. I struggled with myself through many a night here in Richmond Hill. Long hot ones and longer colder ones. It got so the only way to get started was to leave. I went out of Richmond Hill into the city and on to a bus upstate. On past Yankee Stadium and up the Hudson where I realized once and for all I could start out from that point across America and in to that void called life's calling. Destiny.

You ever wonder about destiny Louis?

Louis – Like it was a place in my soul to visit over and over again.

Jack – You know what I learned, Louis? Sometimes you have to leave a place before you can appreciate it. I mean really appreciate it. Like calling home the place where you were born even if you lived in a million other places your entire life. A man who loses touch with his roots has no business talking about freedom.

Louis – Freedom is a place too, hey Jack?

Jack – You know it. It has an address inside you that makes you yearn for something more. A wild man's dream come true each time he wakes up and can taste the fresh air of a new challenge, a new journey and a new beginning. I lost faith in finding that out. I let myself get dragged down by my own lost dreams. The worst thing a man can do is allow himself to become dependent on something. Anything that takes you away from yourself is not worth calling a friend. I fell in love with a bottle, Louis. It was a mistake. I wish someone would have been able to rescue me. In the end you realize something. You can only rescue yourself. You do not need to go on the road to learn these things. In many ways you can sit at home and the truth comes in your window like a warm summer breeze or a cold hard winter frost. I got lost on my highway, Louis; and I never truly found my way back home.

Louis – It's a hard road we travel sometimes, Jack.

Jack – A hard road indeed.

I opened my eyes and looked at the empty seats on the bus. Each seat a shadow of a million lost souls and the wizards of wisdom. I was on my way home to a house where I had never lived before. I stood and held on to the straphanger on the bus and watched out the front window as the bus pulled in to the final stop. I thought of a song the deejay had played the night before, Closer To Home by Grand Funk Railroad. The melody began to take shape in my mind. I was getting closer to my home.

Chapter Five

As I prepared myself to get off the third and final bus along Hempstead Turnpike, a main street in Belmont, I was exhausted from so many memories. As the bus passed a small gas station, I remembered a night like none other as my father made his way to my Uncle's house for a card game. It was a Friday evening and the weather was treacherous. The local highways were closed and the advisories on the radio were asking everyone to stay home. The car had not gone more than five miles an hour from the Queens border in to Nassau, the Long Island borough of New York. As my father's car got to the same light I was now waiting at on the bus he suddenly pulled off the road and into the gas station. In the excitement of watching my father drive I had been so mesmerized that I did not notice the back window was covered in snow as well as the side windows and only a small portion where the wind shield wipers were scraping against ice on the front window. My father opened his car door and casually walked in to where a gas station attendant looked like he had seen a mirage pull in. He and my father came out with huge brooms. My brother and I got out of the car and we could not believe our eyes. The car looked like some kind of sculpture on wheels. Everywhere on the frame of the car snow was iced over, forming an obscurely- shaped igloo. That was what my brother said as he watched my father prepare his broom to brush away the snow. "It looks like an igloo."

Those words seemed to stop my father and the gas station attendant before they cleared the snow away. We stood looking at the car admiring how the snow had fallen in such a way as to create this thing. My brother shouted again, "It looks like an igloo!" Both my father and the attendant started to laugh in unison. The attendant said to my father "No one has come by here all night. You must really need to be someplace ,Mister!" My father approached the car with a broom in his hands and took the first swipe at the massive curved dome on the roof of the car. For whatever reason because of the speed we had traveled and the direction of the wind, the car was a sight unlike anything we had seen before. We had come to Belmont in an igloo on wheels. My father and the attendant swept whatever snow they could from the car's exterior. My mother never woke up during the entire ride and through this episode of a misplaced igloo on the Hempstead Turnpike. My brother and I had the best damn snowball fight ever as my father and the attendant tossed huge bails of snow from the car. My father was happy and was shouting to the attendant "Life's too damn short to lose a precious minute!" The attendant shouted something back "Standing still can kill you!" I remembered this strange conversation as my brother and I were covered in an avalanche of snow tossed by my father standing on top of our car. He and the attendant went back in to the station and they both emerged carrying buckets. When my Dad had gone inside the first time he explained his plan to the attendant who did not hesitate to join in my father's zany plot. I do not know where the heated water came from that they both carried in buckets. They each waited for a moment lifting their buckets in the air and splashed the contents on to the car. For a moment as the heat of the water met the cold ice, smoke began emanating like a fog around us. When the fog cleared the car looked like some kind of crystal ship. As the bus left the light I heard the song Crystal Ship by The Doors echoing in my mind. It was a magical moment lost in time. The bus passed over the Cross Island Parkway, all but closed except for the lights of garbage trucks with massive shovels clearing away the snow. The trucks with their lights on and the swirling storm around them looked like something out of a sci-fi movie. I returned my mind to the present. I checked the address on the paper and knew it was only a matter of time before I would be home. The bus went past Belmont Racetrack on our left with a huge parking lot to our right three football size fields long. I remembered playing in the field with my cousins on days when the adults would take a break from playing cards to rush on over to the track to bet on the horses. We were like one huge caravan of crazed family members rushing to catch the races. I could hear my Uncle Pete's voice yelling as we entered the parking lot "The last race of the day is ours to win!" The adults would all scramble from their cars and go off running through a tunnel that led to the racetrack entrance. My cousins and I would get out of the cars and immediately form sides for a game of tag. "You're IT!" my cousin Michael would scream, and off we would go; dodging in between the thousands upon thousands of parked cars. I thought, as we rolled past the parking lot how we were never bored as children. We always managed to amuse ourselves in one way or another. The bus pulled to a light at the entrance to the racetrack and I knew my stop was closer now. I stood up, and looking out the front window of the bus pulled the cord advising the driver I needed to get off. It was a day of strange revelations and fond memories filled with more question marks than answers. The bus pulled to the side of the road and I got off listening as the air brakes on the bus pressed for a stop. I waited on the corner for a moment looking around, trying to get my bearings. I noticed the pizza place on the corner "King Umberto's" where as a kid my cousins and I would eat slices of pizza and drink our cans of soda feeling like we were royalty. A slice of pizza and a soda cost under a dollar back then, and we would take the excess money given to us by our parents and run off to the pizza place two and three times a day. It was called excess money because there was always a "pot" that the card players would toss money into during their marathon games. The pot was called a "kitty" and it became common to hear one of the adults scream "Take the kitty and get out of here!" to one of my cousins as we ran past the kitchen table on our way to the backyard pool or during a game of hide and seek.

We spoke about the "kitty" as if it were an invisible relative who from time to time would take us all to get pizza. "Did you get the kitty?" someone would yell and off we would run to eat. At home there was always something cooking on the stove, but pizza was the food of kings. We ate our pizza at King Umberto's, where royalty ate in style.

I looked at the changes made to the stores on Hempstead Turnpike and wondered if anyone living here noticed, too; or did you have to leave and come back to fully see the difference? I looked further down the road for another place we used to eat; a place called Hungry Herman's. It was gone now; replaced by the yellow arches of McDonald's. I had nothing against McDonald's, but there were so many of them sprouting up like weeds everywhere. For a moment I thought how the arches looked like manufactured monoliths lost to a future without a heart. They lacked the character of a local place like Hungry Herman's, where the burgers each had a name that made you laugh when you ordered. "Give me Herman!" or "I want a Harry!" were familiar words that echoed in my mind as I made my way down the streets where I spent so many summers long ago. I felt in so many ways that my mother had moved back in time.

Chapter Six

Everyone from our past is connected to a different future. I did not expect to hear certain names again, but sometimes the unexpected happens whether we want it to or not. This is what happened. I was walking in the park one morning when I saw Billy jogging. We stood for a moment looking at one another without saying a word. He casually walked over to me and we shook hands.

"How are you and Gayle doing?" he asked with a knowing look on his face.

"We're doing fine. I'm staying in her basement looking for a job."

"That's interesting. I just saw her walking on the avenue."

"Are you certain it was her?"

"She was with Tommy Hargrove."

"Not a chance. You must be mistaken."

"I don't run that fast. It was her and they both looked......"

"What?"

"They came out of the park walking so close it looked like they were together."

"Which way were they going?"

"Back toward her house; are you sure everything is alright?"

It was an awkward conversation. Billy and I had not seen one another in awhile. I was at a loss to understand what he had seen. I shook his hand and headed back to Gayle's house. I saw her mother and father in their car pulling out of the driveway. I walked towards the house feeling like there was something happening and I had no idea what to do about it. Sometimes drawing conclusions about anything, or anyone, can make life harder than it needs to be. Gayle's sister was standing at the front door when I arrived. "Good morning. You're up early?"

"I woke up when I heard my parents leaving."

"Have you seen Gayle?"

"I assumed she was with you in the basement."

"I couldn't sleep and went for a walk. Billy Moran said he saw her with Tommy Hargrove."

"That's strange."

"Yeah, strange in more ways that I can begin to understand."

She turned from the door as I began to enter. She said in a low voice, "This should be interesting."

"What's that?"

She looked back and then said louder, "Gayle, we were just talking about you."

I entered the living room and Gayle was there looking tired and upset.

"Gayle? Is there something you need to tell me?"

"Tommy Hargrove's in the basement. He needed some place to sleep."

"Excuse me?"

"I am very tired. After I said good night to you I took the dog for a walk. I was standing on the corner when Tommy Hargrove appeared. We started talking. We walked in to the park. I lost track of time."

"That's it?"

"I'm going to bed to get some sleep. Tommy will explain everything."

"Do you have any idea the history between Tommy Hargrove and me?"

"Yeah, you went to the same high school. You live in the same neighborhood all your lives. He's not who you think he is. Talk to you later." She turned to go upstairs.

"This isn't right, Gayle!"

"Make it right, Jonathan. I am too tired to explain anything now."

Standing on the stairs she said, "Trust is something we need to learn. Don't make this in to anything more than what it is."

"Which is what, exactly?"

"Talk to Tommy. He's downstairs."

She went upstairs and both her sister and I could hear the door of their room slam shut.

"What do you make of this?" I asked Lynn, who stood with a bemused look on her face.

"I think my sister is tired."

"Does this make sense to you?"

"I stopped trying to figure out what makes sense when she brought you home."

"Is that supposed to be sarcastic or…….?"

"It's about as honest as I can be. My parents trust her in ways I never thought possible. She has her boyfriend stay in the basement with no real limitations or expectations. I'm thinking if she says there is nothing to worry about between the two of you then you need to trust her better judgment. She has a kind heart. She takes in stray dogs all the time."

"Is that a dig or are you trying to be funny?"

"Lighten up, Jonathan. You're part of the family whether you like it or not."

"You really think so?"

"I know so. My sister loves you. Accept it and accept what she says and does."

"This is the most rational you have ever been."

"I have my good days. It is way too early to test my patience."

"What should I do?"

"Go talk to this Tommy character before she wakes up."

"What do I say to him?"

"I'm certain the both of you will have a lot to discuss."

Lynn went upstairs and I could hear the door to her room shut. I waited in the living room thinking I needed to do one of two things. I could go downstairs and find out what made Gayle bring Tommy Hargrove to her house, or I could go home to my mother's house. Either way I needed to accept certain conditions about Gayle and our future.

I decided to let Tommy Hargrove sleep. I went home.

Chapter Seven

Gayle called me that evening. She told me she knew I would go home. Tommy Hargrove stayed in Gayle's basement for a week. I told her I would see her when she was done taking care of whatever it was the two of them had. She told me it was nothing that threatened her and I; she just had a feeling that some people need friends and that she needed to help him." I asked what her parents thought of the situation. She told me that as far as they were concerned, it was me in the basement and they had no need to know otherwise. I had no idea how she could keep a secret like that from her parents. She said, "It's not a secret, it's just something they don't need to know."

Being home in my mother's new house was strange enough. I saw my brother every day and he could not be more understanding. It was like old times as we spent a few days just being brothers. We caught up on things we might have never discussed. I learned how he was adjusting to life on Long Island. He had found new friends despite frequent trips back to the old neighborhood. I found it comical to hear him calling our home town – "the old neighborhood", but it made sense for him. For the first time I admitted I had no intention of leaving Real and how I planned to one day get married and settle down there. My mother was comfortable in her new house. She never owned anything so spacious and spent her days decorating and re-decorating, painting and re-painting. My brother told me he felt lucky he wasn't blind because she rearranged the furniture so often it made it impossible to not look where you walked. She did not ask once if there was a problem between Gayle and me. The only conversations we had were about meals. "What do you want for dinner?" She would say the moment she came down in the morning. Cooking was a cure- all for everything. She spent the days decorating her new home and planning meals. My years away in the military were never discussed with anyone; it was like they had never happened. It was as if I had never left home; it was confusing and comforting at the same time. I spent the days looking in the paper for a job. I had no idea what I wanted to do. My brother was better prepared to make decisions about his future. He mapped out his future by taking different civil service job tests. He confessed, "I don't know which one will work for me but I'll have options. I like having options." It was a logical mindset and I admired him for it. As the days went by, I realized how much I missed being with Gayle. How much I missed being in Real. The new neighborhood was beautiful with tree lined streets and every house had its own driveway; but it wasn't home to me; I needed a place to call home.

After a week I called Gayle and asked if we could get together. She was happy to hear my voice on the phone.

"Is it alriight to visit, or should we meet some place else?"

She laughed, admitting it would seem awkward with her parents thinking I was in the basement. We agreed to meet in the park. Where else do people who need to talk go?

I had not driven from my mother's new house to the "old neighborhood", so it felt strange to take the highways to get to a place I knew and loved. Once on the highway in my mother's car it felt odd to drive the same roads my father had taken years before when visiting relatives who lived on Long Island. I turned on to Myrtle Avenue for the first time in a car and it felt like I was in the right place. Passing all the old streets even though I had only left a week before was rewarding. I was looking for a ticker-tape parade as I neared the park. In my mind, Gayle and I were destined to be together as long as I could find a job and start figuring out what I wanted to do with our future.

Even as I parked the car on Myrtle Avenue it felt strange to be in two places at the same time. I found myself laughing as I walked in to the park where Gayle sat waiting on a bench; the same bench where we had talked long ago, not knowing that we would become friends for life. I looked at the park benches, thinking if each one could talk they would hold the secrets of a lifetime. They would hold at least the secrets of Real.

Chapter Eight

Gayle did not sit waiting on the bench. She ran leaping in to my arms, offering the hug I longed for. The kiss, too, was reassuring, and we both held on to one another feeling safe.

As we sat on the bench I had to come right out and ask her, "Is he still in the basement?"

She laughed and said that Tommy Hargrove had left to go home earlier in the day.

"Your parents never knew?"

"They were suspicious when they had not seen you for a few days. My Dad asked if everything between us was alright. I told him everything was fine. We were working things out."

"I love your Dad. He's so practical and trusting."

"I never felt a need to let on where you were and who was really downstairs. Lynn accepted it without asking too many questions as well."

"If everyone in the world had a family like yours, it would solve the problems of humanity."

"Let's not get carried away. We have our moments. We're just comfortable with one another."

"So are you going to let me know what's going on?"

She looked down on the ground and off towards the forest behind the bench. We could hear the sound of cars passing on the Interboro Parkway. She had tears in her eyes. I knew enough not to press her. When she started to explain all she had heard and learned in the past week, it was far more than any one person should experience.

"He's not who you think he is Jono. He's had a difficult life. I never expected to hear the things he said.. When he told me what his life was like as a young boy it broke my heart. I promised him I would never tell another person. I suspect he knows that did not include you; and when he spoke about you and your brother, believe it or not he wishes he could have been a part of what you had."

"What did we have?"

"You had a loving family and friends."

"This is bad, isn't it?"

The tears in her eyes swelled and she laid her head on my shoulder. "I cannot imagine it happening to anyone. Do you want the short version or the whole story?"

"I'm not sure. You decide."

She took a deep breath and sighed. "When we walked up here a week ago, I had no idea what I was doing. I knew it had nothing to do with being dishonest with you. It never felt like cheating; I just knew he needed a friend, and I knew you and I were as close to being in love as it is ever going to be. He said he wanted to talk to someone. It was like I was following him in to his past; suddenly I was walking with him and there was no stopping him from letting it all out."

"Letting what all out?"

"Everything he was holding in since he was a young boy.. I know that sounds dramatic, and why he would want to talk to me is anyone's guess. But it was necessary for him to talk to someone, and I know now it was the right thing to do. At first it was small talk and it felt awkward. We stood on the corner while I walked the dog, and he kept looking around like his head was spinning. I even asked him at one point if he was high on something. He thought that was funny for some reason and started laughing. It was very early so I told him we should keep it down, and then he said something that made me realize that his talking to me was no ordinary coincidence. He said, "At least you have friends and parents who love you." It came out of nowhere. It had nothing to do with what we were talking about. I looked in to his eyes and I saw a hurt, Jonathan. A hurt like you said you saw in one of your letters home to me. I didn't understand it when you wrote about it in your letter, and I don't think I understood when I saw it in Tommy Hargrove's eyes. Do you remember what you said in one of your last letters to me? That there comes a time when you realize that someone's life has changed, and won't ever be the same again.

Do you remember why you wrote that letter to me?"

I knew the exact reason why I wrote the letter. I could picture that poor lady's face as I made her toss the suitcase to the ground. I will never forget her eyes. I could not imagine Tommy Hargrove having the same look. I told Gayle, "It can't be as bad as that?"

"Maybe the things that happen to people in one place and time add up to the same horror. I don't know Jonathan. Tommy needed to talk and I chose to listen. We walked from one end of the park to the other. At one point I picked up Penny because she was tired from walking. I held her close to me as he shared his story. I felt more secure having her to hold on to while he spoke. Around 5am w ended up right here on this bench. He was speaking so fast by then I had to concentrate to catch everything he was saying. He and his brother went through stuff that makes those stories about torture we had to sit through in history class sound like cartoons. His mother did things that I still cannot understand. He was shaking when he spoke so much at one point I needed to hug him. I put Penny down and just grabbed hold of him Jonathan like he was a crying baby. His crying was so hard…I was patting his back and he kept saying 'oh, shit!...This is not real…' I had to ask if he meant that what happened to him was not real, or if he couldn't believe he was talking about it. He said his mother would come home after being out late drinking. His father was never home. He did not say why, only that he cannot remember his father ever saying a bad word to anyone. It was his mother he was afraid of. He said he was sorry a hundred times saying "I'm sorry to dump this on you!" I said it was alright even if I had no idea what I was doing here or why it was me he wanted to tell. Then he let it out. The beatings late at night that seemed to last until the sun came up. He had a fear of taking a bath because his mother tried to drown him once when he was really young. He was afraid of toilets for the same reason. My head was reeling trying to grasp if what he was saying could be true. I know his mother. She goes to church. She speaks to my mother after church and they share stories about how proud they are of their children. I have stood there embarrassed when they go on and on about the hopes and dreams they have for us. To think what he was saying could be true made it all the more impossible to understand. He said she owned a belt that she would make him and his brother get. "Get the belt", she would say, and she would force them to lie down after taking a bath and wail away. He told me one day in school a nun noticed blood on his white shirt. Instead of being concerned he was scolded and sent home with a letter for his mother. He gave his mother the letter and she went crazy. He had welts on his back for weeks after that letter. His mother wrote a letter back to the school apologizing for letting him go out of the house looking like that. How insane it that! It got worse than that though when she told him and his brother to kneel. They had to kneel in front of her facing each other with their arms outstretched and their fingers touching. If they let their arms drop even a little bit she would hit them with the belt across their arms. They were forced to do that for hours. He told me how he went to school looking to lash out at anyone he could. He did not care what others thought about him. He made fun of everyone and everything. There were no rules when it came to letting himself go. He was so angry with himself for hurting anyone. He said despite what happened to him, he had no excuse for being an asshole. You ever hear someone admit something like that? He started to repeat stories after awhile, maybe because he wanted to make sure they made sense to me. I think because he wanted to make sure they made sense to him. I don't know what I'll do the next time I see Mrs. Hargrove in church. Hypocrisy is worse than any sin."

I listened to Gayle trying to explain what cannot be understood. I realized there are all kinds of war. There are wars between countries. There are wars between races. There are wars between religions. There are wars between families. There are wars inside our heads we can never win. Gayle had no idea she had summed it all up. Hypocrisy is worse than any sin.

Chapter Nine

In the game of hide and seek the object is to hide and not be found. My cousin Michael was the best hide and seek player that ever lived. He would choose his outfits as we prepared for the game to begin. It was necessary for darkness to arrive before a good game of hide and seek could be played. Sides were chosen and my cousin Michael would disappear before starting. He would put on his hide and seek uniform. No matter the heat of summer or the cold of winter the uniform was always the same. Black plants, black turtleneck sweater and boots. He would then turn in to *Hide and Seek Man.* On some nights members from both teams would be out looking for him. Who ever was on his team would feel proud at how well he was able to hide. Those on the opposing team would be angry because the longer it took to find him chances of their ever getting to hide before kids needed to go in were impossible. If Michael's team hid first, chances were that would be it for the night. Michael took the game of hide and seek seriously. For him, every time out was a challenge filled with opportunities and adventure. He never hid in the same place twice. It was against his code of fair play to consider hiding anywhere that did not break new ground. After the yell would go up on the block that kids needed to go in for the night, Michael would emerge as if out of nowhere, telling everyone the secret of where he had been hidden. A good game started at dusk when darkness was just touching down, and would end as late as 11 o'clock, depending on who was playing and how soon they had to go in. On nights when it lasted longest both teams would end up trying to find Michael. Shouts could be heard up and down the block from those looking for him.

"Not up here!"

"Not over here!"

"He's not anywhere!"

One time Michael's brother Jimmy went inside the house going so far as to check under the kitchen table between the adults' legs and behind their chairs. Jimmy would yell, "No one's this good at hiding! He has to be cheating this time!" It was hard to cheat in a game of hide and seek unless as Jimmy had suspected you went inside a house. The street from top to bottom and the backyards of about 14 houses were considered part of the playing field. There were two houses on the street that no one went near. There was a pink house at the top of the block that belonged to people who we thought had to be part of some kind of gang. The four children from the pink house family never came outside to play with each other no less anyone else on the block. At different times of the day and night strange sounds could be heard coming out of the basement windows. Loud screeching drill-like noises with plenty of cackling laughter followed by what we assumed was a screaming sound. We sat for hours as kids trying to distinguish whether the screaming sound was human or some kind of animal, and we challenged one another to run past the house after dark to show how brave we were. We would run so fast we would lose sight of the turn at the end of the house where huge bushes stuck out from the battered fence that surrounded the home. It was inevitable that some one would return from their run bleeding from their head or on their legs after they were unable to slow down going past the bushes. The other house on the block that no one bothered to include in his or her hiding exploits belonged to Old Man Kunike. That was his official name. Old Man Kunike.

The reason we did not include his yard was for the exact opposite reason associated with the pink house. We just naturally all decided not to bother him. He was too kind to bother or annoy in any way. He had a way about him that made you think old people should live forever. On some nights, if we were out late we would check in on him, since he had a habit of falling asleep in his lounge chair with the TV on. He actually told each of us, my cousins, my brother and I; "If you see the television on past midnight please come on in and turn the stupid thing off." So we did. His house was the smallest house on the block. There was way more property surrounding the house. You walked in to a small living room that included a couch, a lounge chair, a lamp on a table and a small television set on a stand. There was another room off to the side that was Old Man Kunike's bedroom, a tiny bathroom and a little kitchen. Those were the only rooms in the house. There was no upstairs and no downstairs. Old Man Kunike when he was in a good mind to chat would say, "No one needs more space than he can occupy at one time." We were kids and never understood what he meant. I walked past Old Man Kunike's house, stood at the little white picket fence that surrounded his home and wondered whatever happened to the old man with a twinkle in his eye and a smile for anyone who cared to say hello. I thought about a conversation I had with him on a night when the other kids wanted to stay inside to watch "The Wizard of Oz." I could not believe that kids would waste a perfectly beautiful fall night to stay indoors and watch anything on television. Especially a movie everyone had seen a million times. I told Old Man Kunike that everyone was watching television and I thought it was stupid. "They're watching it together is they now?" he said in his singsong voice.

"Yeah, can you believe it? A bunch of kids sitting around watching something they all saw like a million times before."

"I never saw that movie." He said with a touch of curiosity.

"Well it's all kind of fantasy stuff I guess. A girl from Kansas sings this god-awful song about finding some thing over the rainbow. That part of the movie is in black and white. Next thing you know there's a tornado and this girl's house gets lifted right out of the ground and goes flying through time. It crashes on a Witch and kills her! She has her dog with her and they both are terrified about what might have happened. She opens the door to the house and suddenly everything is in like a million different colors. The flowers and the houses are all bright and there's this yellow brick road that they walk on for the rest of the movie."

I turned to look at Mr. Kunike who had been sitting in a lawn chair taking in the quiet of the night sky. He was fast asleep. I thought to myself that I had not even gotten to the best parts.

Those were the two houses that were off limits for good and bad reasons when we played hide and seek. Michael would come out of hiding when the night was done and he would show us where he had hidden. He hid in a tree hanging from a branch with his feet resting on the electrical cables. He would show us how he did it dangling from the tree branch allowing his feet to rest for a moment when no one was passing by beneath the tree. He once submerged himself in the middle of the pool for two hours breathing through a straw and coming up to the surface by peeking through a tube he had carefully left floating on top of the water. With the lights off in the backyard no one would think to look inside a pool. We would stand on the pools deck to scope out other yards and we stood in amazement realizing how many of us had actually walked around the deck of the pool on the night Michael turned in to Navy seal. On another night he hung upside down holding on to the axle of a parked truck. I looked under that truck I believe at least a dozen times. I never saw him stretched on the axle and holding on like some kind of Spiderman. Of all these places he chose to hide the very best in my opinion was in front of our eyes. He lay sideways clutching to a fence in the shadow of an old tree. Everyone must have passed him at least a hundred times during the night. I thought that Michael was the best hide and seek player that ever lived. I wonder if anyone knew where he was as I looked at the address on my paper matching the address on a door. I walked up the steps to the house; I peered through the window and yelled, "Ma! I'm home!"

Chapter Ten

Dear Moron,

Are you still walking around with your head up your ass? If so, please send pictures. There has to be some kind of record with the Guinness people for such things.

Which reminds me, I had to rescue a wounded moose from this patch of ice out on the lake. The moose had wandered out on to the lake which is a very unusual thing mind you; so I had to go on out and try to help. I managed to lasso the moose with a rope after trying for like hours. Next thing I know the moose starts to run. You ever see a moose run on ice? I'm holding on to the rope for some reason because I'm afraid if I let go I might end up being thrown in to a tree or something. So there I was sliding along behind a run away moose on the frozen lake. The moose is making all kinds of strange noises and I was carrying on with a few screams myself. Next thing I know the moose stops dead in its tracks! I can't stop because I'm sliding at full speed. It is pitch black out on that damn lake and before I can even attempt to get myself straightened out I bump right in the rear of the damn moose! Well you might not believe this but with the force my hitting the moose it must have gotten startled or something because it begins to buck like a horse and I leap in the air to avoid being kicked. I leap in such a way that I find myself sitting upright on the moose's back! Now I don't know if this has ever been done before but the moose is in like a state of shock. So I grab hold of my rope and have no idea what to expect next! The moose starts to turn its head trying to stick me with its antlers. But I'm snug deep down against its back and there's no way in hell I was going to let go. After about an hour of fighting the pull of the rope the moose makes this loud snoring like noise. I lean up slowly and try to look around its neck at its eyes. I'm looking right in to two huge moose eyes and what do you think happens next? I realize there is no way you could figure this out so I'll just tell you! The moose sticks out its tongue and licks me in the face! It was the grossest kind of thing ever! I figure the moose is either deciding how I taste so he can eat me when I can no longer hold on, or it's making a truce. Do you believe a moose can make a truce? I didn't think so either but I was willing to believe anything stuck out there in the frozen tundra on the back of a moose! The sun is an amazing sight coming up over the mountains here in Alaska. It catches the glistening snowcaps and sort of gleams in a way that makes everything around you look like your standing in a bowl of cereal. You ever experience anything like that in your life? I doubt it. I bet it only happens here in Alaska. Next thing I know there's a snap, crackle and popping noise on the ice. It sort of echoed through the air and I don't know about you but when you're sitting on a thousand pound moose in the middle of a frozen lake and you hear a sound like that, you think the strangest things. The first thing I thought about was how I could ever let you and Kidd talk me in to moving here! The next thing I thought about was this girl I knew when I was younger. She liked to go ice-skating. It's a strange thing my living here and never once have I put on a pair of ice-skates. It may be why as the sound got louder I thought about leaping from the back of the moose and trying to slide my way to the shore. But you know I was attached to the damn moose! We spent the night together and I couldn't just leave it out there to fall in to the lake that would have nullified the reason I got myself in the mess in the first place! It happened fast and furious! The moose just dropped and my legs were submerged in the lake numb and colder than a well digger's ass! Did you know that moose swim? Let me tell you a thing or two about swimming moose! He was not in the least bit afraid of our predicament. He started swimming with me holding on for dear life. He trudged through the breaks in the ice and casually as if walking on land made his way through the broken ice. He got to the shoreline and I had no idea how tall a moose was once it stood up again on its legs. He stood up and then like any animal began to shrug and turn and twist in really awkward motions. He was getting the ice off his body and again I was holding this rope like it was a lifeline between the now and hereafter. The moose bolted in to a trot and then a full out run! If I had seen the damn branch that low from a tree I would have still been on that moose! The branch hit me in the chest and man did I go flying! It knocked the damn wind out of me and I believe for the first time I knew what it must have been like to be hit by Dick Butkus of the Chicago Bears. I lay there gasping for air. Now I know you're probably thinking I'm lucky to be alive. You're right except did I mention that during the time out on the lake I was afraid of falling off the moose so I tied the rope around my waist? Well I did. It took about a full minute or so before the slack ran out and man there I was being pulled through the damn Alaskan forest by the damn moose! Here's the other strange part that you won't believe but it's true. Because I had been dragged earlier and then got wet when the ice broke – my clothes were like one huge block of ice. I knew it would be a matter of time before the friction of the forest ground wore away the ice on my clothes so I sat up and tried to steer my way making sure not to hit a tree and wind up dead! You already know I'm not dead because you're safe and warm reading this in your nice warm and cozy house! It was a harrowing experience! The moose must have slowed down because suddenly I came to a halt after sliding a few yards. I look up and now the sun is shining the way it does here, like a marginalized version of a flashlight with batteries slowly dying. I start working on the knot tied around my waist hoping to finish before the moose starts up again. I get the rope loosened and let go of the rope. Just as I let go I watch the rope slowly begin to move. For a second or two I thought about getting my rope back! I mean what's a moose going to do with it? I was too exhausted to bother and I watched the rope disappear up the side of a mountain. Anyway, if you still have your head up your ass about whatever it was bothering you, I recommend you try moose skating on a frozen lake in the middle of the damn night. I hope this letter finds you able to breathe. I'll write more once I figure out a way to find my cabin. I've been living with this Eskimo family who promise to get me home once the spring thaw comes.

Keep warm and chill Out
Bob Googenblatt

Chapter Eleven

You can live somewhere and it will never feel like home. Even though Belmont was a part of my youthful memory, I did not feel at home living there. On the first night back in my mother's new home I had a conversation with my brother. He was adjusting to being away from the "old neighborhood", telling me he had already met new friends. I was happy for him, as the friends he had before were not the kind of people he needed to be around. He had a few friends who he knew he would miss; but as he got used to living in Belmont more and more he felt Long Island was where he wanted to stay. I started to look for a job and it felt strange to think that I had left home to be in the Army and yet the only thing I needed was a job. I had learned to do things while in the military that there did not seem to be much of a calling for in civilian life. I sat in the yard behind my mother's house every morning with a cup of coffee, and the Long Island newspaper Newsday. The paper was not like the Daily News as it covered local news for people born and raised on Long Island. I read through the articles and did not feel a kinship to the opinions and ideas shared, and as I searched through the want ads

I felt removed from the concept of working on Long Island. I borrowed my mother's car and drove back to Queens each night when Gayle would be home from school or work. I knew I needed to have a job before I could seriously consider marriage. I had a plan with little way of knowing how to make it work. On the first night home my brother said something that was in keeping with his sense of humor and my inability to feel comfortable at home. He said, "How come you didn't go to war or die or something like that?" I laughed out loud because it was a typical line from a brother who was always a best friend. It made me realize how little we had in common and yet how much I loved him. I wanted to tell him about my exploits and my experience while in the Army but opted to let it go. It felt better to have him think I did nothing. I lay awake that first night listening to my mother's house. Every house has a distinct sound. The radiator in my room played drum-like noises through the night. I thought about an incident when I was in the third grade. A teacher turned from the blackboard and noticed I was laughing. The teacher said, "What's so funny?" I gave the standard answer of any third grader caught laughing in class. I said, "Nothing." She shook her head and told me I had to write a 500-word essay on *Nothing.* I went home and wrote the essay. The next day she had me read my essay on *Nothing* to the class. I concluded, "Nothing was the place in your brain not yet filled with memories." The teacher stood at the front of the class and she was smiling. She told me, "one day you just may write a book."

With the time off while looking for a job I decided on my first night in my mother's new house that I was going to write a book. I did not tell anyone of my intention. I wanted to tell Gayle who would be proud of anything I wanted to do. She was in college studying to be a journalist. I wanted to surprise her with my book when it was done. I told her I was looking for a job and left it at that. Each night when everyone had gone to bed I would sit awake and write the greatest novel of all time. My novel was going to save the world. I was excited about writing and called upon every facet of my experiences to put down on paper what I could remember. I went to the library and took out the books I knew I was supposed to be reading. I read Jack Kerouac's book "On the Road" and was convinced I had no idea what he was trying to say. I read Harper Lee's "To Kill a Mockingbird" and found myself in awe of the written word. I read a Russian writer's book "One Day in the Life of Ivan Denisovich" and was convinced that some people lived lives I would never understand. The Russian writer was named Alekander Solsynitzyn and I yearned to discover more books written by him. I discovered Kurt Vonnegut, Norman Mailer, John Updike, Ernest Hemingway and F. Scott Fitzgerald. The lady at the library questioned me one day on how many books I was reading. She said, "No one can read as many books as you have in the past month!" I assured her that I was discovering something I had never thought to do before and I was happy. She was pleased to see me on a regular basis when I would come in to return my books. She pointed out the latest books that had come in and often she would put aside books she thought I would enjoy. Sometimes the books had explicit sex scenes that she told me about before handing them over. I had never heard a woman talk so openly about such things. The librarian assured me that every book needs sex. She said it with a straight face. She was the only person I had told I was writing a book. She wanted to read it. I told her it was in a highly awkward state and not ready for anyone to read. She found this amusing and I found her reaction comforting. One day I entered the library at closing. She let me in and locked the doors. She said, "I have a few books you might enjoy behind the counter. You can go through the racks of books but be quick about it."

I did not like being rushed to look for something to read. I gave her the stack of books I wanted to return and she placed books on the counter she thought I should read.

I handed her my card and in doing so she held my hand. I had seen men die in battle; I had been exposed to things no one else could understand. I thought I was a man of experience, but the librarian scared me when she said: "The doors are locked and I'm free tonight."

It was an awkward statement and I did not know whether to smile or run through the front glass doors in to the night. I explained to her that I was looking for a job and that when I got the job I was going to ask my girlfriend to marry me. She was not deterred by my reaction. I think it made her feel more comfortable to see me so uncomfortable. She let go of my hand and walked to a back room saying, "Follow me."

I was nervous for reasons I could not fully understand. I stood looking through the books she had selected for me to read. John Irving's "The World According To Garp", and "The Naked Lunch", by William Burroughs. I looked through the small doorway to the room where she had gone. I looked out at the passing cars in front of the library. I went to the doorway and saw she had taken a seat on a small couch. She was smoking a cigarette and had removed her shoes. She said, "Are you going to stand there gawking or help me get out of this dress?" I walked over to her and she stood up turning her back to me as I neared. She lifted her hair away from the back of her dress. I slowly pulled the zipper down and she casually stepped out of it before turning back to face me. She leaned up to take my face in to her hands. The smoke from her cigarette made my eyes squint and I closed them. Her lips touched mine and the taste of her tongue was strange. I told her I knew what to do but did not know how to do it. She told me, "some things come natural to people." I confess to never seeing a woman so naked. I confess to never knowing a woman could be so certain of what she wanted. We made love on the couch. In between our making love she told me more about herself than any woman would ever do again. She told me after we had made love how she had been married. She told me her husband was killed. She told me she didn't know what a woman should do once she reached a certain age and her husband had died. She said, "It's not like I am suddenly too old to enjoy living." I told her that a new man would enter her life and she would feel renewed again. She became quiet taking a long drag from her cigarette before telling me, "I'm not one to forget that I was meant to love only one man."

My night with the sad librarian was not a memory I was proud to remember, nor soon to forget. It would not be repeated. I left the books she had chosen for me on the counter as I left that evening, and I never returned to the library. I began to buy books at stores. I began to build a personal collection of books I enjoyed. I still needed to find a job.

I cannot fully understand why anything happens, but in time if we are lucky answers arrive when we least expect. I could not sit staring at the walls in a house I did not feel was home. I went out for a walk. Walking always clears the mind even when you are going no where fast. I thought about my brother and how he adapted to things better than I could. I kept walking past buildings and images that had little to do with my growing up. The thing about life is sometimes we misinterpret growing up with growing apart. I knew what I had experienced was not easily understood by any one who did not go through the same thing. I did not wish to be with anyone who could understand. Some things need to be left alone. As I walked farther away from the place my mother had chosen to call home I had no destination in mind.. The night air was cold and I was angry with myself for not wearing a proper coat. The cool breeze cut through the jacket I was wearing as I continued going. I walked for hours aware of the coldness, half knowing I should turn around and half wanting to get some place where I could feel comfortable. I did not feel like I wanted to escape as much as wanting to be someplace other than where I was. After hours of walking I stood at the entrance to Forest Park off Woodhaven Boulevard. It was a place where I had felt free as a boy. Looking over at the ball field on the other side of the park I remembered the walk I took with Billy Moran on Freedom Road: a walk that mattered little about where we had been, but more so about what we wanted to accomplish. I walked in to the park and sat down on a bench near a carousel. It was another place in the neighborhood of Real that people took for granted would always be there. I closed my eyes remembering the first time I saw the carousel. My brother and I had gone there with my father. We sat on the wooden horses that went up and down, the music blaring in our ears. My father chose to sit on a bench right outside the gates, and each time the carousel went around we waved at each other. When we could not see my father my brother and I looked at each other laughing. We let go of the pole on the horse and leaned way back on the horses we were riding. The carousel came to slow halt. For a moment when it stopped we were on the far side of the ride not knowing where our father had gone. We untied the strap that held us to the horse and hesitated before getting off. Without saying a word we both felt lost in a strange way. I remember thinking, "Why were we standing alone without anyone to hold our hands?" It was not fear as much as it was awareness. Awareness I did not understand until sitting on the bench years later looking at the shuttered gates of the carousel. The trees were stripped of their summer eloquence and the cold air as morning approached made me realize I was lost in more ways than I cared to tell anyone. I was aware that lost did not always mean geographically; but I still felt lost. I did not feel sad. I remember that it was a sense of confusion about my life and where I wanted to be, but I knew enough to know that there was no good reason to be sitting on a park bench, freezing. I took one more look at the carousel, hoping one day that my life would come full circle as well. I walked further in to the park. I climbed through a chain-link fence in to the golf course, a place all but abandoned in winter. The hills covered in snow looked nothing like a place where people could spend an entire summer day chasing after a tiny white ball. I closed my eyes and took a deep breath. I remembered a past winter's day, and I could hear my brother's voice yelling at me when I destroyed our new sled on the day after Christmas a long time ago. I had taken a dare from some of the park boys to go down a hill called Dead Man's Hill. The hill was steep with trees on both sides. There were dips in the ground that formed treacherous holes. Standing at the top of the hill it was like looking in to a tunnel with no ending in sight. "Don't do it!" my brother yelled at me, "There's nothing to prove!" I knew he was right. But, at the time it was better than hearing I was chicken from a bunch of kids who in retrospect were too afraid to do it themselves. When younger we sometimes think it is worth everything to prove you are better than another. I took a running start and went down the hill. Steering was useless; the hill covered in an icy coating took control of the sled. I leaned several times when I noticed a tree trunk appear. The sled spiraled down the hill on one blade as I shifted my weight. The front part of the sled broke off when it hit a huge ditch slapping me in the face as it ripped off. I was dazed for a moment reaching up to touch my nose and realized that I was bleeding. When it landed with a hard thud I nearly fell off the sled sensing my body going one way and it another. I remember closing my eyes. When the sled came to a stop I opened my eyes to look back over my shoulder. I looked at the hill and then at the top. My brother was jumping up and down cheering. The park boys were standing with their arms folded looking at each other without saying a word. I lay in a pile of snow looking up at the sky. Billy Moran appeared at my side. He stood for a moment staring down at me and then at the broken sled. He said, "You are one crazy bastard, Kidd." My brother arrived soon after looking at my bleeding nose and the busted sled. He asked me if it was worth destroying our Christmas present. Sensing my nose was broken and how I had survived something as stupid as going down a hill no one needed to take I looked at him. As I stood in the cold of the golf course years later I still smiled at my answer that day. I said, "Yes." He shook his head walking away while dragging the broken sled behind him. I stood now years later thinking it was all so surreal. Watching him walking with the broken sled knowing it could never be used again. He pulled the sled up the hill and tossed it at the park boy's feet. He reached over and snatched hold of one of their sleds. He gave them a look and walked out of the park back to our house. It was an act of deviance I never witnessed again. I had done something to prove it could be done and he took home the trophy without caring who it belonged to.

Chapter Twelve

Living on Long Island represented mostly memories of the summers I spent there when I was younger. I had no sense of belonging on Long Island. I would travel back in to Queens on days when everyone I knew was in school or working. I walked along the streets where I had grown up. It's a strange sensation to be in a neighborhood you called your own when you no longer live there. I felt as if I had abandoned the only place I wanted to call home. I would sit in the park on a bench, and watch a new generation of kids playing on the swings and a new generation of kids learning to play ball. A new generation of girls sitting around giggling and gossiping about tomorrow's dreams. I no longer belonged anywhere and I realized unless I found a job and married Gayle, I could never again be in the only place I wanted to be. I watched the buses coming and going on Myrtle Avenue, as they passed by my old house and familiar faces got off the buses hurrying toward home. One day while sitting on the same bench where I had planned out my life as a young boy I saw Billy Moran walking with a briefcase. I wanted him to know instantly who was calling his name. Even though we had lost touch, and I was still uncertain why he needed the time away from our friendship, I was certain I could erase all doubts. I yelled the only thing I knew could rescue us from stupidity. Every friendship goes through a period of stupidity and I wanted to establish that enough was enough. "HEY MORON!" I yelled as loud as I could from the park down on to Myrtle Avenue. Several cars came to a screeching halt. A man walking his dog stopped and began screaming at me; and a woman walking with a bag of groceries dropped the bag and began yelling at the man. I didn't know if Billy had heard me. I stayed on the bench thinking I needed to forget about yesterday and get on with my life, and it was several minutes before I looked up to see Billy Moran with his briefcase standing before me. He was smiling. He said the only thing I could expect him to say "Is there something mentally wrong with you?"

I laughed and grabbed his hand. He sat down on the bench and told me how he was tired of living in the same place where we had grown up. I wanted to tell him how much I longed to get back here, and how I knew since I had left that this was the only place where I truly belonged. Instead, I listened as he told me about his new job. It was a strange sensation to hear a childhood friend talking about things like work and commuting and the way people treat one another in an office. I listened as old friends do. He asked me what I was doing in the park knowing I no longer lived in the neighborhood. I told him how I was looking for a job so I could get married and move back. He said, "Why would you want to do that?"

We laughed knowing without saying it out loud how time changes everything and nothing at all at the same time. We watched as the kids on the swings went higher and higher laughing and calling one another silly names. We watched as kids tossed around a baseball on the ball field choosing sides and taking their positions. In a way it was like watching history repeating itself. We sat on the bench until the sun surrendered and the echoes of kids playing turned in to the sound of crickets and dogs barking in the distance. I told my oldest friend on earth that I had no idea what I wanted to be when I grew up. He shook his head smiling, "Kidd, when you grow up the world will cease to exist."

I loved Billy Moran for understanding what I meant. I knew there was so much we would still experience in life and yet no matter how long we lived, we would always be just two kids sitting on a park bench.

"Billy, did you ever buy those Louis Armstrong records I told you to listen to?"

He told me, "I played them for my father right up until the day he died."

I told Billy that his father was a good man. We laughed about the many things his father said and did that only old friends could appreciate. We both remembered the same conversation his father shared with us one night when we were sitting on his front stoop. His father came out and sat down next to us. No matter how much you know someone's parents it was always awkward when they sat down to talk. Everything you thought you wanted to talk about changed. Billy's father sat in silence for a moment and then said one of the most profound statements we had ever heard. We did not know at the time what he was saying would last a lifetime. Our first reaction as young boys when he said it was to laugh. That's what young boys listening to wisdom do. Maybe it was his delivery. Maybe it was the words and how over time even words take on different meanings. Billy's father sat in silence and then said:

"The fucking you get ain't worth the fucking you get."

We sat now on the bench, with Billy's father passed and my father long gone; aware that we would use this phrase to explain everything that needed to be understood.

Billy shared his thoughts about my finding a job. He told me how everything he learned in college had nothing to do with what he was doing for a living. He told me that despite four years of struggling to pass tests and write all kinds of reports, once out of school everything he thought he had learned was useless. He looked at me smiling and as if on cue we both said, "The fucking you get, ain't worth the fucking you get."

I wanted to ask Billy what was wrong when I had come home that first day. I wanted to understand why he felt angry enough to disappear from our friendship. But I didn't. Instead, we talked about how kids had no idea what it was like to be young. They ran by us on the bench complaining about their parents not buying them the newest sneakers and clothes, and listened as the girls whispered about the latest loves of their young lives, about music and movie stars with 'dreamy eyes'.

Billy and I lived through the 1960s and we came out on the other side, both changed and yet unscathed in ways we couldn't yet know.

I said, "I'm going to get married Moron."

All was well for two friends with years left to discover the meaning of life.

Chapter Thirteen

The interview process was different in the civilian world. In the Army all you had to do was sign your name on a dotted line. Looking for my first job as a civilian proved to be an adventure I would question again and again. I entered the offices of the Human Resource Department at a bank where I was told there was an opening. A Mr. Humboldt Schiltz sat behind a huge oak desk. I was immediately aware the desk was oversized for the room. Mr. Schiltz stood up as I entered the room. I handed him a copy of my resume. Gayle had helped me assemble the sheet of paper filled with bullet points defining my employment experience. I felt it was ironic to hand anyone a sheet of paper with bullet points after serving in the Army for three years.

Mr. Schiltz did not look at me as we spoke. He took the paper, put it down on his desk and began a tedious process of lining the page up with a hole-puncher on his desk. He said, "Tell me something about you not on this resume." I had not anticipated questions outside of the facts of my working experience. I sighed loudly and responded honestly, "If I get this job I can get married."

He shook his head in an awkward manner while lining up the pages of my resume and other documents I had filled out before meeting him. He took a small ruler out of his desk. He leaned his head down until it was nearly resting on the desk studying the exact dimensions of each page and carefully opened the two-hole fastener at the top of a manila folder, checking the holes with the ruler. Without taking his eyes off of the fastener and the holes on the paper he said, "Go on?"

I had not rehearsed any response other than to describe what I had actually done for the past three years. I sat back on a red couch that I realized was out of place in an office so small. "I'm looking forward to sharing what I learned and putting it to good use here at the company." He nodded his head awkwardly saying, "Uh huh."

The words seemed to stay in the air long after he said them; I looked around to see if there was some kind of tunnel attached to the four walls which might create the sensation of an echo. He sat back in his oversized leather chair holding the folder which I assumed was now set up to his satisfaction. The paper aligned just right enabling him to continue our interview. He looked over my head saying, "What do you mean when you say sharing your experience?"

I was confused thinking the statement was easily understood.

"I guess I mean I learned some things that will help make things better."

"You want to make things better?"

"Yes sir."

"Before you even enter a new job, you're saying there are problems?"

"No sir, I guess I feel there is always room for improvement."

"Uh huh."

I felt everything I was trying to say was somehow beyond my control.

Mr. Shiltz in a matter of minutes had made me feel uncomfortable and his attitude seemed confrontational. I tried to remedy the situation by saying "I think experience should count for something."

"Really?"

"Yes sir, I believe I can learn about how things function here."

"Uh huh."

"How long have you been here Mr. Schiltz?"

I had pressed a button. For the first time since entering his office he looked over the top of the folder directly at me. He put the folder down on his desk. He had a slight twitch on his face which I only noticed when he looked directly at me. It was like the act of looking people in the eyes was the hardest thing he could do. He adjusted himself in his chair. He stretched his neck in his collared shirt while reaching up to touch a red and white tie with blue dots. He turned his chair until it was facing the window. A view I could not help but look at in awe the entire time since entering his office. The view encapsulated the beauty of the city as far as your eyes could see. Central Park in its entire splendor stood below us and buildings along Fifth Avenue lined to absolute precision majestically complimented the view.

Mr. Schiltz sighed loudly, "How long indeed?" he said with a sound of exhaustion in his voice. He continued looking out the window as he spoke, "I once tried to document change. It was a hobby of mine. Photography. Once a month for several years, on the 15th of every month –no matter if it was a work day or not – I would take a photo of this view outside my window. It had to be the exact time of day in every photo. At noon, whether it was raining, snowing, sunny or gloomy. At approximately 12'o'clock I snapped the photo. I developed my own film in a dark room. I created the perfect room in my apartment for developing photos. I put every photo in a book. A leather bound book that I discovered on a homeless man's blanket for ten dollars. The homeless man set up his wares every day in the same place." Mr. Schiltz stood up leaning slowly with both elbows on the windows ledge. I could see him on that corner from up here every day. That leather bound journal sold for hundreds of dollars at these high end department stores around here. I saw the exact journal in one of these stores. It sold for $650.00. I handed that homeless guy ten dollars and he took it from me smiling. Every month for close to ten years I carefully glued each photo on to a page in the book. I went several times to the department store gloating about how I found that journal. I would watch the people who shop there hoping to see someone pay $650.00 for something I got for ten bucks. It was a form of perverse entertainment for me. After several visits to the store I noticed how the workers all had an air of superiority. They never followed the customers who shopped there. No, they stood waiting behind these large glass encased counters and their cash registers. It was like they knew everything sold in the store could be had for way less somewhere else. They gloated about it the same way I did over the journal. Ten years. On the day I put a photo on the last page, for the first time, I slowly turned the journal to the first page. I went through the journal admiring the extensive detail I had captured.

It was both rewarding and disgusting at the same time. In ten years, while performing my photographic essay, it was a form of artistic discipline and something more horrible than I could have planned. It was self indulgence taken to a level of embarrassment. I took out a magnifying glass and slowly scanned the photos I had taken. In each one without my realizing it you can see in the distance a bright patch of something. I was so careful to take each photo at the exact time of day; pointing the lens at the exact level and measurements. Upon close inspection you can see the homeless man's blanket laid out on the same street corner. Mr., Schiltz turned from the window with a look of absolute disdain on his face. Do you know what I learned that day?

I robbed a man who had nothing and spent ten years convinced I had cheated a bunch of rich snobs. You asked me, how long have I been here? Long enough to know it was never going to be enough to make a difference." He picked up my resume and scanned it slowly.

"Do you know what your resume tells me?" "No sir."

He grinned and said, "It tells me you were some place where it was legal to kill the enemy."

I did not know how to respond to such an observation. I said, "It was war, sir."

He nodded his head grinning, "War it was, war it is."

"Excuse me sir?"

He tossed the folder on his desk. "The job is yours. It will never pay you what your time is worth. You will learn that people in any corporation have motives. I imagine it is like a foxhole on any battlefield. Some people will share things with you that show they have a life beyond work; but most will expect things from you. Expectation plays a huge role in how you will define success. Success will be laughable at best since it can only be gauged in how much you save the company and never by what you know. Intelligence is a serious problem in any company. There is an old saying, "Knowledge is power!" that is no longer valid. Knowledge makes you dangerous, it makes you expendable. When you leave this office you will need to go through a period of orientation. Everything you think your experience was worth is useless. You will learn to do things our way. This period of adjustment will last 90 days. At that time you will be re-evaluated. If you can live by our standards you will embrace a fine future here. Have a nice day."

I felt uncertain about what I was supposed to do. I wanted to ask about benefits and salary. The things Gayle had told me were important questions. Instead, I stood up and started to leave while Mr. Schiltz stood looking out his window.

"Excuse me, sir?"

Without turning from the window he said, "Any other questions will be answered during orientation."

"Yes sir, but I wanted to ask you something?"

"What is it? I am a very busy man."

I cleared my throat, "What ever happened to that homeless man?"

I sensed a change in his body language. He continued to look out the window. He grunted before saying, "I never took another photo after filling in that last page. I took the journal back to him. When he wasn't looking I placed it on his blanket and walked away."

I opened the door to his office. Before leaving I said, "Thank you for your time sir. It was a pleasure meeting you."

I began my first job on a Monday. I did not stay very long. A year after starting I entered the same office for what was called an exit interview. I needed to move on. I interviewed for another position two blocks away. I got the job. I had somehow given myself a thousand dollar raise in salary. It would have taken me three years to make the money I was offered at the new place. I expected to say goodbye to Mr. Schiltz. Instead, a woman sat behind the desk. Without looking up from the same manila folder Mr. Schiltz had placed my resume in a year earlier, she handed me a bunch of paperwork. She said, "Sign these papers and date each one on the dotted line at the bottom of each." I looked over the papers which were nothing more than short paragraphs advising me I no longer was a member of the company. I signed each one and dated them as she asked. "Do you have any questions?"

She had to look on the folder for my name. "Um, Mr. Kiddrane?"

"Yes I have two questions."

I watched her fake smile turn to a scowl. She looked at me and with an irritated tone in her voice said, "Yes?"

"What happened to Mr. Schiltz? He had this office when I was hired a year ago."

She adjusted herself uncomfortably before responding, "I never met the man. I was told he chose another line of work."

I nodded my head almost smiling with pride for Mr. Schiltz. "The second question is: have you ever looked out the window behind you?"

The question irritated her for some reason. She responded by closing the folder. "The sun is too bright."

I got up from my chair. Before leaving I said, "The least you can do is take a picture of the view. There's more out there than the bright sunshine."

I left the building, walking out on to the city streets. I immediately knew I left nothing inside that building.

I took a long look at the people passing on the street. The vision had been described in so many books; the sea of humanity, the rat race. Standing on the steps of a building I had entered each morning for the past year I could not help but notice the contrast of so many different people. Across the street from the building, there was one of the most extravagant hotels in the world. Limousines and Rolls- Royce's pulled up to the main entrance, one after another. The rich got in and got out of the cars with a sense of privilege. Still, I sensed they detested everyone and everything about the city. To the right of the hotel was the entrance to the world's largest inner city park:. Central Park, in all its grandeur and immensity..

Having made a decision to move on I felt drawn to the park's calming landscape. Once inside the park, I heard music. I watched and listened to a man singing while playing his guitar. His guitar case was open and people passing by threw their spare change and rumpled dollar bills in to it. He sang songs made popular during my youth. I closed my eyes while he sang "Lay Lady Lay" and he sounded exactly like Bob Dylan. He sang an old Everley Brothers song and it surprised me how he harmonized with himself. I took out a five dollar bill and dropped it in his open case. In the middle of a harmonica solo he nodded with appreciation. I walked further in to the park, turning a few times to look at the building where people never bothered to look out windows.

As I neared an entrance to a small bridge, I needed to take a few steps back before recognizing the man sitting on a bench. In front of the man on a bright blue and red Indian rug were dozens of leather journals. I stood for a moment marveling at the journals. I picked one up and paged through the expensive paper. I lifted it up to my nose taking in the smell. "Excuse me sir", I said, "How much are the journals?" Without looking up from a book he was reading Humboldt Schiltz said, "Ten dollars, all genuine leather; each one hand made in Italy. Each one available anywhere you might wish to spend $650.00." I smiled knowing only a few people could recognize Humboldt's statement of irony.

"Mr. Schiltz, it's an honor to see you again."

He looked up at me placing his book beside him on the bench.

"Do I know you, young man?"

"You hired me a little over a year ago at the bank."

"I apologize for that."

I laughed, knowing his statement was authentic.

"On the contrary sir today was my last day. I'm moving on."

"Are you going to another company?"

"Yes, for more money and a better position."

He looked up at the building where we had both once worked and shook his head.

He looked down at his wares on the blanket saying, "The journals are ten dollars each."

"Yes, I am most definitely buying one, maybe two."

"They are genuine leather, hand made in Italy."

"Fantastic. Mr. Schiltz, don't you want to know where I am going? Don't you want to know why I left?"

He looked up at the building and then at me. He picked up his book and said, "No."

It bothered me to see him acting this way. Holding the journal in my hand, I said,

"The lady who has the office you had is a jerk."

He put the book down and smiled. He patted the space next to him on the bench. I sat next to him as two women leaned down to pick up journals from the blanket. The taller of the two looked at Humboldt. Before she could mouth any words he said, "Ten dollars." I could not help but follow his sales pitch with a vibrant response, "They are genuine leather. Hand made in Italy!" She put the journal down and looked at the other woman saying, "Stolen merchandise." They carried on a conversation standing in front of the blanket. "It smells real", the short woman wearing a fur coat said. The taller one responded, "If you want real leather you have to spend the right kind of money."

The fur wearing woman said, "Oh, you are so right. I could not live with myself knowing I spent so little for something so elegant." They walked away.

I looked at Humboldt who was smirking, "Can you believe these people?"

Laughing, he patted my knee saying, "I see it every day. They amuse me."

"How can you stand it? It must drive you crazy?"

"When I stood on their side of the blanket it made me crazy, now it amuses me."

"Are the journals stolen?"

He let out a laugh that seemed to echo with a high pitched crescendo in the air that made people passing by stare at us shaking their heads. "I bought each one at that damn palace of a store across from the bank."

"You spent top dollar and sell them for ten bucks?"

"Sounds insane?"

"Well a lot of people would think so, yes."

"It is my gift to the city."

"But surely you want to do other things?"

"I did other things, it made me sad."

"You mean you are happier giving these things away than pursuing a better life?"

"There is no better life."

"I don't understand."

"Give yourself time. It will come to you."

"You know as I get older, I get more confused."

"Confusion is a good sign. There is hope for you."

"What do you mean?"

"It means you're alive inside. Confusion is a healthy emotion. Too many people accept things on face value. They become robots."

"That can never happen to me."

"It already did. You quit one job to take another. After that there will be another and another. You entered the vicious cycle and just like those women you are convinced you can get better by spending more. Your spending will be represented by time. At first, more money will make you believe you are in control of your own destiny. A new car. A house. It will all be worth your time. Until one day, it fails to match your dreams."

"But those things and getting them is the American dream!"

He looked at me and sighed, picked up his book saying, "The journals are ten dollars each. They are all genuine leather. Hand made in Italy."

I got up from the bench. I handed him twenty dollars after choosing two journals from the blanket. "I wish you well Mr. Schiltz."

Without looking up from his book he said, "Moving out and

moving up are two different things." I nodded my head saying, "Thank you sir. Good luck."

The lessons I learned are not for every one. Louis had told me when I was a small boy, "some people sail through life and others float aimlessly."

Without knowing it, I would discover time and again that sailing through anything was not in the cards for me. I was a floater destined to bounce from one island to another. Floating is not so bad. It's sinking that causes the problems.

I needed to get past the concept of finding happiness in the work place. Instead I needed to focus on finding happiness at home. Through out life this is a difficult thing to manage and everyone may define it differently. On a cold brisk January night I asked Gayle Cooper to be my wife. We had gone out to a local diner to get something to eat after I came home from work; it was in that same diner that years before I had first sat with my parents, and later with Billy Moran and my brother. I decided to ask a question that would represent my life's dedication to one person. I was still in many people's minds too young to think myself ready for such a commitment, but I decided it had nothing to do with age. I remembered Louis telling me one night, "Sometimes you just know!" I just knew it was the right thing to do.

The fact that Gayle was still in college on a four-year scholarship did not discourage me.

Love has a way of making everything rational seem silly. I watched as she got out of her grandfather's car. It was snowing. She ran from the car to the entrance of the diner. She looked back and I told her I had lost my gloves and would meet her inside. She went in to the diner to get a table. I took out the ring I had bought and tied it around the rearview mirror. I went in to the diner and she asked if I found my gloves. I held up my hands showing her my glove-covered hands and we ordered our meals. As I ate my meal and listened to Gayle tell me about her day, I thought about the times I had spent sitting in the diner.

The diner was a special place for us. It was a meeting place for years for many couples and friends going back for many years. When Billy Moran and I would meet here after school we talked about the meaning of life and what we hoped to do when we got older. If the walls in the diner could talk, if the booths could rise up and share what they heard people say, everyone would know how similar they are and how no one gets a free ride without shedding some tears. I thought about games we invented while sitting in the diner, games we played for hours right there at the table. Our games required skill and patience and team spirit. One game required a nickel or a quarter. The object of the game was to push the coin to the edge of the other side of the table without it falling off. If you could get a coin to the edge of the table half-on and half off it was a touchdown, like in football. Another game was something that Billy and I invented that required the entire diner's participation. We came up with it one night when the diner was packed. Every table had a group of people sitting down and going about their business. Billy stood up on top of the table we were sitting at and announced: "EVERYONE! WE ARE GOING TO PLAY JUKEBOX BINGO!" The object of Jukebox Bingo required every table to select a song from the jukebox. Each table would choose a song. They would write the name of their song on a piece of paper. As the songs played, Billy and I would match the table with their song. If we got it right those playing would get free French fries, onion rings or sodas. We never quite figured out why but the owner actually paid for our little excursions and every once in a while the owner, named Bob picked up our tab. He told us "it was good for business." We just wanted to find a way to enjoy the time.

As I sat there listening to the jukebox playing and Gayle telling me about her day at school and then at work, I told myself the next song I heard would become our wedding song. I was amusing myself while trying to be the attentive husband I hoped to become. The song, "Just the Way You Are" by Billy Joel started playing. I asked Gayle if she liked the song. She nodded and continued telling me about her day. We paid our bill and went out to the parking lot. Before getting to the car, I took Gayle by her arm and turned her to face me. Snow was falling and piling up quickly. "Come on, quit fooling around", she said, "we need to get home before the roads get bad." I kissed her wanting to feel in some way as if the kiss would be the last one before we crossed over in to another dimension of our relationship. It occurred to me as I walked from the diner to the car that the instant she saw the ring everything would change between us. That change would be for the better or for worse. That change would be a chance at forever, or one giant mistake both of us would never forget. I wanted it to be perfect. I wanted our future to be built on something more than how much gold we had in the bank or how big a house we owned or what kind of car we drove. She smiled when I looked in to her eyes that last time before everything changed. She opened the door and started up the car. I sat beside her in the passenger seat wondering how could a person drive a car without looking at what's hanging from the rearview mirror. The closer we got to her home and as the time passed by from block to block I understood how nothing can be planned in this life. Life was not like in the movies or perfectly written stories in romance novels.

At her corner as she slowly turned on to her street I asked her if she could see out of the back window. She looked in to the rearview mirror and said it was iced over. I know it was a stupid line but I said it anyway, "If you look closely you'll see it's iced under as well." She looked at me with a strange look in her eyes and then at the rearview mirror. She noticed the ring hanging on a bright red ribbon. She looked again at me nearly taking her hands off the steering wheel. "Hey, watch where you're going!" I yelled, grabbing hold of the wheel. The car came to a stop and she reached out to take a closer look at the ring. "What is this?" she said in a singsong voice. I'm not a romantic but kneeling down in the front seat of a small car was not in the cards. I opened the car door and climbed up on to the hood of the car. The windshield wipers were going full force and I leaned as close as I could get kneeling on the cars hood saying, "Will you marry me?" She was inside the car holding the ribbon in her right hand and tilting her head as she watched me. I yelled, "I'll love you forever just the way you are!" She removed the ring from the mirror and held it in her hand. She opened her car door and looked at me kneeling on the hood. I did not feel the least bit stupid. For the first time in my life I felt like I was in the right place at the right time. She climbed on to the hood of her car with me. I took the ribbon from her hand and placed the ring on her finger. We kissed for the first time as an engaged couple on the hood of her grandfather's old Rambler with snow everywhere falling around us. I could not wait to tell her parents their daughter was giving up her college education to marry me. We had bigger dreams to pursue. I told her I wanted to be, more than anything else, her best friend for life.

Chapter Fourteen

There is no guarantee in life when we will meet friends. Just as friendships might last a lifetime, it is also disheartening to realize that there is no guarantee how long someone will remain a friend. People we have known for many years do not always represent the caliber of friendship we deem worthy of our time and efforts. We can spend an inordinate amount of time sitting next to someone in school, on a bus, a plane or train, in an office or share the same bed and never fully know them. Life can be defined in steps. There are the steps we pursue early on that define who and what we will be, and then there are steps to maintain the pursuit. The maintenance of one's pursuit can be the worse experience or the best experience we go through in our lifetime.

Adjusting to life after the military is a process for anyone, regardless of what period in time it is taking place. Listening to some of the veterans of different wars tell their stories can be enlightening or debilitating, depending on your perspective. I never expected to need an understanding of anyone's experience except my own. I knew only that I wanted to marry Gayle Cooper. I knew only that I wanted to stay in my childhood neighborhood.

I had no idea what it would take to maintain this simple dream.

The friends I thought I had when I left to join the Army changed. Their pursuits had become their own and no one seems to look back on yesterday. It's a code of living that pursuing one's dreams is everyone's right. Watching others climb out of adolescence and young adulthood to find their place in life is a rite of passage. I watched Billy Moran climb from the streets of our humble neighborhood to the heights of college and beyond. I wanted to maintain a simple friendship based on our similar interests and dreams, but those things can change without anyone knowing, until they seem like shadows in a rear view mirror. I thought holding on to some of the dreams was worth everything I ever wanted. Over the years, almost everyone I considered a friend or loved one moved away. I often wonder if they were pursuing a calling or a larger part of a dream they yearned to fulfill, but in some ways I think they surrendered to a larger view of themselves without seeing the merits of maintaining roots in one place. Those who moved on, or moved away, deserved to be happy; no matter how far away they roamed from yesterday. I lost track of more people than I can remember.

Billy Moran and I spoke less and less as time went on. One day I got a call that his mother had passed away. I went to the funeral. I shook his hand and we nodded our heads in understanding. He leaned up and said, "I need your help cleaning out my parent's house. I'll call you." I nodded and went home. A week passed before Billy called me saying he was home. I joined him at his parents' house. We set about the task of cleaning out a person's life. I reminded him of the last time we cleaned out a house when we were younger. It made him laugh remembering Gertrude McGuffey's house. We talked about how the house was torn down because no one could move in to it after she died. There were moments when I knew to leave a certain room or excuse myself, when something was found that he needed to process alone, but as the weekends passed there was less and less to remind Billy of his parents. Carrying furniture no one wanted and leaving it on the sidewalk as garbage added to the reality of the passage of time. As we cleaned out the kitchen, Billy stood for a moment after opening a drawer. Inside the drawer, wrapped in ribbons, were dozens of Googenblatt letters. We sat for a while reading them together; laughing and certifying for the first time that neither of us had written many of them. Billy's father, after all, was a better Googenblatt writer than we could ever hope to become.

With the top floor and main floor emptied of everything, I noticed Billy hesitate at the basement steps. It was the basement where much of what had real value remained. Sentimental value has a weight that no bank can hold. We slowly dismantled the train set his father and uncle had built. The train set was nearly the length of the basement and many times during the Christmas season kids would stand on line to get a glimpse of it. His father and uncle were meticulous in every detail of how it was displayed. They went so far as to have figurines of The Beatles playing in a small park at the center. As we took it apart piece by piece, we listened to Billy's old record collection. The music of Pet Sounds by The Beach Boys, The White Album by The Beatles, Seventh Sojourn by The Moody Blues, Bridge over Troubled Water by Simon and Garfunkel, Blood on the Tracks by Bob Dylan filled the air and we sang along with every song. As we broke apart the wooden structure that held the trains I excused myself several times. The trains were carefully placed in boxes and we carried them to Billy's car parked outside. I removed the posters Billy had on the walls. The last thing I removed from the walls was a life size photo of Farrah Fawcett in a red bathing suit. I rolled it up like it was a famous painting by Rembrandt or Picasso. When it came time to dismantle his father's office in the back of the basement I knew to leave the basement. I sat on the front steps where I knew Billy and I had tried to discover the meaning of life a million times. I sat feeling the presence of his mother who once told us she was having a heart attack because we got home too late. I thought about the things his father told us about his youth while sharing pitchers of lemonade with us. Billy piled his father's things near the basement steps and I carried them outside. Some went in to Billy's car. A lot was left on the curb. I heard Billy yell from the basement he was going to lock up the house. I heard the echo of his footsteps as he closed doors and windows for the last time. I sat on the steps waiting. He came outside and said, "Well that's it Kidd. Everything worth having and saving is in one place and everything else is left for whoever wants it." I nodded my head, knowing not to say anything. I watched after we shook hands the way he walked slowly to his car. I sat on the steps wanting to be the last person to leave. Before getting in his car he yelled to me, "I left something on the basement steps for you!" He pulled away from the curb and I watched his car turn off the block. I went to the basement steps. It was his father's typewriter. On a piece of paper in the roll on the typewriter he had typed:

Write me a story.
Keep Warm and Chill Out.
Googenblatt

Epilogue

Time has a way of begging for interpretation. Memories can get lost in translation.

Stories from our past flow easily for some while others choose to forget. It is interesting how many times I will meet someone from years ago and they will have a different take on what happened. A lot of people adapt or inherit selective memories. They choose to embellish the truth or change the outcome of certain events. I learned over time to let people believe their memories belong to them and should not be disputed or enhanced to create a better story. A lot of people move on with no connection to their youth. I stayed in the same neighborhood because it feels like home.

I return now to the park to walk my dog. It is a ritual that provides solace and comfort. I named my dog Dylan after the folksinger. Bob Dylan changed so many times over the years he has managed to be a voice for every generation since coming on the scene in the early 1960s. My dog is a Labrador-mix and she accompanies me on my walks through the park.

One evening I let her off the leash and watched her enjoying the same space I took for granted as a young boy. I sat down on a bench where as a young boy I had discussed the meaning of life and whimsical theories of the day. The sun was slowly fading behind the trees as I noticed Dylan chasing another dog. I stood up to call her when I saw Billy Moran standing with a leash in his hand smiling.

"Is that your dog?" I hollered to him.

He stood taking a deep breath and shaking his head, yes. He walked slowly toward me looking around at the changes made to the park since we were young boys.

"What are you doing here Billy?"

"I was driving by on Myrtle Avenue when I saw you enter the park. I like to take drives with Elvis. He likes to sit in the front seat and listens to me talking about things no one else wants to hear."

"You named your dog Elvis?"

He sat down on the bench saying, "She's a real hound dog."

"Funny."

"Oh yeah, what is your dogs name?"

"Dylan."

We both laughed realizing we had made a connection to our youth by using the names of artist we enjoyed for our dogs.

I watched as the dogs ran barking and yelping around the park swings and through the forest behind the play area.

"I take her up here so we can feel free."

He nodded his head smiling, "I know what you mean. Fewer and fewer people know how to get away without going away.

The conversation went through a series of memories and challenging interpretations of things we both experienced years ago.

"How is the family?"

"The kids are getting older and growing up fast. The wife and I are happy."

It was nice to hear a friend was happy. I told him how Gayle and I were enjoying life and watching our children get older pursuing their dreams.

Billy looked around the park remarking, "My father introduced me to you right over there."

We both stood looking at the basketball court in silence as the dogs continued to investigate the park.

I knew he was thinking about his father and said, "Your Dad was bigger than life Billy."

He shook his head saying, "You lost your Dad too soon."

Sitting on the bench for a while without talking he began to laugh.

"What's so funny?"

"It just struck me that we're older but not really old."

"Do you know what I hate?"

"What?"

"I am losing hair on my head by the handful every time I take a shower, but now it is growing in places that boggle the mind. No one tells you this is going to happen. When you are young, it is all about learning the limits of how things work and the hush-hush of parents afraid to tell you things you find out any way. Then you get older and again there is hush-hush over stupid things like hair growing out of your nose and ears."

We both sat laughing and while sitting there I felt time has a way of rewarding us with perfect moments. Billy told me about a conversation he remembered we had one night long ago. He said, "You said someone asked you why you were never serious. For some reason that made you furious." He looked at the dogs barking and howling as the moon took its place over the tree line near the highway. He continued, "I thought about that conversation a few weeks ago when I told my wife I was going to retire from my job. She was not thrilled to hear me telling her this, but then I told her about that conversation. The thing is we spend our entire adulthood being serious about making ends meet and doing the right thing. I think I'm tired of being serious."

I did not know what to say to Billy. Knowing we had reached another era in life, talking about retirement and taking things too seriously made me sad.

He shared his plan with me for living life without all the serious commitments of working and commuting. He ran off the number of hours he spent over thirty years sitting in traffic, on a bus, on a train and sitting in meetings with people who knew nothing about him. He was angry and yet satisfied with the ability to feel he could walk away from it all. He finished by saying, "I am finally going to do something I might enjoy."

I told him, "I remember when your Dad retired. That was one hell of a party at Durows. You know that restaurant is gone now. They put up condos and forget about how it looks, it just does not feel right."

"Kidd, a lot is gone from our youth. It is like it never existed."

"It is hard to share with our children how things were when we cannot share it with ourselves."

He agreed saying, "My kids can spend entire weekends staring at a television playing video games or at a computer screen surfing the net."

"We could not stay outside long enough back in the day eh Billy?"

"We sound like two old farts!"

"I think we lived life to the fullest."

The dogs ran around the park until they were done finding new things to entertain them. Dylan sat near me on the bench while Billy threw a stick for Elvis to chase and return.

"I got to get going Kidd. The wife will be getting worried."

"Why not call her and say you met up with me? You can come back to the house and see Gayle. The children will get a kick out of Elvis."

He took a look around the park and said, "I'm going to go home. It was great seeing you." We shook hands which felt awkward for some unknown reason. I watched Billy put Elvis on a leash and walk to the stairway that exited out on to the avenue. It was an exit I saw so many times as a young boy. He got to the stairway and stood for a moment looking at the steps before turning to yell, "Huck you Kidd!"

I laughed yelling back at him, "Go home you moron!"

I don't know anyone's dream except my own. That is how it is supposed to be.

Every so often a letter will arrive in the mail from the great state of Alaska.

It is always signed Bob Googenblatt. Sometimes I think that Bob Googenblatt is more real than anyone I ever knew, and that sometimes we have to invent qualities in a friend.

Finding those people that can travel with you through a lifetime is a quest worth taking if only you allow yourself to believe it is worth the effort.

I look back over the years, and I realize that we cannot control the tides of change no matter how many times we convince ourselves differently. We can embrace our childhood heroes until they are damaged by the deceit and conceit of others. We learn too much about the lives of others; too much information and too much to shatter our illusions. I could fill in so many blanks, if I only knew why it mattered. I could fill up a thousand pages filled with anger and disappointment, but I know now that anger is not worth anyone's energy, and that disappointments are usually based on dreams we thought we deserved. But anger and disappointment are such a small part of life.

I sometimes close my eyes and hear Louis Armstrong's trumpet playing. He comes to me in my dreams. He's always smiling. He brings friends with him that I find entertaining, and I often hear him saying something that resonates with logic.

I remember moments from the past. I hear his laughter and the echo in his voice when he would call my father's name. I hear him telling me things that would take a lifetime to appreciate. I think Louis Armstrong may have known more than he was telling us.

People wake up and they do what they have to do to survive. They do it because that's what they learned to do. Still, very few get to be what they once wanted to be; I remember Louis telling me to always try my best to stay positive, he said once, "Reflection is for mirrors."

I thought about that as I stood out on Myrtle Avenue looking both ways as the morning traffic began to grow in volume. The thing about Louis was that he meant more than what you heard. I walked down the avenue, taking in the changes to a neighborhood I still call home after all these years.

I stood with reverence across the street from a now missing building where I once held my father's hand watching as he stood tall and smiling. I stood on a ball field where I first held a glove and watched the arc of a baseball sail through the air. There are whispers that dance through the trees waiting to be heard. I am trying to understand what they meant, and what they mean.

I once asked my father about jazz. He said, "Jazz is like life, there are more people trying to interpret what it means than can play a single note." I thought about what I wanted to say to people who are confused about where they are going. I wanted them to know that sometimes, being lost is the best place to be. I wanted them to understand everyone feels lost every once in awhile. I wondered where the friends I had as a young boy disappeared to. Maybe they were thinking that it was me who disappeared. Life is funny that way, sooner or later everyone winds up playing a part in a picture show. The difference is that this particular show has no movie stars, and the script is always ad-libbed.

There is no script for daily living. We wake up and do what we have to do to get by. For some, it means doing a job they never thought they would do. For others, it means going through each day like it was a maze bumping in to walls and trying to make sense of it all. A select few seem to skate through life without ever facing real challenges, but I wonder if these people get to a certain age, look back, and cannot make sense of anything that happened to them. . Maybe we need challenges, adversity, to let us know we are alive. The strange thing is that I think most people feel the same way, but they are just afraid to admit it.

If you try hard enough you can remember times when you were so happy that nothing bothered you. But life has a way of changing in a moment. The only thing that really matters is that you never forget those times; and that the memories are what keep us going. Those good times and bad times are playing a role in our minds to keep us on our toes. Louis once said, "No matter how bad you think it is, it's worse somewhere else." I never quite understood what Louis meant but now, when I try to understand, it's almost like he is still standing next to me teaching, without any need for a lesson plan.

Billy Moran is my friend and always will be. Maybe you have a friend like Billy.

Everyone should. Our exploits are the stuff of legend. Maybe just to us, and maybe you had to be there to understand. Maybe your time is now. Take the time to make some memories of your own. Reach out to someone before it is too late.

I will let you go now; life is too short for anyone to lose time. S'all!

LaVergne, TN USA
25 January 2010
171102LV00007B/13/P